Praise for the work of Annie

Christmas in Blue Dog Valley

"The only thing better than a holiday love story is a holiday love story with dogs! That's exactly what Annie England Noblin understands with *Christmas in Blue Dog Valley*, the story of Goldie, an A-list veterinarian who impulsively upends her life to start over in the small farming town of Blue Dog Valley."

—PopSugar

"Noblin brings her trademark charm and humor to the novel. Goldie's romance with Cohen is sweet and natural, but her relationship with the town itself is at the forefront. The small town has an affinity for Christmas, making this a perfect holiday read."

—*Booklist*

"This adorable romance features a big-city vet transplanted to a small town called Blue Dog. Dr. Goldie McKenzie is a fish out of water, but she starts to gain the confidence of Blue Dog residents when she helps cure a sick pup. Cute pups pepper this heartwarming novel, in which Goldie might experience the holiday—and happily-ever-after—of her dreams."

—Retrievist

"*Christmas in Blue Dog Valley* is a sweet tale about new chances, new friends, and a new life far from the glitz and glamour of Los Angeles. Goldie is entranced by the locals who slowly begin to warm up to her. She also gets to meet the local animals: Large Marge, the horse; Alice, the cape-wearing alpaca; Kevin, the "worst sheepdog around" (who knows a good person when he meets Goldie!); and also Airport, the Sphinx cat that Goldie rescues at baggage claim."

—*Romance Reviews Today*

St. Francis Society for Wayward Pets

"Feel-good fiction at its finest. Annie England Noblin has crafted an utterly entertaining tale of unexpected chances and small-town secrets, and it's as sweet and comforting as a hand-knit sweater and a warm puppy in your lap."

—Susan Wiggs, *New York Times* bestselling author

"I was immediately enchanted! Lively and heartfelt, the characters—both human and four-legged—in Annie England Noblin's *St. Francis Society for Wayward Pets* come alive. I adored it."

—Lori Foster, *New York Times* bestselling author

"Noblin's masterful touch hits the sweet spot of humor and tragedy in this heartfelt book about the truest meaning of family, friends, abandoned dogs, and love, amidst a weave of plot-twisting heroics."

—Jacqueline Sheehan, *New York Times* bestselling author

"Annie England Noblin is an incredibly gifted storyteller. *St. Francis Society for Wayward Pets* is heartfelt, charming, and funny."

—Meg Donohue, author of *You, Me, and the Sea*

Christmas at Corgi Cove

Also by Annie England Noblin

Christmas in Blue Dog Valley
Maps for the Getaway
St. Francis Society for Wayward Pets
The Sisters Hemingway
Just Fine with Caroline
Pupcakes
Sit! Stay! Speak!

Christmas at Corgi Cove

A Novel

Annie England Noblin

AVON

An Imprint of HarperCollinsPublishers

CHRISTMAS AT CORGI COVE. Copyright © 2023 by Annie England Noblin. All rights reserved. Printed in the United States of America. No part of this book may be used or reproduced in any manner whatsoever without written permission except in the case of brief quotations embodied in critical articles and reviews. For information, address HarperCollins Publishers, 195 Broadway, New York, NY 10007.

HarperCollins books may be purchased for educational, business, or sales promotional use. For information, please email the Special Markets Department at SPsales@harpercollins.com.

FIRST EDITION

Designed by Diahann Sturge

Bees © 3xy, Maksym Drozd / Shutterstock
Corgi © aksd / Shutterstock
Pickup truck © mart / Shutterstock

Library of Congress Cataloging-in-Publication Data has been applied for.

ISBN 978-0-06-322224-3

23 24 25 26 27 LBC 5 4 3 2 1

For Jack and Will

PROLOGUE

"I just can't handle her anymore," Rosie heard her mother say.

"She's your daughter, Katherine." This from her aunt.

Rosie sat in the kitchen with her uncle, both of them aware of the conversation that was going on in the living room next to them. At first, they hadn't been able to hear them talking, but now, with her mother's and aunt's voices rising higher and higher, it was becoming easier to catch snippets of what was being said.

About her.

"Do you want to go out into the yard?" Rosie's uncle asked, shifting in his seat. He'd poured them both a root beer a few minutes ago, attempting to make jovial conversation until it became clear that Rosie had no interest in responding to him.

"No," Rosie said. She stared at the condensation on the glass and willed herself not to cry.

"You don't need to be listening to this."

Rosie rolled her eyes at him. What she needed was to be back in Houston with

her friends, spending her Saturday at the mall. At fifteen, all she wanted was to be out of her mother and stepfather's house. But two weeks ago, she'd messed it all up by not coming home by curfew, and so she'd spent the night with her boyfriend only for the school's truant officer to come knocking at her mother's work the next day, since getting to school on time or at all seemed to be an issue Rosie faced nearly constantly.

It wasn't that her mother cared what Rosie was doing. She only cared when people noticed and disapproved. And now, she was being shipped off to Turtle Lake, to the end of the world, it felt like, and to people she barely knew, all because her mother didn't want to bother with her anymore.

"We've got a good school here," her uncle continued, failing to notice that Rosie didn't want to talk. "Lots of nice kids here."

"I hate school," Rosie replied.

"I always hated it, too," her uncle said. "But I liked the social aspect of it all."

"I have friends in Houston," Rosie said.

"You could work at the Cove," her uncle tried again. "It gets pretty busy during the season. Make you a little bit of spending money."

"What's there to buy here besides dirt?" Rosie asked, knowing how it sounded. She wasn't angry at her uncle. Not really. He was trying to be nice to her, and honestly, the little bed-and-breakfast-style hotel that her aunt and uncle ran was lovely. That morning when she'd arrived with her mother and stepfather, there had been a just-married couple checking out, giggling and glowing with excitement, and Rosie had felt a pang of jealousy at their happiness. She wanted to be happy. Really, she did. She just didn't know how to get there.

"It won't be as bad as you think," her uncle continued. "You'll see."

It was at that moment Rosie knew she wasn't going back to Houston. The trunk of her mother's car was full of nearly everything she owned back at home. She didn't know why she'd remained so hopeful that this was all some kind of test.

She'd known this was a possibility. Every time she did something her mother disagreed with, her mother threatened to send her down to her "redneck sister and brother-in-law" as punishment. Now that threat had become a reality, and looking around, it certainly did seem like a punishment.

It seemed like hell. She had no reception on her cell phone. Her aunt and uncle had an old rotary phone, a television on the floor with a dial on it, and literally everything was floral. She couldn't live here. She just couldn't.

After a few silent minutes, Rosie's mother and aunt came into the kitchen. To Rosie's surprise, it looked like her mother might have been crying. Maybe Rosie's aunt had said no. That was the only reason Rosie could think of for her mother's emotion. She couldn't remember the last time she'd seen her mother cry.

"You're going to stay with your aunt Mary and your uncle Joe for a while," her mother said, looking past her and out to the Lincoln Navigator where Rosie's stepfather waited, refusing to come inside.

"No!" Rosie said. "No, Mom. You can't! Please!" She stood up, but didn't advance toward her mother, afraid that if she did, she would throw her arms around her and refuse to let go.

"This is what's best," her mother replied. Still, she didn't look at Rosie. "I love you."

"No you don't," Rosie cried, tears streaming down her own face now. "No you don't! If you loved me, you wouldn't make me stay here!"

Her mother made toward the door, and Rosie lunged for her, unable to stop herself. Her uncle caught her by the shoulders and kept her in place as she screamed for her mother not to leave her.

Rosie collapsed onto her uncle, crying loudly even as she heard the car pull away from the house, even as it rolled out of sight and back toward the life she knew she was losing.

CHAPTER 1

Rosie

Rosie Reynolds loved Texas in November. In fact, she loved Texas all of the time, a feeling that was practically required to be a citizen of the state; still, there was just something about Texas in November that made her especially happy. She thought probably it was because by this time in the year, all the tourists had gone, packed up their rented minivans with their hordes of screaming children and hightailed it out of Turtle Lake for the season.

The only sounds she could hear this morning were coming from the beehive in her yard, her little darlings buzzing about as she walked around the hives, preparing for the final honey harvest before winter. This weekend would be one of her last trips to the farmers' market in Austin, where her honey was popular with the locals.

"Good morning," Rosie said as she walked. Now that it was cooler outside, she didn't mind wearing her keeper's getup so much. When it was 99 degrees in July, she often felt like her face was melting beneath the veiled hat.

"I hear ya; I year ya," Rosie grumbled to them. She walked away from her bees and disrobed from the suit. The corgis crammed in closer to her, sniffing the pockets of her frayed jeans shorts.

"Here," she said to them, handing them each a bone-shaped treat. "Now, quit yapping, and let's get to the Cove."

Corgi Cove, often referred to as just "the Cove," was an elegantly situated three-story home on Turtle Lake, just about an hour outside of Austin. For the last twenty years, it had belonged to her aunt Mary and uncle Joe. They'd turned it into a once-popular bed-and-breakfast, but before that, it had been many things. It was first a family home, built during the Reconstruction era after the Civil War. It served that purpose for several decades before it was sold off to a former schoolmarm in the 1950s who wanted to open a sanctuary for wayward teenage girls. The Stillwell House for Girls stayed open until the 1980s when its owner died and the house fell into the hands of distant relatives from the East Coast who wanted nothing to do with it. They kept up with the care from far away until it could be sold. It changed hands a few times, including during the 1990s when its new owner thought she could run her Mary Kay empire out of it, and she painted the entire house pink to match her Cadillac.

Luckily, Rosie's aunt and uncle had rescued it just in time, repainting it yellow and blue and giving it its current name.

Since she was fifteen, Rosie had been working at the Cove at least part-time. There had been a time when she'd been desperate to get out of Turtle Lake. Now, twelve years on, she was still there, and she'd come to enjoy the peace and quiet of life in this sleepy, lakeside town. Of course, over the last couple of years, the peace and quiet had become deafening. This was precisely the reason why Rosie was headed to the Cove so early on a Monday morning, when she'd usually spend more time at her own cottage at the edge of the property with her bees and her garden and her cat, Toulouse. Instead, she was headed up to the big house to await the arrival of a stranger to discuss with her aunt and uncle the sale of their beloved estate.

It wasn't a conversation she was looking forward to, but it certainly wasn't coming as a surprise. They hadn't had a guest at the Cove for months, and even during the busy season, the summer, they'd had only a dozen or so, all stragglers who couldn't get a reservation at the Lake Queen, the luxurious and sparkling new resort on the other side of Turtle Lake. They'd all pretended to be delighted with their stay, but they'd also all checked out early when rooms opened up at the resort, and her aunt and uncle, embarrassed and resigned, let them go with no extra charge for canceling.

Rosie's cheeks still burned when she thought about it.

Followed by the dogs, she let herself into the Cove and winded her way through the empty front room, past the check-in desk, and into the kitchen where her aunt was fixing breakfast.

"Smells good," Rosie said, sitting down at the little table. Even though the larger table in the grand dining room was empty, they'd gotten used to crowding around the smaller one in the kitchen years ago. None of them had ever even mentioned using the formal dining room or table for meals. It felt too much like admitting defeat.

"Over easy?" Mary asked, smiling at her niece. "Cheese grits are on the table."

Rosie nodded and sat down next to Uncle Joe, who was making circles in his grits and not paying any attention.

"Good morning," she said to him.

"Huh?" Joe looked up at her. "Oh, good morning, sweetheart."

"Are you okay?" Rosie asked. "You look . . ."

"Don't say tired," her aunt cut her off. "For the love of sweet baby Jesus, don't say tired."

"Distracted?" Rosie finished, hopefully. "I was going to say distracted."

"No you weren't," Joe replied, sounding only slightly annoyed. "I didn't get much shut-eye last night, is all. I'm fine."

"Good," Rosie said, shoving her elbow into his. "I know today is going to be a . . ."

"Don't say hard day," Mary said.

Rosie couldn't help but grin. Joe and Mary were the closest things she had to parents. She knew her aunt and uncle, who had no biological children of their own, felt like she was their daughter. She'd never known her father, the man who'd only ever given her her last name, and she and her mother had what most people would call a "complicated relationship," which basically meant they only spoke on holidays and birthdays.

"Here you go," Mary said, flopping four perfect eggs over easy onto Rosie's plate.

"This is too much," Rosie said. "I can't eat four eggs."

Her aunt had never learned to stop cooking for a full house.

Beneath her feet, the corgis begged for food, and Rosie snuck them a piece of bacon at the same time Joe did. They looked at each other and giggled.

"Stop feeding them," Mary scolded. "Dr. Bearden said not to feed them at the table."

"But they look so sad," Joe replied.

"And so hungry," Rosie added.

Mary sighed and sat down next to them. "Let's say grace."

Rosie would have preferred not to. She figured if Jesus was listening at all, they wouldn't be in this situation in the first place, but she bowed her head anyway. She didn't want a tongue-lashing from her aunt later. When she opened one eye halfway, though, she found her uncle giving her a wink.

"Hurry up," Mary said after the prayer. "Let's eat so I can get cleaned up before our guest arrives."

Rosie thought the term *our guest* wasn't quite right, but she didn't say anything. In fact, he might be their savior. She'd seen the letters from the bank. She'd been with her uncle when he'd asked for more money to keep the doors open. Hell, she'd asked for a loan herself and been denied by that douche Allan who was still mad she wouldn't go to prom with him their senior year in high school.

Before Rosie had shoveled her second bite of grits into her

mouth, the dogs began barking, and they heard the crunch of tires on gravel outside.

"He's early," Mary said, jumping up and collecting their plates.

"Hey!" Rosie said. "I was eating that!"

"All right," Joe said, getting unsteadily to his feet. "Let's get this over with."

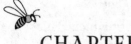

CHAPTER 2

Everett

Everett St. Claire did not want to be in Turtle Lake. In fact, he didn't want to be in Texas at all. What he wanted was to be back in New York at headquarters, but one giant mistake in the form of a stupid argument with his boss had taken him away from the corporate offices, and right into . . . well, whatever this place was. A village? A township? A wide spot in the road, as his grandfather from Missouri would have said. But all he had to do was make this sale. He could make this sale and go back, head held high, and spend the rest of his days in Manhattan. He'd never leave again, if he could only just get back.

Everett knew he was early, but he'd been afraid he'd get lost, driving in the slick, black BMW rental. In fact, he thought he *was* lost until he'd seen a fraying, wooden sign for Corgi Cove, a ridiculous name for a bed-and-breakfast. No wonder they couldn't stay in business.

He got out of his car and straightened his suit, glancing down at the red clay mud that caked his Italian leather shoes as he walked and tried to turn his grimace into a friendly smile. Before he could knock on the door or entirely straighten his face, it swung open, and a tall, ruddy figure appeared before him.

"Welcome," the man said, stepping aside for Everett to enter.

"Thank you," Everett replied. He shifted his briefcase and held out his hand. "I'm Everett St. Claire from the Lake Queen Corporation. It's nice to meet you."

"Pleasure," the man said. "Name's Joe Roberts." He turned and gestured behind him, where a woman about his age, in her sixties, at least, stood next to a younger woman whose expression, he realized, matched his own. "This here is my wife, Mary, and my niece, Rosie."

"It's nice to meet you-all," he said.

The younger woman, whose name he now knew was Rosie, rolled her eyes.

"Would you like a tour?" Mary asked.

Everett glanced around. He didn't need a tour to know that this place needed work or to know that it was incredibly outdated. It was pretty, he had to concede. He knew why the Lake Queen wanted the property. The view was beautiful. It was perfect for one of their resorts, and the bed-and-breakfast, despite its flaws, had good bones. He knew this. It didn't matter, though, because the Lake Queen would just tear it down and build once they took ownership.

"No," he said, finally. "I don't think that will be necessary."

Mary nodded and shot a look at Rosie, whose scowl deepened.

"Let's get down to business, then," Joe said, resigned.

Everett nodded, following the three into a large dining room with an oak table that took up most of the space. He sat down at the one end and opened up his briefcase. "I assume you-all know why we reached out," he said. "Simply put, your business is in trouble, and we'd like to help."

"Take advantage is more like," Rosie mumbled, and her aunt, the one called Mary, elbowed her in the ribs.

Everett looked at Rosie and tried to smile. He thought he was mostly successful. Despite her obvious hostility, she was really quite attractive, with long dark hair and green eyes. She wasn't his type, not really, in her jeans shorts and ratty tank top, but if he'd seen her in a bar on a Saturday night, he definitely would have looked twice.

"What we want," Everett said, tearing his eyes away from Rosie and setting them back onto the older couple, "is to *help*. We both have the same goal, and that's to get you out from under the stress of this business."

Joe nodded. "All right," he said, sitting down next to Everett. "Let's hear your pitch."

Everett explained most of the details while the three sat quietly and listened. It wasn't a final offer, and it wasn't an official offer. It was simply a longer version of what he'd explained over the phone.

Rosie was sitting at the opposite end of the table staring at him, and it made him slightly uncomfortable, although he tried not to let it show. He'd seen this kind of behavior before from people who weren't ready to admit that their business was failing or who weren't ready to let go of their dream. He felt bad for her, but this was business.

"So," Rosie said finally, leaning back in her chair. "If my aunt and uncle were to sell to the Lake Queen . . ." She said the last two words as if they were dirty. "If they were to sell, what would you do with the property?"

"We'd open a new hotel," Everett said smoothly. "It would look a lot like the one on the other side of the lake."

Next to him, Joe took out a handkerchief from the pocket of his overalls and wiped his face, despite the relative coolness of the room.

"Are you all right, honey?" Mary asked.

"Fine, fine," Joe grunted.

Rosie slid her eyes away from her uncle and set them once again on Everett. "What are your plans for the house?" she asked, moving her arm around to gesture at the room. "What about the cottage down the road?"

"We might keep the cottage," Everett replied. "Sometimes those are nice for people who want to get away, but I'm not an architect."

"What are your plans for the house," Rosie repeated, as if she hadn't just heard him.

He shifted in his seat. He didn't want to lose control. It was one of the reasons he hated going out into the field. People were so emotional. Why couldn't they see that he wasn't out to get them. He didn't even *know* them.

"We'll tear it down," he said finally.

"You can't!" Rosie said, standing up. "It's a historical home!"

"I didn't see anything about it being on the historical register," Everett said, giving a cursory glance through his paperwork.

"Well, it should be! You can't tear down the Cove."

"Rosie," her uncle said.

"No," Rosie replied. "No, Uncle Joe, I don't want to hear it. We can't sell to the Lake Queen. They'll destroy this place."

"Rosie."

"They'll build some gaudy building where you can get hot stone massages and a pool with a cheap swim-up bar, just like the other one," she continued, ignoring her uncle. "They want this place because it's on the outskirts of town, and they won't have to pay city taxes, and nobody in Turtle Lake will benefit. It's a death sentence!"

"Rosie!"

She looked over at her uncle. Her name had come out strangled, as if he were on the verge of crying. But he wasn't crying. He was swaying back and forth, his skin sallow, with one arm clutched to his chest.

"Joe!" her aunt screamed, rushing over to where her husband had crashed to the floor. "Oh my God, Joe!"

Rosie stood there, frozen to her spot. She looked over at Everett, silent pleading in her eyes. *Help,* she seemed to say.

"He's having a heart attack," Everett said, springing into action. "Here." He threw his phone at Rosie. "Call 911."

Rosie did as she was told as Mary knelt beside Joe.

Everett took off his jacket and knelt as well, gently moving a hysterical aunt out of his way so he could inspect the man on the floor.

As Rosie gave the information to the 911 operator, Everett said, "I don't feel a pulse. I'm going to start CPR."

Rosie stayed on the phone until they all saw the lights and heard the wail of the ambulance. The nearest hospital was not far, just a few minutes' drive, especially for a speeding vehicle, but it felt like hours to Everett.

The paramedics took over for Everett while Rosie went to her aunt to help her up off of the floor. She clung to Rosie as if she, too, might collapse at any second.

"He's breathing," Rosie's aunt whispered. "I saw him breathe. Please, God, don't let him be dead."

Rosie wrapped an arm around her aunt's waist and said, "It's okay. It's going to be okay."

Everett wasn't sure if she was right, but he hoped her words rang true.

"I'm going with him," Rosie's aunt said, breaking away from her grip and hurrying out the door.

"Ma'am," one of the paramedics said, holding up his hand. "You need to stay back."

"Roger Young," Rosie's aunt said, swatting his hand away. "I changed your diapers at church. Move."

Roger looked at his counterpart and shrugged. "Fine, get in."

The ambulance wailed away, and Rosie stared after it, looking dumbfounded. Eventually, Everett reached out and touched her shoulder, which caused her to jump away from him.

"Sorry," he said, quickly removing his hand. "I, uh, well, are you okay?"

She looked up at him. "I should get to the hospital," she said. She started toward the front door and then paused. "I should lock up. Make a sign for the door. I don't know why it would matter; we don't have any guests right now. Where are my keys? Oh, damn it, I forgot. Tommy's got my truck down at the shop." Her sentences bumped into each other, crammed close together.

"I can drive you," he said.

Rosie considered this. He could tell she wanted to say no but she also knew that it might be the fastest way to the hospital.

"Fine," she replied at last. "Thank you."

Everett, who'd collected his suit jacket, put it back on, and now looked as if nothing at all had happened to ruffle his feathers, pulled the door open and replied, "Let's go."

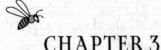

CHAPTER 3

Rosie

Uncle Joe was going to live. By the time Rosie got to the hospital, her uncle had already been prepped for surgery. He would need a bypass to help improve blood flow to his heart and time to heal, but as her aunt explained it to her, it wasn't as grim as it looked when they'd left Corgi Cove.

To Rosie's surprise, Everett hadn't merely dropped her off at the hospital, but he'd followed her to the inquiry desk and walked with her to the waiting room. He'd stayed there until Aunt Mary wandered out an hour later, looking exhausted, and he brought her aunt a cup of watered-down coffee, for which she was grateful.

"Thank you," Mary said to Everett. "You saved his life, you know."

"I'm just glad he's going to be all right," he replied.

"We aren't out of the woods," Mary said, more to herself than to anyone else. She was looking down into her coffee cup. "But it could have been so much worse."

Rosie knew that her aunt was right. If not for Everett, it certainly would have been worse. Still, she couldn't avoid thinking about how if he hadn't come to Corgi Cove in the first place, perhaps her uncle wouldn't have had a heart attack. If *she* hadn't been arguing with *him*, maybe . . .

"Rosie!"

Rosie looked up to see her best friend, Susannah, striding toward her. She embraced Rosie, pulling her in close.

"I came as soon as I heard," Susannah said. "How is he?"

"He's in surgery," Rosie replied. "They think he'll be okay."

"Thank *God*," Susannah said. "What happened?"

"Heart attack," Rosie said. "Who told you?"

"Hmm?" Susannah was looking down at her phone, furiously typing with her thumbs. "Oh, Tommy told me."

"Well, who told him?"

Susannah shrugged. "The ambulance drove straight through town. I'm sure everybody figured out pretty quick where it was headed."

"Great," Rosie muttered. Tommy was Susannah's brother, whom Rosie had dated on and off since high school. They'd been off for years, but since he was Susannah's brother, they stayed close. She also knew everybody in town would be checking in on her uncle, which was nice, but she also knew it would be overwhelming for her aunt, who was an introvert. It was Uncle Joe who was the more gregarious of the two, and Aunt Mary would have trouble keeping up with the barrage of questions from well-meaning friends and townspeople.

As if on cue, Mary tapped Rosie on the shoulder and held out her phone. "Can you please respond to these for me? I just can't right now."

"Of course," Rosie said, accepting the phone.

"Hey, Mary," Susannah said, reaching out to embrace Rosie's aunt. "Is there anything I can do for you right now?"

"Oh, honey, thank you," Mary said. "Could you run by and check on the dogs on your way home?"

"You got it," Susannah said.

As the three women stood there, Everett approached them and put his hand on Mary's shoulder. "I should probably head back to Austin," he said to her. "I'll be in touch."

Mary gave him a weak smile. "Thank you again for everything you did today," she said. "I'm sure this wasn't how you expected to spend your afternoon."

"Not quite," Everett said with a laugh. "But I'm glad that Joe is going to be all right."

Rosie narrowed her eyes at Everett. She didn't like the familiarity with which he was addressing her aunt and uncle. Like they knew each other. Like they were old friends.

"I figured you were staying at the Lake Queen," Rosie said, trying and failing to keep the tone of her voice civil.

"I thought about it," Everett replied. "But the Queen has an apartment in Austin for people who might be here . . ." He trailed off. "Longer term."

"We'll let you know when we're home, and ready to continue

our conversation," Mary said. "In the meantime, if you have questions or anything, you can reach out to Rosie."

An amused smile appeared on his lips, but all he said was "Will do" before waving at them and striding across the waiting room and out through the double doors.

"Who was that?" Susannah wanted to know.

She was a little breathless, and Rosie knew what that meant—she thought Everett was hot. That's how Susannah always got when she was in proximity to an attractive man.

Rosie resisted the urge to elbow Susannah in the ribs. Instead, she just said, "That's the guy who wants to buy the Cove."

"That guy?" Susannah asked. "He looks like he should be in an office somewhere crunching numbers. Very sexy numbers."

"Do you need some water?" Rosie asked her. "You seem pretty thirsty all of a sudden."

"Oh, like you're not?" Susannah retorted. "What's it been, Rosie? Two years?"

Rosie scowled at her friend. "It wouldn't matter if he looked like Jason Momoa," she said. "He's trying to take the Cove."

"I know," Susannah said. She reached out and hugged Rosie. "Try not to worry about that right now."

"You know?" Rosie asked.

Susannah looked embarrassed. "I mean, I'd heard maybe Mary and Joe were thinking of selling."

"And you didn't say anything to me?" Rosie demanded.

"I thought you knew!"

"Of course I knew," Rosie grumbled. "I just didn't know *everybody* knew."

"Look, we'll talk about this later, okay?" Susannah asked. "It's been a tough day for you, and I didn't mean to upset you."

Rosie walked over to a nearby chair and slumped down into it.

"This has been the worst day," she said.

Susannah sat down beside her and took her hand. "Joe is going to be okay, and everything else will be, too."

"It's my fault," Rosie continued, close to tears. "I started a fight with that stupid man, and if I hadn't, I bet nobody would be here right now."

"That's not true," Susannah replied. "Come on. You didn't cause his heart attack. That's not really how it works. You told me last week you thought your uncle wasn't feeling well. And you've seen how he eats."

Rosie mustered a smile. "He does eat pretty bad."

"Like a linebacker for Texas A&M," Susannah said.

"Thanks." Rosie tried to control her breathing. All she really wanted to do was curl into a ball and cry, but she couldn't, wouldn't do that. Her aunt needed her. Instead, she pulled her phone out of her pocket and opened the last text message from her mother, the one sent just a couple of months ago, the day of Rosie's twenty-seventh birthday.

She looked over at her aunt, who stood just a few feet away, and locked the phone again. Her aunt would be furious if she told her mother without permission. Their relationship with each other was even more complicated than Rosie's was with her mother. Half sisters, they'd been raised in two completely different homes until they were teenagers. As long as Rosie had known them, which was obviously her whole life, they'd never gotten along.

But she knew that there had been a time, when they were young women, that they'd been quite close.

It wasn't until Rosie's mother, Katherine, met Rosie's father that the rift began. Mary hadn't liked Rosie's father at all, and in the end, she'd been right. Rosie always thought that it was the fact that Mary was right and not that she hadn't liked Katherine's choice in husbands that Rosie's mother couldn't quite forgive.

Katherine Reynolds, now Katherine Hanson, had to be right in all things.

Rosie sometimes wondered how much of that piece of her mother she'd been given. There were days when she was easygoing like Mary, but there were days like today, in that argument with Everett, that she felt more like her mother. Keeping the peace was difficult, especially when threatened. And it didn't matter how many flashy smiles and placating words Everett St. Claire used. He was absolutely a threat.

CHAPTER 4

Everett

Everett sat in his car in the parking lot of the hospital and stared out the window, thinking. This had *not* been the way he'd envisioned this day going. From start to finish, it had been a complete disaster, and now his potential client was laid up in a hospital bed, fighting for his life, and his obnoxious niece wanted to eat Everett alive—she probably would have, had she been given the opportunity.

This was not going to look good back at headquarters.

His boss was going to be furious when he called her to tell her he'd not even gotten close to coming to an agreement. She didn't like him, anyway. He'd been demoted and then thrown at her like a wounded puppy, and she would have much preferred to make a coat out of him than help him get back to New York. Of course, they'd both known it might take more than one meeting, but he'd at least hoped to return to her with some sort of encouraging news. Now it just looked like he was trying to kill people.

He'd been led to believe that this would be easy, a cakewalk, he'd been told. Most people in the area *wanted* to sell. That's why his boss Francesca had given it to him. Despite the fact that she was unhappy with having him as her charge, it still looked good to make a sale. And the people here were either close to retirement age or had taken over the family business and were ready to be out from under it. At least, that's what Francesca *and* the report he'd read had both said. He hadn't anticipated a fire-and-brimstone twentysomething running in to rage against the machine. God, she was irritating.

He thought about Rosie, the way she'd looked at him when she realized why he was there visiting with her aunt and uncle. He'd seen the betrayal and hurt on her face, and while it was probably true that her anger was directed more at the situation than at him, he didn't like it. Everett wasn't used to being on the receiving end of that type of disdain. His whole life people had loved him— that's why he was so good at his job at the bank where he'd been poached by Francesca. People *liked* him, even when they were being denied a loan. He just had one of those faces. His sandy blond hair was thick and full, his green eyes twinkled, and—most importantly—he smiled easily.

Right now, however, he wasn't smiling. He was trying to figure out where exactly he'd gone wrong and how to fix it. He needed this sale. He needed to impress Francesca. He needed to check Corgi Cove off his list so he could go home.

Everett looked down at his phone. He'd had a nice conversation with Mary the week before when they'd scheduled the meeting. He hadn't had to tell her anything she didn't already know—Corgi Cove, their beloved mom-and-pop B and B, was in trouble. In fact, it had been in trouble for a number of years, and Mary explained to them their unsuccessful attempts to revive it, none of which included pumping any money into it, primarily because they didn't have any. What she hadn't mentioned, or rather who she hadn't mentioned, was Rosie.

Rosie.

Damn, she was pretty. Everett knew that shouldn't matter, not with the task at hand, but he couldn't help but think it. She *was* pretty. Even though she hated him, or maybe because of it. It was hard not to notice a woman with long brown hair and a creamy complexion, with eyes that were just a little bit too big for her face. She looked surprised nearly all the time, which made him want to laugh, but not in a cruel way. It was more in a way like when a person saw something that they weren't expecting, and that delight bubbled over into a giggle.

And Everett, as easy to smile as he was, did not giggle.

He started his car and backed out of the parking space, preparing to make the forty-five-minute drive back to Austin. He'd speak to Francesca later. He needed time to think. He needed time to plan and, most of all, he needed to come up with a way to make Rosie like him so that by the time the ink was dry, she'd be thanking him.

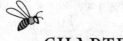

CHAPTER 5

Rosie

Rosie was exhausted by the time she got home. She'd retrieved Bonnie and Clyde from the Cove, and although they seemed confused about going with her, they didn't hesitate. It was well past their dinnertime.

Rosie felt guilty about leaving her aunt at the hospital, but she knew that they both couldn't stay. Someone had to get back to Corgi Cove just in case any wayward travelers stopped in, however unlikely that scenario might be. She left a note on the front door with her number. She could have spent the night there, and she might do that in the days to follow. But tonight, at least, she wanted to go home to her cozy cottage and collapse.

She didn't want to think about the day anymore. She'd known the Cove was in trouble—of course she had, but she hadn't

realized how dire it was until she'd seen Everett pull up in that shiny black BMW, even though she knew he was coming. Her aunt and uncle, bless their hearts, still thought of her as a lost fifteen-year-old girl, sent to live with them because her mother no longer wanted the burden of being a parent, and while Rosie loved them for trying to protect her, she wished they'd been more honest about how desperate things had gotten. Until today, Rosie thought selling was just one option of many. Now she was starting to see that it might be the *only* option.

Rosie set her keys down on the end table by the door and wandered to the kitchen to feed the dogs. Somewhere, her cat, Toulouse, was hiding, no doubt annoyed that her sanctuary had been invaded by Bonnie and Clyde. They'd had, the three of them, something of an acrimonious relationship since Clyde sat on Toulouse's head when Bonnie and Clyde were puppies. Now Toulouse regarded them with suspicion if he had to regard them at all.

After Rosie made sure all the animals had their food, she settled on the couch with Bonnie and Clyde. Toulouse meowed at her and ate with one eye on the dogs.

"Sorry, buddy," she said to him. "They're here for the night."

She'd taken approximately one bite of her grilled cheese sandwich when her phone rang. When she saw it was her aunt, Rosie answered without even so much as a hello.

"Is everything okay? How's Uncle Joe?"

"Well, if you'd let me catch a breath, child," came the reply from her aunt.

"Sorry," she said. "Sorry, I'm just worried."

"Everything is the same as when you left," Aunt Mary said.

"Vitals are good. Everything looks as good as it can look right now, given the circumstances."

"Okay," she replied. She let out the breath she'd been holding. "Do you need me to bring you anything? A change of clothes or something?"

"No, Irene already went by the house and did that," her aunt said. "She said you'd taken the dogs, that old busybody. Thanks, sweet pea. I didn't think to ask before you left."

"Of course. We're having grilled cheese sandwiches for dinner."

Mary chuckled. "I'm sure they're loving that."

Rosie thought that even her aunt's laugh sounded tired, and she considered yet again phoning her mother and once again decided against it.

"I'm calling because that young man who was here today called to say he'd left his briefcase at the Cove. I told him he could pick it up tomorrow when you'd be there," her aunt said. "And, Rosie?"

"Yeah?"

"Be nice to him. I mean it."

"I will be," Rosie replied, trying to sound offended and knowing Aunt Mary had every right to say what she had. "I promise."

"Good," her aunt said. "Because right now he might be the only hope we have left."

CHAPTER 6

Rosie

Rosie woke up the next morning in the same spot on the couch where she'd fallen asleep. This meant that some portion of her body was bound to be sore when she stood up, and she inwardly cursed getting older. It didn't seem fair. Teenagers didn't even appreciate waking up feeling refreshed.

She checked on Toulouse and moved his food bowl closer to his hiding spot and out of reach from the nosy corgis. Then she took a shower, threw on the least wrinkled clothes she could find in her closet, and headed out the door, Bonnie and Clyde at her heels and a piece of toast with honey in her hand.

This was the path she'd been walking every day for the last twelve years, since she'd been a troubled fifteen-year-old from Houston. She knew it so well by now that Rosie figured she could probably make it there with her eyes closed and her hands tied behind her back. Now she was wondering how much longer she'd be able to say that.

She stopped in front of Corgi Cove to look at it. She knew why it was often overlooked for bigger and brighter hotels like the Lake Queen. It still looked like it had looked when her aunt and uncle bought it in the nineties. It was cute, yes, and the name was even cuter. Tourists often got a kick out of it and took pictures in front of the sign. Rarely did they stay for the night.

Not anymore.

Not since luxury hotels like the Lake Queen moved in just outside of town nearly five years ago. The area turned from a quaint little lakeside town to a genuine tourist trap, and Rosie tried not to grit her teeth in anger when she walked through the door of the Cove and saw Everett's briefcase tipped over on its side on the floor, forgotten in the chaos of the day before.

She took a deep breath. She would be nice to him. He'd saved her uncle's life, after all. Of course, maybe he'd also caused his heart attack . . . or maybe they'd caused it.

Rosie shook those thoughts from her head and proceeded to get ready for the day. Lights, vacancy sign, and coffeepot on. Corgis settled in their beds behind the front desk. She resisted the urge to call her aunt so early in the morning for an update, and instead busied herself dusting and vacuuming, the latter an act she'd forgotten Bonnie and Clyde hated until they both began to howl.

She'd just turned off the vacuum when she saw a small group of people huddled outside the door, peering inside. They were earlier than Rosie expected them, but she'd known they were coming. She waved at them to come inside.

"I tried to keep them out," Tommy said, his voice muffled in the back of the group. "Nobody would listen."

"It's okay," Rosie said. She wrapped the vacuum cord around the hook and did her best to smile. "I know everyone is just worried about Uncle Joe."

"Well?" Irene, a tiny woman who owned the liquor store on the corner and always carried her pistol on one side and her Chihuahua, Coco, on the other, asked. "He gonna live?"

Rosie nodded. Irene already knew he was going to live if she'd taken clothes to her aunt the night before, but she didn't mention it. "He was stable when I left last night, and I haven't heard from my aunt yet this morning, which I'm taking as a good sign," she said instead.

"Thank God for that," Connie, the town florist, said. "I wasn't itching to prepare a funeral arrangement for old Joe just yet."

"Like hell you weren't," Irene snorted. "Every time someone in this town dies, you make a mint."

"Not everyone wants to be buried with a forty-ounce Bud Light and a pack of Virginia Slims," Connie shot back.

Tommy pushed his way past the two women to where Rosie stood. "We heard there was some guy here when it happened," he said. "Actually, I overheard Susannah telling Mom."

He looked so sheepish that Rosie didn't have the heart to be annoyed with Tommy *or* Susannah for telling their mother, the town gossip, about Everett.

"Yes," Rosie replied. "He was here on business."

"What kind of business?" Irene asked.

"None of yours," she replied.

"I'll just call—" Irene began, but Rosie cut her off.

"You will not call my aunt," she said. "She's got enough stress right now, and she doesn't need *you* nosing around asking questions."

She nearly sighed with relief when Irene's reply was concealed by the dinging of the bell at the front door. She was slightly less relieved when she saw that it was Everett, come to retrieve his briefcase.

Tommy, Irene, and Connie all swiveled around to see who it was.

Everett gave them a broad smile. "Good morning," he said.

Rosie gave Tommy a look.

"All right," Tommy said, herding Irene and Connie toward the door. "We'd better get going. Rosie does have a business to run."

"But I've still got questions," Irene replied.

"I'll have my aunt call you later," Rosie said to her, using her best customer service voice, which only barely covered her annoyance. "I promise."

"Fine," Irene grumbled.

Connie stopped in front of Everett and looked up at him. For a moment, Rosie thought the older woman might actually reach out and touch him. Instead, she turned around and winked at Rosie before allowing the door to clang behind her on her way out.

"Angry mob?" Everett asked once they were alone. "I've gotta say, they don't look very tough to me."

"You don't know them," Rosie grumbled, handing over his briefcase.

"That's true," Everett agreed. "You didn't look quite as terrifying as you turned out to be."

"I'm feral when threatened," Rosie replied, trying not to smile.

"I wasn't threatening you," Everett said. "I'm trying to help."

Rosie rolled her eyes. "Sure you are."

"I am," Everett continued. "Corgi Cove is in trouble. If you didn't know it before yesterday, you know it now."

"You're looking for cheap land to bulldoze," Rosie said. "Don't try to act like you're being philanthropic. We both know that's a lie."

"Look," Everett said. He glanced around the lobby. "We might not have to tear this place down *completely*. It's quaint, and with some work, it could be cute. It's not what we usually do for Lake Queen properties, but who knows what might happen."

"That's reassuring," Rosie said. "Anyway, it's not up to me. It's up to my aunt and uncle, and they're a little tied up right now."

"I know," Everett said.

"Don't bother them at the hospital." She looked up at him. God, he was tall. He'd be a lot less imposing if he weren't so damn tall. "I mean it."

"I won't," Everett said. "Do I look like a complete asshole to you?" He took a step back from her, set his briefcase down, and raised his hands up into the air.

"Yes," Rosie replied before she could stop herself.

Everett sighed and sat down on one of the battered couches.

It was Bonnie and Clyde who broke the silence by clambering out of their beds and jumping up on either side of him. Bonnie, curious as she was, began to lick one of his hands.

Before Rosie could tell her to stop, Everett laughed and gave the top of her head a ruffle. "My mother had a corgi," he said. "When I was a teenager."

"You must not be a total asshole, then," Rosie said. "They don't like just anyone."

"Can I be honest with you?" he asked.

"I'd prefer it," Rosie replied.

"I don't want to be here any more than you do," Everett said. "I don't enjoy this, if that's what you're thinking."

She went over to the coffeepot and poured him a cup of coffee into a white Styrofoam cup. "What did you do before this?" she asked.

"I've worked for the Lake Queen for five years. But I was in the corporate office in New York City."

"What happened?"

Rosie watched him consider the question, and then he said finally, "Politics."

"Well, we don't play a lot of politics here," she said, which was a complete lie, and they both knew it. "You aren't going to get anywhere with the people here if you aren't a hundred percent honest."

"Well, in the spirit of honesty," Everett replied, "if you want to help your family, you need to encourage them to sell."

"I appreciate the advice," Rosie said coolly. "But I don't even know you, and you don't know this place." She gestured to the Cove. "This place *is* my family."

"It's just a house," he said.

"It's everything," Rosie said. "Don't you feel that way about your home? At least about the home where you grew up?"

"I grew up everywhere." Everett shifted a bit in his seat.

Rosie moved Clyde onto the floor and sat down next to Everett. "My aunt told me I needed to be nice to you today, so I'm trying, but again in the spirit of honesty, you're making it very difficult."

Everett laughed. She thought that he probably didn't do this very often, and she wanted to tell him that it made him look much less like an asshole, but for once, she kept her thoughts to herself.

"Well," he said. "I promise I'm not trying to do anything to hurt your aunt and uncle. They're in trouble, and I can help."

"You keep saying that," Rosie muttered.

"They may lose it all if they don't find a solution to their debt," Everett said matter-of-factly. "If they sell, they don't have to leave Turtle Lake or the state of Texas. Just the property."

"Or what's left of the property," Rosie grumbled.

"Properties change hands all the time," Everett said.

"Not around here," she replied. "Not unless you count the Lake Queen snatching everything up for themselves. Most of the people who live here have owned businesses here for decades."

"Were the people here earlier business owners?" Everett looked skeptical.

"Actually, yes," Rosie said. "Irene owns the liquor store, and Connie owns the flower shop. And Tommy . . . well, Tommy doesn't own anything except a guitar and a pair of work boots, but his dad owns the auto repair shop."

"Owning a bed-and-breakfast isn't quite the same as owning an auto repair shop," he replied. "Especially not in a resort town."

"That's not the point."

"What is the point, then?"

Rosie stood up. "It's about the community. What it's like to live here. Who we are. You aren't from here. You said yourself, you're from New York, which is about as far away from Texas as you can get. You don't know how this town works."

"Why don't you show me?" Everett asked. "Introduce me to your town. It might help for me to know a little bit if your aunt and uncle decide to sell."

"*If*," she snapped.

"That's what I said."

Rosie thought about it. It might be a good way to buy time while she worked to come up with a solution that didn't involve selling. And maybe, just maybe, she could convince the town to work with her to show Everett that he didn't want to buy Corgi Cove. They already hated the one Lake Queen hotel enough. If she could convince everyone that two hotels would be completely unbearable, she could run Everett off. It might even be easy.

"Fine," Rosie said at last, sticking out her hand to shake his. "You've got yourself a deal."

CHAPTER 7

Rosie

The Corgi Cove Canine Club met every Tuesday, rain or shine, on the grounds of the bed-and-breakfast. Most weeks, Rosie didn't attend. It was more her uncle Joe's club than anything else, and she preferred to keep to herself at her cottage with her bees and Toulouse. But Aunt Mary had called and asked her to contact every member to request they still meet, despite the fact that Joe was in the hospital. "It's what he would want," Mary had said.

They'd all agreed to come, and Rosie approached the group with Bonnie and Clyde at her heels. The group was already deep in conversation.

"I'm just sayin' I don't think it's right that I can't take Tilly into the beauty salon," Cleo Jones was saying when Rosie walked up to the group. They were all standing around the side of the

Cove, where it was nice and sunny and the dogs could run around. "What do they want me to do? Leave her in the *car*?"

"Maybe they're worried about toxic fumes?" Marty Weiss asked, gripping the leash of Otis, his basset hound, tighter.

"No, that can't be it," Cleo replied. "Otherwise, they wouldn't allow people in the salon."

"It's too late for us," Marty continued. "We're already half-lizard."

"Nobody is half-lizard," Rosie said, bending down to give Otis's long ears a scratch.

"True," Marty agreed, solemn. "You're either full lizard like the king of England or not at all."

Rosie rolled her eyes. "You need to stay off of the internet," she said. And then, turning to Cleo, replied, "You can't take her into the salon because it's a health hazard. You know if Susannah could let her in, she would."

Cleo sighed. "Well, how's your uncle?" she asked. "I heard he was doing better."

"He is," Rosie agreed. "He's at least feeling well enough to protest everything the doctors want him to do, like change his diet and exercise more."

"Them Corgis give him plenty of exercise," Marty said, pointing down to Bonnie and Clyde who were, at the moment, taking turns jumping over a now snoring Otis. "They ain't like my boy here."

"Uncle Joe pretty much just lets them wander while he sits and reads the newspaper," Rosie said. "It's Aunt Mary who takes them for walks in the mornings."

"I guess now that duty falls to you?" Marty asked.

"I'm more like Uncle Joe in that respect."

There were six members of the group, not including Uncle Joe and Aunt Mary. Cleo and Marty were two, and Connie and Irene were two. Rosie's favorite two members, however, were Elizabeth and her dad, Justin. Justin was the assistant principal at the local high school, and Elizabeth was his thirteen-year-old daughter. They had a boxer named Mando that was, in Rosie's opinion, the cutest dog in the entire world. Their ages combined barely reached the age of everyone else in the club, but neither of them seemed to mind that. They still came every week to hear about Cleo's beauty salon woes and Marty's latest conspiracy theory.

Rosie waved at them and jogged over, Bonnie and Clyde at her heels. They liked Elizabeth and Justin best, too.

"Hey," Justin said, unclipping Mando's leash to allow him to run off with the corgis. "How is everything going?"

"It's going," Rosie replied. "I'm holding down the fort, so to speak."

"How's Uncle Joe?" Elizabeth asked.

Rosie smiled. She liked the way Elizabeth had, ever since she was a little girl, called him *Uncle Joe*. "He's doing a lot better," she said.

"We heard a rumor there was a man at the Cove the day of the heart attack," Cleo said, tottering up to them and then leaning in closer to Rosie. "What was that all about?"

Rosie had known this was coming. It was one of the reasons her aunt Mary had agreed that the group should meet. It would be easier for everyone if Rosie could just get it out of the way early and clear the air. She waited a few minutes while they all gathered around to listen. "The man who was here that day works for the Lake Queen. They want to buy the Cove."

There was an audible gasp from the group.

"No wonder old Joe went and had a heart attack," Marty said.

"Are they selling?" Cleo asked. "Are they going to sell Corgi Cove?"

"I don't know," Rosie replied. "But it might be the only thing left to do."

"Why didn't they say anything to us?" Cleo asked.

"Would you say anything if your business was in trouble?" Justin asked her, giving a sympathetic smile to Rosie, who honestly just wanted to throttle Cleo.

"The Gas Stash has never *been* in trouble," Cleo said, puffing out her chest so far that Tilly nearly fell from her arms.

"That's because it's one of two gas stations in town," Rosie pointed out to her. "There are nearly a dozen hotels here, and everybody, vacationing or not, has to buy gas."

"I'd be happy to give them some tips on running a business," Cleo continued, ignoring her. "If you think that might help."

"I think we're beyond the point of business tips," Rosie replied.

"What do Mary and Joe say?" Marty asked. "What do they want to do?"

"I don't think they *want* to sell," Rosie said. "But I think they believe it might be the best thing to do given the situation. Maybe especially since Uncle Joe's heart attack. I don't know."

The group was silent for a long moment.

"Had Joe been feeling sick or something?" Marty asked at last, clearly concerned. He was a few years older than Joe, and Rosie wondered if maybe he thought heart attacks were contagious.

"He wasn't feeling great that morning," Rosie admitted. "He just said he didn't sleep very well. You know Uncle Joe. He wouldn't tell my aunt Mary anything that might worry her."

"Well, we're all sure sorry," Justin said, a clear attempt to turn the conversation to something else, and Rosie was grateful.

"Thanks," she said. "Let's get the dogs out here and get them running around. I'll go back inside and bring out the lemonade."

"It's November," Cleo said, wiping the sweat from her brow. "Can't we have hot chocolate?"

The rest of the group hooted.

"It's 85 degrees!" Justin said.

"Iced coffee, then." Cleo pouted.

Rosie looked down at Cleo's tiny bichon, every bit as neurotic as Cleo. Tilly preferred to be carried around in Cleo's purse, and wasn't particularly fond of the other dogs. More than once, she'd growled at Bonnie, who wasn't nearly as good-natured as Mando.

"Do you want the lemonade or not?" Rosie asked, looking back up at Cleo.

There was a resounding "Yes!" from the group.

Cleo nodded her agreement. "I'm sorry, sweetheart," she said to Rosie. "I guess maybe I'm more upset about all of this than I'm willing to admit. I just don't want Joe and Mary to lose this place. We all love it so much."

Rosie reached out and rubbed Cleo's arm. "I know," she said. "If there was anything I could do to fix it, I would."

"Is it really too late?" Elizabeth asked. She looked close to tears. "Isn't there anything we can do?"

They all looked at each other.

"Maybe there's somethin'," Marty said. "Somethin' we ain't thinkin' of."

"If you think of anything," Rosie said, "anything at all, let me know because I am fresh out of ideas."

"We'll all think on it," Irene said. "Because we just can't lose this place."

The group nodded in agreement.

Rosie smiled. She felt bad for not wanting to have the meeting today. They were good people, and they truly cared about her family. She didn't know what any of them could do to save the Cove, but it made her feel good that they wanted to try.

"I'll go in and get the lemonade," she said at last.

She didn't realize that Irene and Connie were following her until she heard them bickering behind her. She turned around to face them once she got to the steps of the Cove.

"What is it?" she asked them.

"We need to check out the competition," Irene said, putting her hands on her hips.

"What?" Rosie asked. "What are you talking about?"

"Have you ever been to the Lake Queen?" Irene asked.

"No," Rosie replied, wrinkling her nose. "Why would I go there?"

Irene sighed. "To check out the competition!"

"They're not exactly competition if there aren't any guests at the Cove," Connie pointed out.

"Thanks," Rosie muttered dryly.

"You two aren't listening," Irene continued. "We need to go over there and check it out. Do a little spy work."

"Now you sound like Marty," Rosie said.

"Fine," Irene said, shrugging. "I'll take Marty with me." She turned around and began stomping off.

"Irene!" Rosie called, running after her, the lemonade forgotten. "You can't just go to the Lake Queen and *check it out*. You have to be a guest, and besides, the Cove doesn't need you getting arrested and blaming it on us later."

"I'm not going to get arrested," she replied, indignant.

"You will if you take Marty," Connie muttered.

"Fine. You two go with me, and I won't ask Marty to go."

"I feel like I'm being blackmailed," Rosie said.

Irene rubbed her hands together. "I'm driving."

CHAPTER 8

Everett

Everett didn't know why he'd asked Rosie to get to know the town. He knew that they'd tear the place down the minute the ink was dry, and there was really no incentive for him to get to know the townspeople. It didn't matter what they were like. It was the customers who mattered. The Lake Queen was about modern comfort and style. Rosie had been right about the hot stone massages and swim-up bar—not something he particularly enjoyed, but they were favorites among the Midwestern travelers who frequented the resorts scattered across the South.

"If the bank takes possession before we're able to secure the sale," Francesca was saying, "that will complicate matters greatly . . . hello? Everett? Are you still there?"

"I'm here," Everett replied. "Sorry, I'm just reading through some paperwork."

"That's something you should have done already," Francesca said.

"I did," Everett replied. "I mean, I have, but it doesn't hurt to look over it again."

"This should be a simple sale," Francesca continued. "The . . . what's it called again? The Corgi Cove is practically destitute. And I'm not surprised with such a ridiculous name."

"Oh, it's not that bad," Everett heard himself saying, even though he'd had that same thought only just the other day.

"Agree to disagree."

"Anyway, that's why I'm calling," Everett said. "Things have gotten complicated."

"How so?" Francesca asked, sounding as bored as Everett was sure she looked. "Out with it. I'm late for a lunch meeting."

"One of the owners had a heart attack yesterday at our meeting," Everett said as quickly as possible. Best to rip the Band-Aid right off.

"What the fuck?" Francesca replied. "Did he die?"

"No," he said. "No, nothing like that. But he's still in the hospital, and he may be there for a while."

"Can he still sign his name?"

"I don't know," Everett said. "But I can't accost him after major surgery to find out."

"I don't see why not."

"I have to form a relationship with these people, make them trust me," he said. "It's not as simple as a signature."

"Yes," Francesca replied. "It is."

Everett rubbed his right temple with his free hand and sighed.

"You've got one month," she said. "And then I'm pulling the plug and sending someone more experienced in to work with these . . . *people*, and you can explain your failure to the higher-ups."

"Understood."

"I'm going to make a call over to the Lake Queen," his boss continued. "It just so happens that I know the sales rep in that area. I'm going to set up a meeting so he can help you strategize some ways to close the sale."

"I don't think that will be necessary," he replied.

"I didn't ask you what you thought," Francesca said coolly. "I'll text you with the details."

Everett pressed END CALL and set his phone down on his coffee table. This was an absolute disaster. He had to get a grip on the situation, and fast.

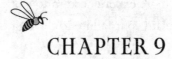

CHAPTER 9

Rosie

Rosie was glad that her aunt was at the hospital with her uncle, because if she knew that she was about to get into a car with Irene and Connie and go to the Lake Queen to spy . . . well, Rosie couldn't even begin to imagine her reaction.

"What are you waiting for?" Irene hollered after the meeting, honking her horn at Rosie, who was trying and failing to get the dogs to stay in her cottage.

"Stop honking!" Rosie yelled. "You're freaking them out."

"Listen," Rosie said to them. "If you'll stay here, be good, and not terrorize Toulouse, I'll bring you a snack when I get home."

Bonnie and Clyde stared up at her, their heads tilting back and forth from one side to the other.

She sighed. "Fine, just don't eat my couch."

She shut the door behind her and ran out

to Irene's car, literally the most conspicuous car anyone could take to a stakeout—a 1970 Oldsmobile 442 convertible. It was avocado green. Aside from the liquor store and her dog, this car was Irene's pride and joy.

In fact, Irene's dog, Coco, was sitting right in the front seat between Irene and Connie.

Rosie climbed into the back seat and prayed that she'd survive the short drive to the Lake Queen on the other side of town. It was far enough outside of town that nobody had to see it unless seeing it was your mission. Rosie had chosen to ignore its existence, but she did know what it looked like. It was gorgeous. Everyone in town knew it.

"Look at this place," Connie breathed. "I forgot how pretty it is."

"The last time we were here, they'd invited all the business owners to a luncheon," Irene said, parking the car in a side parking lot reserved for employees. "Remember, Connie? They said they wanted to get to know us all so they could do business with us and then went with cheaper shit from God knows where and called it a *corporate decision*."

"Oh, I remember," Connie said, pursing her lips. "I made all these sample arrangements and then they sent an email to tell me they'd gone with another company."

"The Cove would never do that," Rosie said. She squinted at a group of people walking into the hotel. They were laughing and pointing to the lake as they rolled their suitcases inside. They looked like they were having a good time.

"Come on," Irene said, cutting the engine. "Let's go inside."

"Absolutely not," Rosie replied. "You said we were just driving over to look at the place."

"I changed my mind," Irene said. She picked Coco up and put her into her handbag so that the top of Coco's head was sticking out. "They won't know we're not guests."

"We know we're not guests!" Rosie protested, but Irene and Connie were already out of the car and motioning for her to follow them.

Rosie sighed and climbed out of the car, hurrying along behind them. The last thing she wanted to do was go inside. She didn't want to see it. She didn't want to have a visual in her head of why people were flocking to the Lake Queen over Corgi Cove, even though she already had a pretty good idea.

The lobby was huge, with marble floors and a fountain in the middle. Off to the side were plush couches and a bar behind which led to an overlook where guests could sit and enjoy drinks while taking in the scenery of the lake.

Rosie resisted the urge to order the strongest drink she could get and scanned the lobby for Connie and Irene. She found them speaking to the person behind the counter on the opposite side.

"What are you two doing?" Rosie asked, hurrying up to them. "Why are you talking to people?"

"Look at these spa options!" Connie gasped, pointing to a brochure in Irene's hands. "Oh, I love Swedish massages."

"Do you think we have time for that?" Irene asked, squinting down at the pricing. "It's not that bad for half an hour."

Rosie cleared her throat.

They looked up guiltily.

"Why don't you two get a room while you're at it?"

Irene closed the brochure. "We weren't really going to get massages."

"We weren't?" Connie asked, her tone disappointed.

Irene elbowed her in the ribs.

"It's fine," Rosie said, walking over to one of the plush couches and sitting down. "This place is amazing. I can admit it. I don't know how we can compete."

"You don't have to compete," Irene said. She pulled Rosie up and steered her toward the bar.

The bartender, who was wearing a crisp white shirt and black vest, smiled at them. "What can I get for you lovely ladies?"

"Vodka soda," Irene said without asking Rosie or Connie.

"Do you have your drink tickets?" the bartender asked. "They should have been delivered with the rest of your room package."

Irene patted down her pockets and checked her purse, pretending to look for the tickets. "You know what, sugar? We don't," she purred. "I'm old, and I guess I forgot them. Could you do me a favor and let me run up and get them later?"

"Of course," the bartender replied, smiling broadly. "What kind of vodka?"

"Whatever's the most expensive," Irene said with a wink.

After they got their drinks, which Rosie had to admit tasted better knowing they were essentially stolen, they went out onto the balcony to sit down.

"This vodka soda is awful," Irene said.

"No it isn't," Rosie said. "Nothing here is awful, and like I said, the Cove can't compete."

"And I said the Cove doesn't have to compete," Irene replied.

"I don't know what you mean." Rosie took a gulp of the vodka soda.

"Do you remember when that new liquor store opened up a few years ago? It was over in Wood Grove," Irene said.

"Yeah," Rosie replied. "I remember. They had wine from around the world or something."

"That's the one," Irene said. "Well, I was worried that they might take my business, especially since wine isn't really my thing, but do you know what I did?"

"What?" Rosie asked.

"I just made sure that everybody knew I had the best liquor. I had the best beer. Go to Wood Grove for the wine. Come to Turtle Lake for the other stuff," Irene said. "It worked, and that place was out of business within a year."

Rosie set her empty glass down. "That's a really nice story. But the Lake Queen isn't going anywhere, and we've already lost business. We're going to have to do something . . . something big if we want to keep the Cove." She looked around the balcony. "I just don't know what."

As she scanned the tables full of people eating lunch and enjoying the view, her gaze snagged on a table at the far left of the balcony—on a face she recognized.

It was Everett.

He was digging into a salad and nodding along to whatever the person he was sitting with was saying. Whoever they were, they clearly worked for the Lake Queen as well. Both men were wearing suits.

When Everett looked up to catch the attention of a waiter, he caught Rosie staring at him. He looked confused and then annoyed to see her there, which in turn confused and annoyed Rosie. She glared at him and turned her body away, trying to decide if Irene might be able to get away with ordering one more free drink.

"I've got to go to the bathroom," Rosie mumbled, getting up from her chair. "I'll meet you out front."

She hurried off of the balcony and back into the lobby, wishing she could just take a flying leap right into Turtle Lake.

CHAPTER 10

Everett

Everett caught her just outside the bathrooms in the lobby. She was scowling, and that didn't change when she saw him heading toward her.

"What are you doing here?" he asked. Okay, it was more of a demand, but he was annoyed.

He couldn't help it. He hadn't been expecting to see her there, and seeing her sitting there, with her drink in hand, looking all . . . well, he didn't know. But he didn't like it. It distracted him.

"What are *you* doing here?" Rosie retorted. "I thought you said you were staying in Austin, or was that just a lie so that I wouldn't associate you with this place?"

"Why would I lie to you about that?" Everett asked. "I'm having lunch with a . . . colleague."

"Discussing ways to get Corgi Cove bull-dozed before Thanksgiving?"

"If that's what it takes," Everett said through gritted teeth, and then he instantly regretted it. Rosie's face fell, and for a second, it looked as if she might burst into tears.

"Get out of my way," she said finally. "I've got to go to the bathroom."

Everett held up his hands and let her pass. This was not how he'd planned their next interaction to go. He'd been planning on using the tentative truce they'd seemed to have to get her to listen to him, to agree with him about the sale. What he hadn't expected, however, was that she'd show up right when he had one of Francesca's minions so far up his ass that he'd nearly forgotten what he was trying to do in the first place.

He'd taken it out on her, and he shouldn't have.

Still, he couldn't understand what it was she was doing here. Surely she hadn't known he would be there, too. The meeting had just been set up.

"Were you seriously just standing there waiting for me to come out?" Rosie asked Everett when she reappeared a few minutes later. "That's weird."

"Is that your friend over there, letting her tiny dog drink out of the fountain?" Everett asked, pointing to where Irene stood, holding Coco over the fountain while two Lake Queen employees hovered around her, attempting to get her to stop.

"I've gotta go," Rosie said. "Enjoy your lunch or whatever."

"I will," Everett replied. "See you soon, Rosie."

"Lucky me," Rosie muttered, rolling her eyes.

She walked away toward her friend, who was now arguing with an employee and yelling something about drink tickets, which

Everett knew she didn't have, since she wasn't, you know, a guest. But he smiled at the way Rosie put her arm around the woman and led her outside while the dog yipped and tried to get back to the fountain.

He had to admit—that wasn't something you saw every day, not at the Lake Queen.

CHAPTER 11

Rosie

"Tell him he *has* to stay," Rosie said into the phone, switching ears as she spoke. "The doctors made that decision, not us."

On the other end, Rosie could hear her aunt and uncle quibbling.

"Here," Mary finally said to Rosie. "*You* talk to him."

After a few seconds, her uncle came grumbling onto the phone. "Hello?" he said. "Tell your aunt she ain't the final word."

"I'm not going to tell her anything," Rosie replied. "Besides, she isn't the one who told you that you had to spend two weeks in rehab before coming home. That was your doctor."

"They're conspiring against me," Joe grumbled. "Everybody's old here."

"You sound like Marty," Rosie said. "And I hate to break it to you, Uncle Joe, but you're also old."

"I'm the paterfamilias," Joe said, a dry laugh escaping his throat. It was his favorite joke to make whenever Rosie and Mary disagreed with him. "You can't talk to me that way."

"Oh, really?" Rosie asked. "Then act like it."

The front door jangled, and Rosie looked over to see Everett enter, in his black tie and carrying his black briefcase. He looked all business; he was not smiling, which Rosie guessed was fair given their last interaction at the Lake Queen.

She held her finger up to him.

"I miss the dogs," Joe continued.

"They miss you, too," Rosie said. "But they'll be much happier if you come home and don't immediately drop dead because you are a stubborn old man who refused to do what the doctors ordered you to do."

From the doorway, Everett raised an eyebrow.

"Fine," Joe replied with a sigh. "Fine, I'll stay."

"If you're nice," Rosie began, "a pretty, young nurse might give you a sponge bath."

"I heard that!" Mary called in the background.

"I love you both," Rosie said. "Be nice."

"We love you, too," Joe said. "But I can't make any promises."

Rosie clicked END CALL and released Bonnie and Clyde from behind the desk so they could run out to sniff Everett's shoes.

"Your uncle having trouble?" he asked.

"Not physically," Rosie said. "His doctors say he's doing great, but they sent him to a rehab facility today, and he doesn't want to stay."

"I don't blame him," Everett replied.

"Me, either, really," Rosie said. "He misses the dogs, and he misses being here, but this is what's best for him."

"Can't you take the dogs to visit him?" Everett asked.

"I don't think pets are allowed," Rosie said. "If they were, I'm sure he would have demanded I bring them."

"We could always sneak them in."

Rosie looked up at him. "What?"

"I bet we could fit them in a couple bags and carry them in. Nobody would even notice," Everett said. "I used to take my grandfather's cat to his nursing home all the time."

Rosie laughed. "You're serious!"

"Why not?" Everett asked. "They're not that much bigger than the cat."

"You're going to drive to the rehab facility with two ill-tempered corgis, stuff them into a bag, and take them to see my uncle?" Rosie asked. "Why?"

"To be nice?"

Rosie narrowed her eyes at him. "Yeah, I'm not buying it."

"Look, I'm sorry for the way I acted," Everett replied. "I was just surprised to see you there, that's all. You act like the Lake Queen is a cancer on society, and then I see you there having drinks. It was weird."

"It was totally weird," Rosie agreed.

"So what were you doing there?"

She shrugged. "I don't know. Connie and Irene talked me into it. I just wanted to see what it was like, I guess."

"And was it as terrible as you thought it would be?" Everett asked.

"No," Rosie said, deflating. "It was amazing. The Cove can't compete." She looked up at him. "Is that what you wanted to hear?"

Everett set his briefcase down. "No, that's not what I want."

"I don't believe you," she replied. "You're trying to buy the Cove on *behalf* of the Lake Queen."

"Not today," Everett said, giving her a lopsided smile. "Today, I'm taking two lovable corgis on a road trip, and I promise not to try to make a sale while I'm there."

"Just butter them up to make a sale later," she said. "Smart."

"Oh, come on. Let's call a truce. Just for today."

Rosie considered this. In her experience, anyone who said they weren't a bad guy usually was. Still, she knew her uncle would love to see the dogs, and if that would make him happy, maybe it was worth it.

"No sales," Rosie said finally. "And you have to carry the bags."

"Both of them?"

"Both of them."

The Road to Recovery Rehab Center was located nearly half an hour from Turtle Lake, and Rosie was impressed with how well the corgis rode in the back seat of Everett's sleek BMW. They'd never been particularly good riders before, but Rosie guessed that they hadn't ever ridden in style, either, and even though they were dogs and not people, Rosie figured they probably liked the smooth ride over the bumpy, dusty ride in the truck.

She did, that was for sure.

"It's a company car," Everett said as if reading her mind.

"It's nice," Rosie conceded.

"It's all right," he replied.

"Driving it around Turtle Lake will get you noticed for sure," Rosie said.

"In a good way?"

She shrugged. "I guess it depends on who you talk to."

"I don't usually drive myself when I'm in New York," Everett admitted. "I'd forgotten how much I enjoy it."

"You don't usually drive yourself?" she asked, unable to keep the tone of incredulity out of her voice.

"The company has a car service," he replied. "And in the city, you can walk a lot of places."

"You can't walk anywhere in Turtle Lake," Rosie said. "Well, you can in town, but most people live out of town, so we have to drive everywhere."

"I've noticed." Everett pulled into the parking lot of the rehab center and turned around to face the corgis in the back. "All right," he said. "You two need to be nice and quiet when we go inside. No barking."

"You think they're going to listen?" Rosie asked, laughing. "They don't even listen to Uncle Joe."

"I guess we'll find out," he replied. "So, here's the plan—I'll carry the bags in, and you'll tell the person at the reception desk that we're here to see your uncle and bring him a few things from home."

"That's not technically a lie," Rosie said.

From the trunk, Rosie pulled out the two bags they'd chosen to hide the dogs. Clyde went in without a fight and even seemed to enjoy being inside the bag. Bonnie, however, nearly wiggled her way out twice, and Everett nearly zipped her nose.

"Make sure you leave a little open so they can breathe," Rosie said to him as he struggled to contain Bonnie.

"I'm the one who can't breathe," he said. "How can a dog this little be so aggressive?"

Rosie reached into her pocket and gave Bonnie a treat.

"You had treats in your pocket the whole time?"

"I forgot about them." She shrugged.

Maybe it was because Rosie knew what was in the bags that Everett was carrying into the building, but it genuinely surprised her that the receptionist didn't even ask when Rosie signed their names in to the visitors' list. The story she'd practiced in her head all the way there about *bringing a few items from home* wasn't even necessary.

Her aunt Mary, however, knew something was amiss immediately when she saw that Rosie and Everett were there together.

"What are you two doing here?" she asked. "Did you call?"

"We thought we'd surprise you," Rosie said, rushing Everett inside. "We brought something for Uncle Joe."

"What is it?" Mary asked, looking down at the now wiggling bags. "Is it . . . alive?"

At that moment, Bonnie popped out of the bag. She stood very still for a few seconds on her little legs, sniffing the air.

"Bonnie!" Mary exclaimed, waking Joe up with a start.

Bonnie, upon hearing her name, burst into action, first running to Mary and then to the bedside, as a more lethargic Clyde emerged, looking as if he, too, had been asleep.

"What . . . what's going on?" Joe asked, sitting up. "Bon-bon! Clyde-boy!"

Everett, who hadn't said a word since they entered the room, lifted the dogs, one by one, onto Joe's bed.

"You said you missed them," Rosie said.

"Is this allowed?" Mary whispered.

"Well." Rosie hesitated. "Nobody told me it wasn't."

Mary looked as if she might scold her niece, but when she heard Joe laughing with joy at seeing his dogs, she changed her mind. Instead, she reached out and gave Rosie a hug. "Thank you."

"It was Everett's idea," Rosie replied, not sure why she said it. She hadn't meant to give him credit.

If anything, she'd wanted to keep him as far away from any credit as she could. She wasn't looking to endear him to her aunt and uncle. She wanted them to look at Everett for what he was—a suit trying to take their home. Still, it had been his idea, and it was a good one. She never would have thought about it, or been able to carry it through, on her own.

"Everett?" Mary asked, raising an eyebrow.

"Mr. St. Claire," Rosie said, correcting herself.

"Well, thank you," Joe said in between licks to the face from Clyde. "This right here makes my whole day."

"It was nothing," Everett replied.

"Nothing compared to you saving my life from what I hear," Joe said. "I'm sorry my damn heart decided to quit working the day you came to call. I hadn't exactly planned for it."

"I'm glad it wasn't more serious," Everett said.

"We all are," Mary said, looking fondly at her husband. "Now Joe will have to start taking it easy like I've been asking him to do for years."

Joe grumbled, but he didn't protest, and Rosie realized just how tired her uncle really looked. More than anything, he looked his age—nearly seventy. He hadn't ever looked old to Rosie, not really. Or maybe he'd always looked old, and she hadn't noticed. She wasn't sure. It was hard to look at him in the modified hospital bed, fragile and pale. Just a week ago, he'd been up on a ladder cleaning out the gutters. She doubted he'd be doing anything like that anytime soon.

And if her uncle couldn't . . . or shouldn't do the things he'd always done around the property to at least keep it up and running, would selling really be such a bad thing?

She shook those thoughts from her head. *NO—stay the course.* Everett was the enemy. Sure, he'd helped with this one thing, but that didn't mean he wanted the best for Rosie and her family. He didn't even know them.

Just then, the door to the room opened, and an unassuming nurse walked in, pushing a cart with plates of jiggling, cubed Jell-O. Her mouth made a little O when she saw the dogs perched on top of Joe.

When Bonnie saw the nurse, she jumped down from the bed, raced over to the cart, and then without warning, continued running—right out the door and into the hallway.

Clyde, sensing this opportunity, followed suit.

"Bonnie!" Rosie yelled, running after them. "Clyde! No!"

The problem, she realized too late, was that the nurse left enough opening in the doorway for the dogs to escape but not for a full-size human. Before she could stop herself, Rosie banged right into the Jell-O cart, knocking herself, and all of the bowls of Jell-O, onto the floor.

The crash was so loud that Rosie forgot for a second why she'd even been trying to leave.

"This is why pets aren't allowed!" the nurse said, moving the cart out of the way so that Everett and Mary could get into the hallway and chase after the dogs. "This is why!"

Rosie looked down at herself and tried to decide if she should get up or just stay right where she was. Maybe if she stayed down on the floor long enough, she could transform into Jell-O and pretend that this mortifying turn of events never happened.

Instead, she got herself up, tried in vain to rid herself of Jell-O remnants, and followed the noise.

There was a LOT of noise.

Rosie tried to hurry, but there was Jell-O on the bottom of her shoes, and it was both slippery and sticky, and she didn't even want to think about the trail she was leaving behind her.

She found the source of the noise: the corgis, Everett, Aunt Mary, and a crowd of people in the cafeteria, where Bonnie and Clyde were licking the plate clean of a very confused-looking man who had to be at least 110 years old.

"I'm so sorry," Rosie's aunt Mary was saying. "I didn't know . . . I mean, I didn't mean for them to escape."

"It's fine," the old man said with a chuckle. "I ain't seen dogs this fat and sassy in years. Not since my Zoey girl left me."

"It is most certainly *not* fine," said a woman in scrubs standing next to Everett. "Who authorized this?"

"I'm so sorry," Rosie said, echoing her aunt. "This is all my fault. I didn't mean for the dogs to get loose. My uncle just missed them so much. I thought it would lift his spirits."

"You're a good egg, kid," the old man said, petting the top of Clyde's head.

The woman in scrubs glared at Rosie. "We do not allow pets on the premises unless they are certified service or emotional support animals." She gestured over to where Bonnie and Clyde were still licking the old man's plate. "It's clear they are not."

Rosie felt herself bristle, despite the fact that she knew her cheeks were flaming with embarrassment and she was covered in Jell-O. "They could be," she said.

"I doubt that very much," Scrub Woman replied. "And, anyway, I know they aren't approved guests."

"We'll take them home," Everett said, speaking up. "Again, we're really sorry."

"I hope they've had their rabies vaccinations," Scrub Woman continued. "Can you provide proof of that?"

"Can you?" Rosie shot back.

Beside her, Everett touched her elbow. "Why don't you go and grab the bags. I'll get the dogs."

"Fine." She trudged back to Uncle Joe's room with her aunt at her heels.

"You're dripping Jell-O," Mary said. "Oh, Rosie."

"I'm sorry," she said through gritted teeth. "I didn't mean to get you in trouble."

"Who's in trouble?" Uncle Joe asked.

"We are," Mary replied. "Bonnie and Clyde ate an old man's dinner in the cafeteria, and Rosie asked the director of nursing if she'd had her rabies shot."

"Well?" Uncle Joe asked. "Has she?"

Rosie couldn't help it. She giggled.

"You two deserve each other," Mary muttered, but she was smiling.

"I promise not to come visit again," Rosie said, collecting the bags. "I really am sorry."

"Don't apologize," Joe said. "This is the happiest I've been since before the heart attack. Thank you, sweet girl."

"I love you," Rosie said to him, bending down to peck his bristly cheek. "You could use a shave."

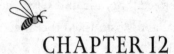

CHAPTER 12

Everett

"I can't believe that went so wrong so fast," Everett said as they drove back toward the Cove. He couldn't decide if he was annoyed or amused with the way things had gone at the rehab facility. He'd wanted to have a few minutes to speak to Mary and Joe, especially since Francesca had reminded him more than once that time was of the essence. His decision to take the corgis for a visit hadn't been one he'd really thought about until it came out of his mouth, and it irritated him that he'd made such a decision without weighing the consequences.

He'd planned to show up and talk some sense into Rosie, to plead with her to encourage her aunt and uncle to sell, and to show her the reality of what their options were. Without the Lake Queen, they'd lose the property to foreclosure in a matter of months. Instead, he'd walked in and seen her on the phone, and he couldn't bear to get into another argument with her.

"I thought we were going to get arrested," she admitted. "That nurse was not amused."

"No, she wasn't," he agreed. "She might've been more understanding if you'd been even a little sorry."

"I said I was sorry!" Rosie replied. "She wasn't having it."

"Can you blame her?"

"This was your idea!" Rosie said, turning around in the front seat to check on the dogs in the back. "My uncle really enjoyed it, though. So, thank you, I guess."

"I should have made you sit on a towel or something." Everett glanced over at her. "You're . . . sticky."

"I need a shower," she replied. "And probably to burn these clothes. I never want to look at another jiggly food for as long as I live."

By the time they got back, Bonnie and Clyde were over their adventure and ready to be out of the car. They jumped out the second Rosie opened the door and ran straight toward her cottage.

"They're hungry," she explained. "I should have fed them at least an hour ago."

"So have I passed your test?" he asked.

"What test?"

"You know, the one where I prove to you that I'm not an ogre who wants to ruin your life?" What he wanted to add was that it would be so much easier if she'd just give up on trying to save Corgi Cove. It was hopeless.

"Do you still want to buy the Cove?" Rosie asked him, jogging after the dogs.

"Yes," he replied, going after her. "That hasn't changed."

"Then, no," she said.

"Oh, come on," Everett continued. "I drove you all the way to the rehab facility with two slobbering dogs in the back."

Rosie turned around to glare at him. "I knew it," she said. "You didn't do this out of the goodness of your heart. You did it because you were trying to butter up my aunt and uncle."

"No," he corrected her. "I was doing it to butter *you* up. It's pretty clear that the only way this is ever going to work is if you give your approval."

"I wish that were true," Rosie grumbled. She put her hand on the gate. "Go home before I command my bees to sting you."

Everett stopped. "Do they listen to you without your costume?" He gestured to the discarded clothing on the porch.

"It's not a costume. It's a beekeeper's outfit."

"How long have you had them?" he asked. He'd never known anyone who kept bees.

"A couple of years."

"How do you even get into something like that?" Everett wanted to know.

"Kind of by accident," she admitted. "They originally belonged to a woman who had a hobby farm just outside of town. When she died, her family didn't want them, and the people who bought their house didn't want them. They were going to be destroyed. So I took them."

"The dogs don't bother them?" Everett asked.

"Did you see them run right up to the porch?" Rosie said. "That's because they know better than to get too close to the hives. Clyde learned the hard way. His nose was swollen for a week."

They stood there for a few seconds, neither of them knowing what to say. Everett knew that he should say his goodbyes and be on his way, but he didn't want to. He wasn't sure if it was because he was still desperate to convince her to cooperate or if he simply didn't want to leave *her*. The thought was unsettling.

Finally, Rosie sighed. "If I let you come in, that doesn't mean we're friends," she said.

"Absolutely," he replied. "Not friends in the slightest."

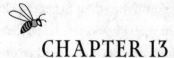

CHAPTER 13

Rosie

Rosie left Everett in the living room with the cat while she took a shower. She wasn't really sure why she'd invited him inside. Even though it was pretty obvious that he'd helped her take the dogs to visit her uncle to make himself look better, she still appreciated the gesture. Her uncle had been so happy. In fact, he'd texted her a few times since she'd left with Bonnie and Clyde to tell her thank you.

Toulouse followed her into the bathroom and meowed loudly at her for taking a shower before feeding him, but her only objective was getting Jell-O out of her hair. When she emerged twenty minutes later, she found Everett in the kitchen with a bag of cat food in his hand.

"He was meowing at me," Everett said, sheepish. "And his bowl was empty."

"It's fine," Rosie said. She pushed the

towel wrapped around her head behind her ears. "Just so you know, he's not starving."

"I can tell," he replied.

"Do you . . . want something to drink?" Rosie asked. "I have water and a week-old bottle of wine in the fridge."

"I'm all right," he said. He looked around her small space. "How long have you lived here?"

"Since I was eighteen," Rosie said.

Everett stared at her. "Did your aunt and uncle raise you?"

Rosie raised an eyebrow. "What's with the twenty questions?"

"Nothing," he replied. "Just curious."

"They took me in when I was fifteen." She guessed it didn't hurt to tell him. "My mother lives out of state with my stepfather. We didn't . . . we don't have the best relationship."

"Gotcha," he said, looking slightly uncomfortable. Then, after a few tense seconds, he said, "My mother died when I was twelve."

"I'm so sorry," she said.

"It's fine," Everett said, waving her off. "My dad remarried the next year, and my stepmother is wonderful. I miss my mom, of course, but I'm lucky when it comes to family."

"And where do they live?" Rosie asked.

"In Connecticut," he said, a genuine smile spreading across his face. "My sister has three kids, and they moved there from New York to be closer to them. My dad is retired military, so we spent most of our lives moving around. I think they're all happy to be settled."

"I understand that," Rosie said honestly. She'd never felt settled before she came to Turtle Lake. And until recently, she thought she was settled forever. "It's nice to have a place to call home."

Everett seemed to consider this.

"I've had a lot of time to settle in," she continued, unable to stop herself. "When I moved here from Houston when I was fifteen, my uncle Joe started working on this place for when . . . if . . . I graduated from high school. The deal was that if I graduated and didn't get into trouble, I could live here."

"What kind of trouble were you getting into?" Everett wanted to know. "You don't look particularly dangerous."

"I had a nose ring when I was fifteen if that helps." She laughed. "The truth is I was getting into a lot of trouble at my mom's house, and she thought it might be better if I got out of the city. I always hate admitting this, but she was right."

Everett nodded. "I understand why you're so attached to this place, then."

"I'm attached because it's my home," Rosie replied. "It's my aunt and uncle's home. I can't stand the thought of some big company coming in and leveling it, all to build a gaudy hotel that has no personality and no . . . charm."

"But think of the revenue for the town," Everett countered. "Turtle Lake's tourism has been dwindling year by year, and that's because it's one of the only lakeside communities *without* the draw of a large hotel."

"The other lakeside communities aren't reaping the benefit of hotels like the Lake Queen. They always build right outside of town, so the people don't profit. That's why you want the Cove. We aren't inside city limits."

Everett didn't respond.

"You know I'm right."

"My dad used to say, when we were moving around a lot," Everett began, "that it's not where you live that's home. It's your family that makes a home what it is."

"And do you think your dad still feels that way?" Rosie asked. "Now that he's settled in Connecticut close to your sister and his grandchildren?"

"Probably not."

"I don't know where we'll go," Rosie continued. "My aunt, uncle, and I. I mean, I know we'll stay here in Turtle Lake. I'm sure we'll find something. But I can't imagine my life away from this place."

"I'm sorry," he said. "I know that none of this is easy."

"Is this the part where you say it's not personal; it's business?"

Everett laughed. "No, because I know it's personal to you."

"But not to you," Rosie said, pointing at him. "To you, this is just a place to mark off your list. It doesn't mean anything. It's all paperwork."

"I didn't say that," Everett said.

"You don't have to." She turned her back on him to put the cat food back into the cabinet.

"I'm just trying to do my job."

"Please stop saying that," Rosie replied, not turning around, not facing him.

"I think I should probably go," Everett said finally.

"I agree," Rosie said.

"I'll be back," he said. "You know as well as I do that if your aunt and uncle don't find a solution to their financial situation, they'll lose the hotel to the bank by the first of the year. I'm just trying to prevent that."

"Out of the goodness of your heart," she quipped. "Absolutely."

Everett didn't say anything as he left, but Rosie thought that the tires of his BMW squealed just a little too loudly as it roared down the gravel road and back toward town and left her alone once again.

CHAPTER 14

Everett

Everett brooded all the way back to Austin. He'd planned for the day to go better than it had. The dog idea was genius, and until they'd gotten back to the Cove, Rosie seemed appreciative. Then he'd had to go and mess it all up. He didn't even know why he was worried about what she thought of him. Her opinion had no bearing on whether or not her aunt and uncle needed to sell, but he worried it might influence whether or not they *would* sell. He doubted she truly realized how dire it really was. If she did realize, she wouldn't be so obstinate about it all. She'd be *grateful* he was swooping in to save them just in time. After all, targeting Corgi Cove had been his idea. There were plenty of other prime real estate opportunities in the area—it was just that Corgi Cove was, in his opinion, the best deal, even with the old hotel standing there. Well, at least for now.

He missed New York. He missed his apartment back in New York. He liked the clean lines and the way the sun streamed into his bedroom in the mornings, waking him up just before his alarm. He liked the way his suits fit into the closet and the proximity of his couch to his television set, but it still hadn't felt the way he hoped it would. It hadn't felt the way Rosie's house felt the minute he stepped inside, warm and inviting.

Maybe, he thought, he needed to get a cat.

Of course, he wasn't home enough for a cat or even a really, really hardy fish. Everett thought about how, as a child, he'd always wanted a dog, but his father refused. They moved too much, his father said, and if they had to move overseas, the dog couldn't come. Still, he'd begged and begged.

It didn't matter now. None of it did. Everett was an adult, and he understood more about why his father said no so often. Living beings, especially pets and people, were a lot of work.

What he didn't need, as he pulled into the parking garage of the bleak apartment building the Lake Queen had set him up in, was any more work.

This had been his mantra for a long time. It was one of the reasons he'd never really had a serious relationship as an adult. Sure, there had been women he'd been interested in, women he'd dated, and a couple of women he'd thought about telling his family about, but none of them had ever worked out. It wasn't their fault—it had been his. He knew that. He wasn't an easy person to deal with. His whole life centered around work and work and work. It was easier that way.

Maybe that was something Rosie sensed about him, why she'd

suggested he didn't really understand a town he didn't think he had any interest in understanding. Turtle Lake was a small place, the kind of place where everyone knew everything about each other.

Everett inwardly shuddered. What kind of people wanted to live so . . . close to everyone else? It sounded awful to him. No, he was much more comfortable knowing people at a distance, and this stunt he'd pulled today brought him closer than he'd wanted to be, getting to know people in a way he wasn't comfortable with.

He was going to have to be much more careful from now on.

CHAPTER 15

Rosie

Word had gotten out about the possible sale of Corgi Cove, and Rosie found herself fielding questions as she made her way around town delivering honey to a few of the local businesses. The flower shop was by far the best seller, and Rosie guessed it had something to do with the fact that flowers just went well with honey. Connie kept a small section of the store expressly for local businesses. The honey and Leona Lee's goat's milk soap were favorites.

"I was wondering when I'd see you," Connie said when Rosie came through with a basket full of honey. "We've had people asking."

"I'm sorry," Rosie huffed. "I meant to come in earlier, but I took the dogs to visit Uncle Joe."

"Is that allowed?" Connie asked. "I can't imagine that would be allowed, especially for two heathens like Bonnie and Clyde."

"No," Rosie said, trying not to grin. "Not really."

"Were Bonnie and Clyde well-behaved?"

"No," Rosie said again. "Not really."

"Well, anyway," Connie continued. "It's not the honey they're after." She picked up a jar and squinted at it. "Although it does look lovely."

"What is it, then?" Rosie asked. "I know Aunt Mary started a phone tree to keep everyone updated about Uncle Joe, so nobody should be wondering about that."

"No, it's not that," Connie replied. "It's about the . . . you know . . . the Cove."

"What about it?" Rosie asked, although the sinking feeling in her stomach told her she knew exactly what.

"Word's gotten out," Connie said. "People are talking."

"I knew it wouldn't take long," Rosie said.

"It was Irene," Connie said. "I know it was. She's always the one to open her big, fat mouth."

"Like about Pastor Dave?" Rosie asked.

"That was different," Connie replied, stiffening. "He was taking money from the collection plate!"

"To give to the Methodist shelter in Austin," Rosie pointed out. "He was hardly stealing."

"I saw him with my own two eyes," Connie replied.

"I know," Rosie agreed. "You did."

Pastor Dave had moved in from another parish in Texas and had lasted exactly six months before Connie and Irene had gotten him so twisted up around town that he had to move out in the middle of the night. In fact, that was how she'd ended up with

Toulouse. Pastor Dave left him behind, and for that, Rosie would never forgive him.

"Anyway," Connie continued. "People are asking what your aunt and uncle plan to do."

"I don't know," Rosie said. "We haven't really discussed it much. They've got other things to worry about, and I'm doing my best to keep the Lake Queen from coming in and stealing out from underneath them, like I told you."

"That's not what Leona tells me."

"What do you mean?" Rosie asked. "How would she know anything about it?"

"She said she saw you heading out of town yesterday in that fancy car with that fancy man," Connie said.

"That wasn't what it looked like," Rosie replied.

"No judgment," Connie said. "I saw the man. I don't blame you."

"It was his idea to take the dogs to visit my uncle," Rosie said, both annoyed and embarrassed she had to explain herself.

"Uh-huh," Connie said, nodding. "I figured it was something like that, and that's what I told Leona."

Rosie doubted Connie had said anything at all like that to Leona, and she wondered who else Leona had spoken to. It reminded her that she needed to go and see Susannah. If anybody knew anything about the gossip, it would be Susannah. She heard everything at the salon.

"Anyway," Rosie said. "Here's five jars. I'm sorry I couldn't bring you more, but I need to save enough for the farmers' market in Austin this weekend."

"That's okay, honey," Connie replied. "I know you can charge double, and those dumb city folks will gladly pay it."

Rosie grinned. Connie was right. She could charge nearly twice as much in Austin. "I'm making some bee salve this time, too," she said. "It was a hit last year. People think it cures rheumatoid arthritis."

"Of all the nonsense," Connie huffed. "You know my sister Janice has had rheumatoid since she was twenty. Ain't nothing cures it."

"I tell them that. But I guess it does some good for pain, and people like that."

"Bring me a pot if you've got any left over," Connie said. "I'll pass it along to Janice."

"Will do," Rosie said, waving at her as she left.

It really was a gorgeous day outside. Although Rosie liked the quiet of the off-season, she did think that it was a shame that more tourists weren't around to witness the weather. The tourism board of the lake country advertised during the winter months, but this time of year, people were concentrating on their holiday festivities in their own towns, with their own families. Rosie realized she ought to drag out the Christmas decorations from storage to decorate the Cove. It was usually something she did with her aunt and uncle, but she wasn't sure if either one of them would be in much of a mood to do it—especially with everything else that was going on, on top of her uncle's heart attack.

Her first Christmas in Turtle Lake, her aunt and uncle had tried their hardest to get Rosie into the Christmas spirit, but she'd repaid them by getting herself suspended the week before the

Christmas holiday. She expected that she'd suffer a long lecture from them, but instead, her uncle had taken her out on his johnboat and taken her fishing. They'd had a talk, and Rosie promised she'd try to make friends and wait at least six months before getting suspended again. In return, her uncle had promised her the cottage.

Not long after that, Rosie met Susannah in English class. And Susannah in turn introduced Rosie to her brother, Tommy, who became Rosie's first real boyfriend. There were so many people in this town Rosie loved, and even if she couldn't live in her beloved cottage, maybe she'd still be able to stay in town. Maybe she'd still be able to make herself useful.

"What are you doing just standing around like that?" Susannah asked from the salon entryway. "You're making the old ladies nervous."

"I always make them nervous," Rosie said. She hadn't even realized she'd walked all the way to Susannah's salon, which was aptly named Curl Up and Dye.

"They'd like you better if you'd let me give you a haircut," Susannah said, beckoning her inside.

"No," Rosie corrected her. "*You'd* like me better."

"Well, I've got time today," Susannah said. "Come have a seat in my chair."

Rosie groaned. She hated having her hair cut. She hated having anything done to her hair. She was so tender headed that even brushing it hurt, and Susannah was always threatening to cut it all off and give her a pixie cut just like she had. Besides, Rosie liked her hair just the way it was—long, brown, and out of control.

"Oh hush," Susannah said. "If you want to talk, I need to look busy."

"Fine," Rosie replied, relenting. "But no color."

"No color," Susannah agreed.

Rosie sat down. "I'm sorry I haven't called you back," she said.

"Or texted or come by or even sent out a smoke signal," Susannah said.

"Or any of those things, either," she agreed.

"I'm not mad about that," Susannah said. She took out a brush and began to run it through Rosie's hair.

Rosie winced.

"I'm mad that you didn't tell me what was going on at the Cove," her friend continued. "You could have told me you were in trouble."

"I didn't know," Rosie replied. "I mean, I knew, but I didn't know it was so bad. I didn't know they were thinking about selling."

"I don't blame them for not telling you."

"Why?" she wanted to know.

"Did you freak out when tall, dark, and handsome paid a visit?" Susannah asked. "Sit still. You're making this worse."

"No," she said.

"Really?"

Rosie sighed. "Okay, maybe a little."

"That's what I thought," Susannah said. "Okay, to the bowl to wash before your cut."

Rosie stood up. God, she hated the way she looked in salon mirrors. "I just wish there were something, some way to fix it."

"Sounds like selling would fix it," Susannah said.

"Without selling," Rosie said, sitting down and leaning back into the bowl. "Use that tea tree oil stuff you used last time."

"Got it," she said. "And I know. I know that's what you wish, but what can you do now?"

"There has to be something. I just haven't thought of it yet."

"Tommy says Connie and Irene were drooling over the guy working for the Lake Queen," Susannah continued. "What's his name?"

"Everett," she replied. "And they were."

"Irene hates everyone, so he must be good-looking."

"He's all right," Rosie said. "But he's the enemy."

"Of course he is," Susannah agreed. "Okay, get up. Back to my chair."

"Not too short," she reminded her friend. "Just trim the ends."

"Can I put a pink streak in?"

"No way."

"Fine," Susannah said. "You're no fun."

"I'm serious," Rosie warned.

"I know," Susannah replied. "You always are."

CHAPTER 16

Rosie

Rosie left the salon pleasantly surprised with her hair. This time, she'd actually let Susannah cut her bangs, and she knew her aunt would be thrilled that Rosie didn't have to constantly brush them out of her eyes.

"Hey!" Susannah called after her, charging down the street. "I remembered something!"

"What is it?" she asked, turning around. "I tipped you, I swear!"

"Not . . . that . . ." Susannah huffed. "God, I need to go back to the gym."

"That's what you remembered?" Rosie asked, grinning.

"No," Susannah said. "Look!" She produced a magazine—one of those magazines that everyone forgets exist until they're sitting in a beauty salon or a doctor's office.

"*Texas Southern Living*?" Rosie asked.

"Yeah," Susannah said, excited. "Turn to the back. Page 144."

Rosie did as she was told. At the bottom of the page, there was an ad that read "Discover Texas Diamonds in the Rough."

"It's a contest!" Susannah continued. "The magazine is advertising for readers to submit businesses that they think should be featured in the magazine. It's specifically for those that have fallen on 'hard times' and need a little work. First prize is a hundred thousand dollars and a Christmas photo shoot."

Rosie thought about it. "That's amazing," she said, finally. "But I don't know if that amount would save us."

"It might keep you afloat long enough to figure something out," Susannah countered. "And the publicity alone would probably drive some traffic your way."

"It might."

"Just think about it," Susannah said. "It's better than nothing, which is what you have right now."

"It says we'd need to submit an essay and photos of the business," Rosie replied. "I haven't written an essay since high school."

"I bet Justin would do it," Susannah said. "He's got to be a decent writer. He's a principal."

"We'll need to hurry," Rosie said. "The submission deadline is in two weeks, just after Thanksgiving."

"All right," Susannah said. "You talk to your aunt and uncle and see if they'll go for it. I'll talk to Justin. I have Elizabeth's dad scheduled for a color tomorrow after school."

"Thanks," Rosie said, reaching out to hug her friend. "You're the best."

"I know. Don't forget it."

Rosie rolled the magazine up and slid it into her bag.

When she got home that afternoon, after she'd tended to the bees and the dogs and of course Toulouse's incessant meowing until she fed him, Rosie sat down on the couch and flipped through the magazine. She had a vague recollection of seeing the exact same issue in the lobby of the Cove, but she couldn't be sure. She hadn't truly read a magazine since the prom issue of *Teen Vogue* her senior year in high school.

The contest sounded pretty straightforward. She'd need to write a short essay about why the Cove was a true diamond of Texas, and she'd need to send pictures of the Cove. The whole point was to show that the B and B had potential, even though it needed work, and Rosie thought there were probably plenty of ways she could show the charm of the place.

All she had to do was figure it out, and she had to convince her aunt and uncle not to sell in the meantime. Her uncle had a little more time before he was allowed to come home, which meant she could practice what she was going to say to them. If they truly wanted to sell, she'd know it by their response.

Rosie stood up and looked around her living room. The cottage was small—a kitchen and a living room that seemed to run together, a bedroom, and a bathroom. It was originally meant to be an extension of the Cove, a place people could rent to be near the amenities of the hotel but far enough away from everyone to feel private. It had needed work, though, and Rosie's uncle refused to hire anyone to help. After Rosie moved in with them, she helped him on the weekends and after school sometimes. Together, they'd ripped up the old shag carpet and sanded the hardwood floors underneath, replaced the windows, and given the outside a fresh coat of paint. She'd insisted on a light pink, which she thought at the time made the cottage look magical—like a fairy hideout in the middle of a forest. Uncle Joe hadn't protested. They'd driven to Austin one afternoon and bought the paint, which was the exact color of a house she'd seen on the Florida coast one summer on a trip with her mother and stepfather.

Her mother.

Rosie sat back down onto the couch with a thud. They rarely spoke, and when they did, the conversation was never pleasant. Her mother, Katherine, was Aunt Mary's younger sister by five years. They couldn't have been more different people. Katherine was pushy and demanding in all the places Mary was soft and understanding. They both had a temper, to be sure, but Rosie had only seen her aunt's temper flare once or twice in her whole life, and it was never directed at her. Katherine, on the other hand, seemed to save her temper for Rosie. At least, that's how Rosie had seen it as a teenager.

Now their conversations centered more on her mother's despair that Rosie hadn't gone to college and resentment that Rosie treated Aunt Mary more like a mother than she did Katherine. Rosie knew that her mother had aspirations for Rosie that centered around her only daughter going to a good school, earning an MBA like she had, getting a high-paying job, and starting a family so that Katherine could be the doting mother she'd never been to Rosie.

Instead, Rosie was single, still living on her aunt and uncle's property, and selling honeybee products that scarcely earned her enough to get by. Still, it was the life Rosie had chosen, and she was proud of it. She knew who she was, even if her mother didn't understand.

For a moment, Rosie was tempted to pick up her phone and call her mother to tell her about the trouble at the Cove. She knew that her aunt Mary hadn't told her. Their relationship was about as strained as Rosie and Katherine's, but Rosie also knew that if she told her mother that they needed money, she'd offer it up. There would be strings attached, of course, but if they could keep the Cove, wouldn't it be worth it?

Her right hand hovered above her phone. She could call. It would only take a few minutes to explain. Then she thought about the look on her aunt's face when she told her she'd called Katherine for help and thought better of it. If her aunt wanted to call, that was one thing, but Rosie knew it wasn't her place. The only thing she could do, she knew, was to figure out another way to help—without telling her mother.

As if on cue, her phone began to ring. She stared at her mother's name on the screen, paralyzed.

"Hello?"

"Rosie!" her mother said. "What in the *hell* is going on in Texas?"

"What?" Rosie asked. "Nothing! What do you mean?"

"I just got off the phone with Mary," her mother continued. "Why didn't you call me about Joe?"

Rosie hesitated. Why hadn't she? There were a couple of reasons, she guessed, neither of which she wanted to tell her mother. Firstly, she didn't want to, and secondly, she didn't think Aunt

Mary wanted her to. "Well," Rosie said, finally. "I didn't really think it was my place."

"You're supposed to keep me informed!" Katherine replied. "You know they're getting older."

"Mom," she said, already feeling a headache coming on. "You're only five years younger than both of them."

"I've always been in perfect health."

"I know. You're perfect."

"Don't get snotty with me," her mother said. "I'm just calling to check on things. You know Mary downplays everything."

"Uncle Joe is going to be okay," Rosie said. "Really, he is. They moved him to a rehab facility for the next week or so, and then he gets to come home."

"Mary didn't tell me any of that," Katherine said. "She told me he was going to live, and she got off the phone with me as quickly as possible."

Right then, Rosie wished she knew how to get off the phone with her mother as quickly as possible. Instead, she just said, "Well, now you know everything that I know."

Her mother sighed. "Rick said we could get in the car right now and drive down there tonight if you need us to."

"I don't think that's necessary, Mom," Rosie said, feeling panic rise in her throat. "Really, I don't."

"Who's taking care of the bed-and-breakfast while this is happening?" Katherine continued. "You?"

"Yeah," she replied. "Yes, I'm taking care of it."

"You don't sound very sure about that, sweetheart. Are you sure you don't need help?"

There was no way Rosie was going to let her mother come to Turtle Lake and allow her to see the nearly abandoned Cove. She'd just make a huge deal out of it and try to fix it, and all that was going to do was put Rosie's aunt in the hospital bed next to Uncle Joe.

"I'm sure," Rosie said. "It's not quite the holidays, and we don't have many guests right now, anyway. I'm fine looking after Corgi Cove by myself for the time being, I promise."

"Will you please keep me updated?" her mother continued. "I don't think your aunt will tell me the truth about anything. She never wants me to worry."

Worry wasn't the term Rosie would have picked, but she was going to go with it. "I will," she said. "I love you."

"I love you, too, honey," her mother said.

Rosie collapsed onto the couch as soon as the call was over. Bonnie and Clyde, who'd been asleep by the door, woke up when Rosie sighed heavily, and the two of them pranced over and jumped up on either side of her. Toulouse eyed them warily from his position on the floor in front of the fish tank.

"It's fine," she told him. "I'm allowed to love them, too."

Toulouse sneezed in response.

In some ways, she wished she could tell her mother about the Cove. She wished she could tell her about the way business had fallen off over the last few years, about the wear and tear, and about the way they were so close to losing it all. She knew in her heart that her mother would figure out a way for them to stay, but at the end of the day, her aunt Mary would never stand for that. It wasn't a pride issue, not really. It was just that if her mother fixed it, if she took out a loan or gave them money, or anything like that, then they'd all be indebted to her forever. She'd have a say, an opinion, and Katherine always had opinions about everything. Besides, just like it wasn't her place to tell her mother about Uncle Joe, it wasn't her place to tell her about the Cove. For now, she'd just have to let it be whatever it was going to be.

And that's when she remembered the magazine that Susannah had given her. She reached over to the end table and snatched it up, flipping through the pages until she got to the information about the contest.

It was interesting, that was for sure. The concept was to entice older, historic hotels to enter to win a "diamond in the rough" contest. "Find the quaint and the charming!" the advertisement read. "Discover old Texas!" The rules were simple—each business that chose to enter had to send in a video and several photographs of the building, along with an essay about why it deserved to be selected as a finalist. The entries were due by December 1, which by now was less than a month away. The three finalists would be featured on the magazine's website for people to vote for their favorite, and the winner would be selected and announced on Christmas Eve. The winner, the advertisement read, would receive a "dream makeover" and a one hundred thousand dollar cash prize, plus free advertising for a year.

Rosie read the article over and over until she had convinced herself that the Cove could win. This was something she was going to have to pitch to her aunt and uncle—something that she would have to convince them they had a chance to win, if they could just hold off on signing anything until the first of the year. Surely, she thought, that could be done.

Absently, she stroked Bonnie's head, and Bonnie whimpered a bit in her sleep. Rosie knew that both of the dogs missed her aunt and uncle and that she was a poor substitute. She hated not being able to explain to them why they were staying with her and not at home with their custom-made dog beds that Uncle Joe made and lovely manicured yard. She liked to pretend that they annoyed her, but the truth was that she found them comforting, especially right now. They were like snoring, weighted blankets. When they went home next week, she'd miss the way they slept right next to her.

At least they all, she and the dogs, had a home, and if she had anything to do with it, she'd keep it that way.

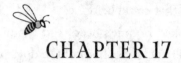

CHAPTER 17

Everett

In Everett's dream, he was in a boat with his father somewhere in Michigan. The dream was a memory from when he'd been seventeen years old. His father, Ralph, had taken him out to tell him that he was planning to get married to the woman he'd been dating for the last year, and he'd wanted to tell Everett first, to see what he thought, before he told Everett's younger sister, Celine.

The dream was different, though, because in his dream, there was a storm brewing in the distance, and Everett knew that day had been sunny, gorgeous. Nothing about the dream felt right. As the clouds rolled in, Everett tried to convince his father that he was perfectly fine with his would-be stepmother, but his father just kept telling him over and over that Nadine would never be his mother but that she was good for the whole family.

Everett agreed. Still, it didn't matter what he said. The closer the storm got, the more frantic his father became.

When he woke up, Everett was in a cold sweat, the covers bunched around his feet at the base of the bed. He always had bad dreams when he was under stress, ever since he was a teenager. An ex-girlfriend, who also happened to be a psychologist, told him that it was because he didn't express his anxiety and frustration on the outside as much as he should.

He'd thought, quite stupidly, that spending a little time outside of New York City, even though it wasn't his choice, might be relaxing. He thought he could make an easy sale and then take some time for himself, but the reality was, even on Saturday, he felt like he needed to work. He hadn't heard from anyone at the Cove since the day he'd taken Rosie and the corgis to see Mary and Joe, and he was beginning to get anxious, especially with Francesca breathing down his neck.

He got out of bed, made himself a cup of coffee, and showered. Afterward, he felt better and decided it might be a pretty good idea to reach out to Mary, just to check in. He wouldn't talk business—he'd just see how they were doing.

Mary answered on the first ring.

"Mr. St. Claire," she said. "How are you doing?"

"Oh, I'm good, Mrs. Roberts." Everett smiled into the phone. He genuinely liked her. "I can't believe it's so warm out. I'd be dressing for winter in New York."

"Are you missing home right now?" Mary asked.

"Nah," he replied, even though he was, in fact, missing home. "I'm enjoying the warmer weather."

"Texas is the best," Mary said, her voice full of pride. "And please, if I haven't said this before, call me Mary."

"Call me Everett," he said. "I'm sorry to bother you this morning, but I just wanted to call and check on Mr. Roberts and see how he's doing. I should also apologize for the Jell-O incident last time."

"No apologies necessary," she said. "It was all in good fun, and the nurses have mostly forgiven us."

"That's good to hear." Everett hesitated, trying to decide if he could shift the conversation, even though he'd told himself that he wasn't going to discuss business.

"Is there something I can help you with, hon?" Mary asked.

"Well, I know it's Saturday, but I thought if you'd like, I might bring you some paperwork to look over, since I didn't have the opportunity to leave you any during our first meeting," Everett replied, hoping he sounded nonchalant. He didn't want to seem pushy, and something about this phone call felt risky.

"That would be just fine," Mary replied, much to his relief. "But you know, Rosie is going to be in Austin today for the farmers' market. Why don't you just take it to her while she's in town?"

Shit. Shit. Shit. The absolute last thing he wanted to do was take any paperwork to Rosie. "Okay," he said. "That sounds great."

"She won't bite," Mary said with a laugh.

"I don't know about that." He wondered how Mary knew that the thought of seeing Rosie made him more nervous than he was willing to admit.

"I'll make her promise," Mary said. "And I'll send her a text to let her know you're coming."

"Great," Everett said, ignoring the inner voice that told him this was a mistake. "I'll make sure she gets the paperwork today!"

CHAPTER 18

Rosie

Although Rosie's primary bee product was honey, there were bees-wax products besides the arthritis salve that she took with her to the Austin farmers' market once a month. She also made scented wax melts, body butter, and sometimes beard wax. In truth, she'd started making the beard wax to lure the cute goat farmer over to her booth. She'd already bought more woolen mittens than she'd EVER need to wear in Texas. Now it was his turn.

"I'm not going to be gone that long," she said to the dogs. They were watching her from behind the screen door. "I'll bring back treats!"

Their ears perked up slightly at the word, but they started barking when she turned her back to begin load-ing the truck. Right now, she wished she had her uncle's muscle. He always helped her load the truck before she went to Austin. It made her miss him and then, for some reason she couldn't explain, Rosie wanted to sit down and cry.

"I thought you might like an extra hand."

Rosie turned around to see Tommy standing there, awkward, with his hands in his pockets.

"Hey!" she said. "Thanks, Tommy. You're a lifesaver. I've got about three more baskets in the house, but I'm afraid if I go in there, the dogs will tie me up and make me stay home."

"Kinda hard to do without opposable thumbs," Tommy joked.

"You underestimate them," Rosie said to him as he jogged up the steps of the front porch. "Be careful."

Tommy returned a few minutes later with all three baskets perched precariously on top of one another. "You were right about the dogs," he said. "They're monsters."

"They licked your jeans, didn't they?"

Tommy nodded. "They licked my jeans."

Rosie laughed. She knew the dogs loved Tommy. Truthfully, there was a lot to love. He was kind and fun, and he was nearly always in a good mood. Sometimes she wondered why things hadn't worked out between them, but even when he was being cute and helpful like he was now, deep down she knew why—they didn't love each other. Not like that. Sure, Tommy thought he loved her, but he didn't, not really. What he loved was the idea of the two of them together, high school sweethearts, raising a family.

That wasn't what she wanted . . . at least, not with Tommy.

"Do you want me to go with you?" he asked, breaching her thoughts. "I'm free today. My dad's got the shop closed so he can remodel the kitchen."

"And you're telling me Tom Sr. didn't tell you that you had to help him?" Rosie asked.

"Oh, he told me I had to help him," Tommy replied. "But I told him that I couldn't because I had to go to Austin with you."

"Nice try," Rosie said.

"Please," he begged. "I have to listen to him bitch at me all week at the shop. Don't make me spend my Saturday doing it, too."

"Go help your dad," she ordered. "Go on."

"Fine," Tommy said, releasing a long-suffering sigh. "But I'm not going to like it."

Rosie laughed and pulled her phone from her pocket when she heard the ding of a text message. It was from her aunt, and Rosie's heart leaped into her throat, thinking maybe something awful had happened with Uncle Joe.

Everett St. Claire is coming by the farmers' market to bring you some paperwork. Be. Nice.

Rosie stared at the message. Just great.

What kind of paperwork? Rosie typed back.

Just be nice.

Rosie shoved her phone back into her pocket and started up the truck. She wasn't going to promise anything.

The farmers' market was buzzing by the time Rosie got her booth set up. Her friend Miranda, who sold cheese and butter from her small hobby farm, was full of farmers' market gossip.

"Did you hear that Mac and Libby are getting a divorce?" she asked Rosie. "Apparently, Libby was 'crystal healing' with some-one else."

"What?" Rosie asked. "Who?"

Miranda shrugged. "I don't know. I've asked around, and ev-eryone seems to think it was Mark, the ostrich jerky guy."

"That's going to make the vegans really mad," Rosie replied, stacking her body butters into a pyramid on her table.

"You're telling me," Miranda said. "She's going to have to move over to their side if she's not careful."

"I remember when that happened to Clarence," Rosie said. "Remember, he had to set up between Mark and Tony."

"Who's Tony?"

"You know him He's the guy who has the pickled pork."

"That's right!" Miranda exclaimed. "Poor Clarence. He never sold a thing after that."

"I know," Rosie said with a shudder. "Don't mess with the vegans."

"Oh my God, Rosie," her friend said, scurrying over to Rosie's booth and gripping her arm. "It's him. It's the HGF."

Rosie craned her neck to look past the crowd and four booths to the right. There he was. The Hot Goat Farmer in the flesh.

"He's so hot," Miranda said, using a flyer for Rosie's honey to fan herself. "You should go talk to him."

"You go talk to him," Rosie replied. "I did it last month."

"You didn't talk to him. You bought more mittens."

"I told you never to speak of that," Rosie said. "Besides, back in September, you bought two scarves. Who needs *two* wool scarves?"

"I'll buy whatever he's selling." Miranda smirked. "All right. I'll go. Mama needs a new scarf."

Rosie laughed as her friend walked toward HGF's booth. The two had been lusting after him for nearly a year, but in truth, she hoped Miranda had a shot. She'd gone through a divorce not long ago, and now she was a single mom with two little girls and a farm to run by herself. If anybody deserved a Hot Goat Farmer, it was her.

"Excuse me?"

Rosie looked away from her friend and focused on the woman standing in front of her, holding up a pot of the body butter.

"I'm sorry," Rosie said. "I didn't see you there."

"That's okay." The woman looked flushed. Like she'd been rushing around. "Can you tell me the ingredients in this?"

"Oh," Rosie said, taking the pot and turning it upside down. "The ingredients are right here on the bottom."

"Thanks," the woman said. "Sorry."

"That's okay," Rosie replied. "You look hot. Do you want a bottle of water or something?"

"That would be great," the woman said. "I feel like I might pass out."

"Come sit down," Rosie said, directing her behind the booth. "Take a minute to cool off."

"I can't sit here for too long," the woman said, looking around, her voice anxious.

"Carrie!" came a voice, rising up amidst the throng. "Carrie! Where are you?"

"Oh shit," the woman said. "That's my boss."

"Carrie!" A tall redhead stomped up to the booth. "What are you doing back there? And, oh my God, is that *bottled water* in your hand?"

"I'm so sorry, Breezy," the woman said. "It's just so hot today, and I . . ."

"It's fine," Breezy said, waving her off. "But I'm in a hurry, so if you didn't find anything, please put that cancer bottle down and let's go."

She didn't even look in Rosie's direction, but for a second, Rosie thought she looked familiar. Like someone she'd seen somewhere, but she couldn't figure it out. Maybe she was a regular at the farmers' market or something.

Poor Carrie looked so exhausted that Rosie felt bad for her. "Is there something in particular you're looking for?" she asked. "Maybe I can help you."

"I doubt it," Breezy said. She glanced over Rosie's wares and continued. "I'm looking for something *all natural,* and from the look of these plastic containers, you can't help me."

Rosie worked very carefully not to roll her eyes. "Actually," she replied, "these containers are completely biodegradable, and the beeswax products inside of them are one hundred percent all natural and organic."

From the corner of her eye, Rosie saw Breezy's assistant take a sip of the bottled water.

"Oh really?" the redhead said, slightly more interested. "What does it smell like?" She picked up a container and popped the top off, ignoring the tester Rosie set out. She put it up to her nose. "Not bad."

"The body butter is a customer favorite," Rosie said. "I usually sell out just an hour or so after setting up."

"I'll take them," Breezy said, snapping at her assistant, who hopped up. "How many do you have? Is this it?"

"You want them all?" Rosie asked, shocked. "There are twenty of them."

"Are you sure you don't have any more in the back somewhere?" Breezy asked.

Rosie turned around. She wasn't sure what "back" Breezy was referring to, but all she saw were the empty baskets she'd used to haul her products. "No," she said. "This is it."

"Do you take special orders?"

"Not this late in the season."

"So, this is it?" Breezy asked. "Nobody else will be able to buy these from you?"

"Not until the spring," Rosie replied, furrowing her brow.

"Exclusive," Breezy said, gleeful. "Perfect."

Rosie looked over at the woman's assistant, but she only shrugged and said, "Do you take cash or card?"

"Uh, either one," Rosie replied, calculating the expense in her head.

"Great," Breezy said. "Carrie, give her my Amex."

Carrie did as she was told, and Rosie's eyes widened when she took the black Amex from the woman's hand and put it into her Square reader. While Breezy signed the receipt, Rosie bagged up all twenty of the body butters and slid one of her cards in with them.

"Thank you," Rosie said. "I hope you two have a great day."

"Thanks for the water," Carrie said, giving Rosie a small smile as she hurried after her boss and disappeared into the crowd.

"Holy shit, Rosie, do you know who that was?" Miranda asked, trudging up to her, a fuchsia woolen scarf in her hands.

"Who?" Rosie asked. "That woman who just bought *all twenty* of my body butters?"

"She bought them all?" Miranda replied, incredulous. "Wow."

"Who is it?" Rosie asked. "She looks familiar, but I can't place her. Does she have a booth here?"

"That's Breezy Cole," Miranda hissed through the gap in her front two teeth. "She's *famous* here in Austin."

"Why?" Rosie asked. "Is she on TV or something?"

"She's an influencer," Miranda replied. "You know, like on social media, *and* she has her own decorating show on Austin public television. She's a big deal here."

"I thought she looked familiar," Rosie mused. "But I couldn't figure it out."

"Big. Deal," Miranda repeated.

"Well, she bought all of my body butter," Rosie replied. "So, I guess I should be excited."

"Oh!" Miranda squealed, grabbing Rosie's hand. "Maybe she'll feature you on her show or her blog or her Insta!"

"Maybe," Rosie said with a laugh. Then, looking past Miranda, she saw HGF heading in their direction. "Hey, why is Hot Goat Farmer walking toward us?"

"Huh?" Miranda turned around.

"You forgot your receipt," HGF said, hurrying up to them.

"Oh," Miranda said, blushing. "Thanks, uh, Dillon."

"Dillon?" Rosie mouthed to her friend.

Miranda shrugged.

"Hello," Dillon the Hot Goat Farmer said to Rosie. "I remember you. You always buy my mittens."

"I have an aunt in Vermont who loves them," Rosie said, feeling gross for lying and relieved she thought of it.

Miranda elbowed her in the ribs, but she ignored it.

"That's great," Dillon replied. He flashed the women a perfect smile. "I appreciate my loyal customers."

Rosie could see that Miranda was about to melt into a steamy puddle of water right in front of them, and just as she was about to crack a joke, she saw another familiar figure in the distance. This time, however, there was no question about who the person was—it was Everett, and he was headed straight for them.

CHAPTER 19

Everett

Everett saw Rosie before she saw him. She was right where her aunt Mary said she would be—in the far corner of the market, honey glistening in glass jars on her table. At present, Rosie was talking to another woman and a man, all three of them engrossed in a conversation, and Everett could see the way the other woman was looking at the man, as if she wanted nothing more than to devour him for breakfast.

He couldn't tell what Rosie's face looked like. He could barely make out her profile, and she had her arms crossed over her chest. As he walked closer toward them, he could see that her expression was one of amusement, and for some reason, he much preferred this over the lustful expression of the other woman.

When Rosie saw Everett, though, her expression changed to one of annoyance.

She seemed to be silently asking him, *What the fuck are you doing here?* Even though he knew that she knew why he was there. He held up the folder to her just to make sure.

"Hey," he said, trying to sound casual.

Rosie narrowed her eyes at him.

"Rosie?" Miranda asked. "Who's your friend?"

"He's not my friend," she said.

"That's hurtful," Everett replied. And in truth, it was a little bit hurtful. It was true, they weren't friends, not technically, but she didn't have to say it like that. He stuck out his hand to the woman. "Hi, I'm Everett."

"Miranda," she said, smiling.

"And I'm Dillon," the man said. He'd been silent until now. "But I better get back to my booth." He handed Miranda a scrap of paper with scribbles on it. "Here's your receipt." He gave them all a short wave and trotted off in the opposite direction.

Miranda looked down at the receipt. "His phone number is on it!" she gasped.

"What?" Rosie asked, snatching the receipt from Miranda's hands. "Oh my God, it is!"

"How long do I have to wait to call him?" Miranda asked. "Can I do it right now?"

Rosie laughed. "Maybe wait a day or two."

"Fine," Miranda said, pouting. "What if he changes his mind?"

"He won't," Everett said, speaking up. "If he gave you his number, he isn't going to change his mind."

Miranda looked up from the receipt to Everett. Then she looked over to Rosie, who was trying to look anywhere but at him. "So, this man isn't your friend?"

"We're business associates," he said quickly.

Rosie made a noise that sounded a little bit like a sneeze and a little bit like a cough. "Yeah," she said, finally. "Sure, we're *business associates*."

"I'm confused," Miranda said.

"He's just here to give me some paperwork." She held out her hand.

Everett didn't hand it over right away. Instead, he stood there smiling at her. "This is a nice place," he said. "I might have to take a walk around and see what's for sale."

Rosie squared her shoulders at him territorially.

New understanding dawned on Miranda's face. "You're that guy!" she exclaimed. "The guy who's trying to steal the Cove."

"I'd pay for it, I assure you," Everett replied smoothly. He didn't want to show Rosie and her friend how much that comment annoyed him. "Rather, the company would pay for it."

"Nobody's paying for it," Rosie said.

"Nevertheless," Everett said, dismissing her, "I have paperwork I need for you to take to your aunt and uncle. They said the fax machine at the Cove is broken and, for some reason, they don't have email?"

"I have email," Rosie replied. "But we don't have an official email for the Cove."

"It's the twenty-first century," Everett said. "How does a business not have an email address?"

"We got one a few years ago," she explained. "But my uncle . . . well, he let his friend Marty convince him to send money to a Nigerian prince, and my aunt banned them both from the computer."

Everett's lips twitched, but he managed to keep his smile hidden.

For a moment, they were both silent, and Everett was keenly aware that Rosie's friend Miranda was watching their exchange with great interest. He liked Rosie, even if she didn't like him, and he told himself that maybe if they'd met under different circumstances, they could have at the least been friends.

Everett didn't have very many friends, especially female friends, but that didn't stop him from wondering if Rosie might like him if she only got to know him.

Miranda cleared her throat. "Um, we should get back to our booths," she said.

"Right," Rosie replied, almost as if she'd forgotten all about it. She looked at Everett.

He looked down at his folder and frowned. "Shit, this is the wrong one," he said. "I'll go and grab the right one from my car."

Rosie turned around and walked toward her booth, and Everett set off in the other direction, headed for where his car was parked at the other end of the farmers' market. Finding parking had been a bear, and he was embarrassed to realize when he arrived that he'd never considered coming to the farmers' market before today, even though it was just a few blocks from his apartment.

Admittedly, he thought, he hadn't been doing much with the exception of working. He liked the convenience of his apartment—

close to nearly every amenity the city could offer him, including nightlife. It was rare that he went out after making it home, however. The Cove was his top priority, and he'd been focusing all his energy on it in the hopes that he could get back to New York mostly unscathed. Still, he liked the warm sun on his face as he walked, and he liked the way everyone here seemed so laid-back, like they weren't really in a hurry to get anywhere. It was so opposite of what he was used to that it had taken him a while to understand that the people in Texas weren't trying to annoy him by their pace, they were simply unbothered.

Everett opened up his car door and pulled out the manila envelope containing the documents he needed to give to Rosie. They weren't anything official, just a proposal for Joe and Mary to look over. He didn't want to rush them, had no intention of rushing them, but they knew just as well as he did that they'd be in fore-closure by the New Year if they didn't agree to the sale. Getting an email address would help, he thought, finally allowing himself to smile, but there wasn't anything that could fix the dire situation at Corgi Cove that wasn't short of a miracle.

And he didn't deal in miracles. He dealt in cold, hard truths. He dealt in facts. He dealt in numbers, and he dealt in *reality*, a place Rosie clearly didn't live in if she thought she had time to do anything that would save the hotel.

As he neared her booth, he watched her laughing and smiling with her friend and passersby. He had never seen her like this. She looked relaxed and happy—a far cry from the way she looked when they'd interacted. He looked down at the envelope he was carrying and was tempted to take it back to his car. If he handed it to her, she'd stop laughing and smiling, and for some reason, the thought bothered him.

But he couldn't do that. He was here to do a job, and that job involved delivering paperwork. Miranda saw him first, and she nudged Rosie as he continued moving toward them. Rosie's smile faded, but it didn't go away completely, and Everett sighed with relief.

Rosie looked away and back at the customer standing in front of her, who was counting out crisp bills.

"I'm going to give each of your jars their own bag," Rosie said, sliding a jar of honey into a paper bag labeled *Rosie's Honey Pot* in light pink lettering. "If you bring the jars back to me, I'll give you a 10 percent discount on your next purchase."

"Great," the woman in front of Rosie replied. "I'll be sure and do that."

"Have a good rest of your day!" Rosie said cheerily.

Everett picked up a jar of honey and inspected it. "How much?" he asked.

"Usually, it's ten dollars a jar," she replied. "But for you? Twenty dollars."

He looked up at her. "I'll take one," he said. "Do you take American Express?"

Rosie rolled her eyes. "No."

"Yes you do!" Miranda exclaimed. "You just took . . ."

Rosie gave her a look, and her friend clamped her mouth shut, amusement dancing in her eyes.

Everett reached into his wallet and pulled out a twenty-dollar bill. "Here," he said.

Rosie accepted it, and when she didn't even attempt to give him change, he chuckled. "You weren't joking," he said.

She was about to respond when the sky, which had been clear minutes earlier, clouded over and there was a clap of thunder in the distance.

"Is it supposed to rain today?" Miranda asked, looking up.

"I don't think so," Rosie said. "At least, my weather app didn't alert me."

"Do you think we should close up?"

Rosie shrugged. "I don't know. I don't have a ton of product left, anyway."

"I do," Miranda said, slightly deflated. "But if it starts to rain and we don't pack up, everything will be soggy. Nobody wants to buy soggy cheese."

When the first fat raindrops began to fall, nearly everyone at the farmers' market decided to pack up, and it was a frenzy of breaking down stands and loading up vehicles. Everett helped Rosie and Miranda get as much as they could out of the rain. Most of what Rosie had could be put into the front of her pickup truck, and when they were finished, they were all three soaking wet.

Miranda waved at them as she drove off, and Rosie, water dripping from her bangs and eyelashes, gave him a curt nod.

"Thanks," she said. "I should really get going."

"I left the paperwork in the truck," Everett said.

Rosie slid into her truck, and he waited, as was the gentlemanly thing to do, for her to pull away. He watched as she tried to start the truck, listened to the sounds of the engine attempting in vain to start over and over before he finally knocked on her window.

For a moment, he thought she was going to ignore him, and he felt annoyance rise in his throat. Here he was, standing in the rain, trying to help her, and she wanted nothing to do with him.

"It does this all the time," Rosie said. "Especially when it rains."

"I can take you back to Turtle Lake," Everett said. "Come on."

She shook her head. "I just need to wait for it to stop raining."

"Get out of the truck, Rosie," Everett replied. "Come on, let me take you home."

"But I—"

"Fine," Everett said, cutting her off. "If you want to sit here for the rest of the damn day, be my guest."

He was at his limit. He'd tried being nice, and she wasn't having any of it. If she wanted to be ridiculous, he didn't have to stick around for it.

He turned on his heel and began to walk away. Just before he was out of earshot, he heard her yell, "Fine!"

She got out of the truck and slammed the door behind her, scurrying toward him.

"Change your mind?" he asked.

"I can't just leave the truck parked here," Rosie said. "Not for too long."

"We can figure that out," Everett replied, stepping up his pace as the rain began to fall faster and harder. "Let's just get out of the rain."

"Where are you parked?" she asked.

"On the other side," he replied. "Come on."

"I cannot believe this," Rosie said once they were in his car. "I cannot believe this is how my damn day is going."

"Lucky I was here," Everett said, only half joking.

Rosie looked over at him. He could tell she wanted to be mad, wanted to say something snarky to him, but she just didn't have it in her. He liked this weary expression she was wearing even less than he liked it when she was being rude to him.

"Yes," she said, finally. "Thank you."

"Hey," he said, resisting the urge to reach out and put his hand on her shoulder. "It'll be okay. We'll get the truck towed back if we have to, but we'll figure it out."

"We?"

Everett gave her a lopsided grin. "We're stuck in this together," he said. "Like it or not, at least for now."

CHAPTER 20

Rosie

Rosie felt her spirits begin to lift as they drove toward Turtle Lake. The day hadn't turned out like she'd hoped, but she'd sold more than she thought she would, and even though it wasn't much, it was something more than she'd had when she woke up that morning. At least, that's what her uncle Joe would have told her if he'd been there. He always tried to look on the bright side of things, even though it wasn't in her nature. She was more like Aunt Mary, expecting the worst and secretly hoping for the best.

Her uncle kept them both on an even keel, a lifeboat when Rosie felt like she might drown. She'd be lying to herself if she couldn't admit that without him, no matter how temporary, she felt lost. Without them both, it felt like chaos.

"Are you all right over there?" Everett asked her. "You look like you're really thinking about something."

"I'm fine," Rosie said automatically. "I mean, I'm soaking wet, and I've probably ruined your seats." She smiled. "I'm actually all right now that I think about it."

"My seats will be fine," he replied. "Hope that doesn't, uh, dampen your spirits too much."

"Hilarious," Rosie quipped. "Oh, hey! Hey!"

"What?" Everett asked. "What? What's happening?"

"Pull over up here," she said, pointing just ahead of them.

"Where?"

"On the left," Rosie said, continuing to point. "Oto's Diner. See the rooster?"

Everett turned into the parking lot of a ramshackle building with a giant rooster statue off to the side. The red paint was peeling in strips from its comb.

"Is this place open?" he asked, peering through the rain. "It looks abandoned."

"The parking lot is in the back," Rosie replied. "Drive around and then ask me if it's abandoned."

Sure enough, when Everett drove around to the back of the diner, the lot was completely full, and he had to squeeze between two rusted pickup trucks to park.

"They have the best pie in the state," Rosie said when Everett still looked doubtful. "Just trust me."

"What kind of pie?" Everett asked.

She eyed him. "When was the last time you ate anything that even resembled a home-cooked meal?" she asked.

"Um, 2003?" Everett replied.

Rosie laughed. "You're going to love it here."

When she pushed the door to the diner open, the smell of food filled her, and she nearly cried with happiness. She always tried to stop by Oto's on her way home from the farmers' market, but she didn't always make it, and this time, it had been two months since her last visit.

"They're staring at us," Everett whispered to her.

"No," Rosie replied. "They're staring at you. You look like the city."

She nearly giggled when Everett looked down at himself in confusion. Then she heard a booming voice from behind the counter yell, "Rosie! My Rosie!"

A man, who was not nearly as big as the giant rooster, but filled the room nonetheless, approached Rosie. He was wearing a hairnet and carrying a spatula, a gold-capped smile stretching across his face.

"Oto!" Rosie exclaimed, opening her arms wide to hug him. "I've missed you, old man!"

"Old man?" Oto asked, feigning irritation. "What old man? I see no old man here!"

"You better find a mirror quick," she joked.

"How is Joe?" Oto wanted to know. "I text him, but Mary respond to tell me he is asleep."

"He's doing better," Rosie replied. "He should be home next week."

"That is good." Oto looked from Rosie to Everett and then said, "I have two more questions for you." He held up two fingers on a three-fingered hand—the hand not carrying the spatula. "Who is this, and where is my honey?"

"Oh!" Rosie reached down into her bag and pulled out a jar of honey. "I put one for you in my bag this morning so I wouldn't forget."

"Thank you," Oto said. "And your friend?"

"He's not—" Rosie began, and then stopped herself. "This is Everett."

"Nice to meet you," Oto said. His tone wasn't exactly friendly, but Rosie had never known Oto to be particularly friendly to anyone he hadn't known for at least a decade.

Everett looked down at Oto's three-fingered hand, but he didn't hesitate to shake it, much to Rosie's relief. She'd seen Oto physically throw men out for staring too long or making an off-handed comment. The rumor was that he'd lost his fingers in a bar fight in his home country of the Czech Republic, but her uncle Joe told her Oto lost them in a tussle with a gator a few years before the diner opened. Rosie had always thought that was a much better story.

"Sit down, sit down," Oto directed them. "Tell me what you wish to have."

"Do you have a menu?" Everett asked.

Oto raised an eyebrow.

"We'll both have the chicken fried steak," Rosie said. "And two pieces of pecan pie."

"Good," Oto replied, not taking his eyes off Everett. "Menu," he muttered. "*Směšný.*"

"He seems like a sweetheart," Everett said once Oto walked away.

"You asked for a menu," she replied. "Oto doesn't do menus."

"How is anybody supposed to order?" Everett asked. "I've never been here before."

Rosie shrugged. "Oto doesn't get a lot of outsiders. If you don't already know what you want to eat, then you're probably here by mistake."

"You could have warned me," he grumbled.

"I'm sorry," Rosie said, not sorry at all. "But you'll like the chicken fried steak. It's his specialty."

Everett sat back in his seat and surveyed his surroundings, and she watched him. He didn't look nearly as uncomfortable as she would be in such a situation, and she was impressed. He looked out of place in his khakis and crisp white shirt, but he didn't look like he *felt* out of place.

"So is this one of those places where everybody knows everybody?" Everett asked.

Rosie nodded. "For the most part. My uncle and Oto have known each other for years. Oto worked at the Cove before he opened his restaurant."

He looked over at Oto, who was back behind the diner counter. He was an imposing figure, tall and broad. "Was he security or something?"

"No," Rosie said with a laugh. "He mostly did odd jobs around the hotel. He helped Uncle Joe fix up the cottage for me. He's a good guy."

"A good guy not to cross," Everett replied.

"Maybe I should tell him you're trying to shut us down," Rosie said, only half joking.

Everett quirked an eyebrow. "I *will* leave you here."

"No you won't. Because for some reason, you think you need me on your side to convince my aunt and uncle to sell."

"I don't need you on my side," he said. "It would be nice, but I don't need you."

Rosie sat back as Oto brought their food and set it in front of them. It smelled so good, she nearly forgot how irritated she was that Everett had the audacity to think he didn't need her, even though she knew he was right.

"Eat," Oto commanded.

"Thank you, Oto," Rosie said, beaming up at him. "It looks great."

"Less talk. More eating."

Rosie picked up her napkin, unrolled her silverware, and placed the napkin in her lap. "Try it," she said to Everett.

He did as he was told. Neither one of them spoke again until they were nearly finished.

"You were right," he said finally. "This was very good."

"I told you so," Rosie replied, pleased with herself. "You should taste his Thanksgiving meal. It's like winning the food lottery."

"Thanksgiving is coming up," Everett said. "I'd almost forgotten."

"Me, too," Rosie admitted. "There's been so much going on that I haven't even thought about it."

"Do you have a big dinner with your aunt and uncle?" he asked.

Rosie nodded her head. "Yes. Every year. In fact, Oto cooks, and we have a few people from town over to the Cove." She paused for a minute, unsure if she should say the next part. "It's the only time the place has been full for the last couple of years."

"I will come this year," Oto said, appearing in front of them. He had a plate of pie in each hand.

"I'm not sure if my aunt and uncle will be up to it," she replied.

"We must," Oto said. He set down the plates. "Joe will not go hungry."

Rosie smiled up at him. "Okay," she said. "Maybe seeing everyone will be good for Uncle Joe."

Everett stuck his fork down into the pecan pie and said, "I love pie."

Oto let out a rare laugh. "It is the best, yes?"

"Yes," Everett agreed, his mouth full.

"You will come to Thanksgiving," Oto said. It wasn't a question.

"He lives in Austin," Rosie said, answering the non-question for Everett. "I'm sure he has his own plans."

"Actually," Everett said, lifting his napkin to his mouth, "I don't have any plans for Thanksgiving. I'd love to come."

She narrowed her eyes at him, but Everett was pretending not to notice. What was he doing? He couldn't come to Thanksgiving. Especially not with half the town there. It wasn't a day to do business, and she knew that the second he felt like he had an opportunity to get her aunt and uncle alone, he would. She couldn't let that happen before she had a chance to tell them about the contest. There was still hope.

"Listen," Rosie said, digging into her pie a little more ferociously than she meant to. "You can't come to Thanksgiving."

"Why not?" he asked.

"You know why not." She took a bite and chewed. "My uncle

will only have been home for a few days. Thanksgiving dinner isn't the place to discuss it."

"When would be the right time to discuss it?" Everett asked. "After we're all dead?"

"That would be fine with me," she said.

"I'm not the bad guy here," Everett said, leaning in closer to her across the table. "You have to know that."

"I don't *have* to know anything," Rosie replied.

"I don't think you understand the dire situation Corgi Cove is in," he said as if he hadn't heard Rosie. "Your aunt and uncle *will* lose the property if they don't catch up on payments by the first of the year. Is that what you want? For your aunt and uncle to go through that heartbreak?"

"No," Rosie began.

"Don't you want them to get out while they still can—while they can still make a profit?" Everett continued. "Or would you prefer they live in abject poverty for the rest of their lives, in debt with no credit?"

Rosie sat back, fighting tears. Of course she didn't want that.

"This isn't going to go away," Everett said. "I know you want it to, but it isn't."

"What if I could save it?" Rosie asked, her voice just above a whisper. "What if I could save the Cove?"

CHAPTER 21

Everett

She was out of her mind.

That was the only explanation Everett could think of for what Rosie had suggested. He glanced to the magazine that now sat beside him on the passenger's seat. Rosie left it for him to read over, urging him to consider what she'd proposed.

Save the Cove. Of all the ridiculous . . .

Everett shook his head. There was no way this idea of hers was going to work. It would be a long shot even if the contest didn't require entries to be submitted by the first of December. As it stood, Rosie had only two weeks to get everything ready to submit to the contest, and there was no guarantee they'd even get picked to move forward, let alone win.

What did she honestly think was going to happen? At best, it was a distraction from the inevitable and, at worst, it was false hope—something he thought he'd stressed that her aunt and uncle didn't have time for. Surely they wouldn't be on board with it.

Once he was back at his apartment, he put in a call to Francesca. He'd run this past her first before he said anything to Rosie. When she'd initially told him about it, he'd stayed quiet, murmuring only that he'd take a look at the contest when he got the chance.

"That's absurd," Francesca said. "They'll never win."

"I know," Everett replied. He stared into his empty refrigerator. "But their niece, Rosie, thinks there's a chance, and she's willing to do anything it takes to keep the Cove from selling."

"She's the one who gave you trouble before?" Francesca asked.

He bristled at the word *trouble*. He didn't like the idea that anyone would give him trouble or that Francesca might think he couldn't handle the assignment.

"She's opposed to her aunt and uncle selling," Everett said, finally. "But she doesn't really pose a threat. She doesn't own the estate."

"Could she continue to make things difficult for us?"

"I guess she could," he replied. "Especially if she's dead set on this idea of winning a contest."

"Why don't you go along with it," Francesca said.

"What?"

"Make a deal with her," she continued. "Tell her that you'll help her with this silly little fantasy if she promises she won't stand in the way of the sale when she finally comes back down to reality."

"Do you think that's a good idea?" Everett asked. "This could take another month, maybe two by the time it all shakes out."

"The bank won't foreclose before the first of the year, and they'll hold off a little longer if they know a deal is pending," Francesca replied. "I know we both thought this would be a fast sale, but things are more complicated than we anticipated. Make her think you're on her side. Earn her trust."

Everett mulled this over for the rest of the evening as he tried and failed to watch television, tried and failed to read a book, and finally, tried and failed to go to sleep. Eventually, he rolled out of bed to get some work done on his laptop. But his thoughts kept drifting back to Rosie. He didn't like the idea of tricking her into trusting him.

But would it really be deceiving her if he offered to hold off until the beginning of the year in exchange for her submission to an inevitable, at least in his mind, sale? It didn't sound so bad when he thought of it like that. He could help her, even, all the while knowing that there wasn't a chance in hell that Corgi Cove would be selected.

What did it hurt to humor her in the meantime?

It didn't, he decided, shutting his laptop. He was doing his job, and there was nothing wrong with that. Francesca was right. This *was* the easiest way. In fact, he was annoyed with himself that he hadn't thought of it. All he had to do was get through the next few weeks, play nice with Rosie, and by the first of the year, he'd have a signed deal in his hand and a happy boss. He'd be well on his way to a bigger, and much better, he told himself, life.

CHAPTER 22

Rosie

The members of the Corgi Cove Canine Club stared at Rosie expectantly. They weren't sure why they'd been summoned, without their dogs, on a day that wasn't usually reserved for meetings.

"I'm sure you're all wondering why I called you here," Rosie said.

"I'm not joining another cult," Marty said, crossing his arms across his chest.

"Me, neither," Irene agreed. "I just barely made it out of that Heaven's Gate mess."

"Nobody's joining a cult today," Rosie said. "I think I might have a solution to the Corgi Cove problem."

She passed around copies she had made of the contest from the back of the magazine.

"What is this?" Connie asked. "Some kind of contest?"

Rosie nodded. "And before any of you say anything, I know that it's a long shot. I know that the deadline is coming up, and we'd basically have a week to prepare, but I still think it's worth a shot."

"Why are you telling us?" Irene asked.

"Because I can't do it without you," Rosie replied. "Especially not with Uncle Joe out of commission. He'll be home soon, but he and Aunt Mary won't be able to help."

"Do you think this is actually something that might keep them from selling the Cove?" Connie asked.

"I don't know," Rosie said honestly. "But it's all I've got right now."

"Have you talked to your aunt and uncle about it?" Justin, who'd been silent until now, chimed in. "Are they on board?"

"I sent a text to my aunt, but she hasn't replied," Rosie admitted. "I'm going to talk to them about it once Uncle Joe is settled back at home."

Justin nodded. "Okay, well, if they're in, I'm in."

"Me, too," came a chorus from the rest of the group.

Rosie clapped her hands together and said, "Really? Oh, this is great! Thank you!"

Buoyed by the response from the group, Rosie was excited to talk to her aunt and uncle. She spent most of the afternoon preparing for them to return home. Their house was just feet from the Cove, and it was easy to keep an eye on it in the unlikely event someone wanted to check in.

Rosie cleaned their house, made sure the dogs were settled,

and even brought in some leftover honey on toast—one of her uncle's favorite breakfasts.

When Mary and Joe arrived back at the house, Rosie was thrilled to see how good her uncle looked, considering all he'd been through. Though he was still a bit pale and gaunt, he was smiling, and he made his way into the house mostly unassisted, with Mary clucking her tongue behind him about "being careful" while walking up the steps.

"Mary, I swear on Bonnie and Clyde that if you don't stop barking orders at me, I'm going to lie down right here and die," Joe grumbled.

"I just want you to watch where you're walking, that's all," Mary argued.

"It's hard to concentrate with you flappin' your gums."

"All right," Rosie said, taking her uncle's arm. "That's enough, you two."

Bonnie and Clyde came crashing into the living room when they heard Mary's and Joe's voices, and Rosie only just got her uncle situated on the couch before the slobbering beasts were upon them, licking Joe's face and barking for attention.

"I've missed you rascals," he said, burying his face in Bonnie's soft coat. "I've missed you so much."

"They missed you, too," Rosie said, sitting down next to him. "I was a poor substitute for you and Aunt Mary."

"You've just gotta know the right places to scratch," Joe replied, rubbing Clyde's belly in a way that made the dog's left leg move up and down in a furious motion.

"Thank you for taking care of them," Rosie's aunt said, coming into the living room with a fresh cup of coffee for herself and herbal tea for Joe, who sniffed the concoction and then set it down on the side table without taking a drink. "We appreciate everything you've done while we've been gone."

"It was nothing," Rosie said.

In truth, it hadn't been nothing, but it hadn't been much, either. It wasn't like the Cove needed a lot of attention. It was mostly wrangling the corgis and making sure they stayed on the opposite end of her small cottage than Toulouse. Rosie wished that she could tell them that they were booked up for summer, that all of their problems were solved.

"Well, we appreciate you," Joe said, pulling her out of her thoughts.

"I want to talk to you about something," she said. She anxiously laced her fingers together.

"What is it?" Lines of worry started to appear on her aunt's face. "Are you okay?"

"I'm fine," Rosie assured them. "This isn't about me. Well, it is, but it's not." She took a deep breath. "Okay, let me just show you."

She handed them each a copy of the magazine, earmarked to the page she wanted them to read, and waited.

"I don't understand," her uncle said finally, turning over the magazine in his hands. "You want us to enter this contest?"

"Yes," she said simply. "I do."

"But, honey," Aunt Mary replied. "I know that the thought of selling the Cove upsets you, but I'm sure you know by now that we don't have any other choice."

Rosie sat down on the arm of the couch closest to her uncle. "Do you want to sell?" she asked. "Truthfully, do you want to sell?"

Her aunt and uncle looked at each other.

"If you want to sell," Rosie said, "I won't say another word about it. I know I've already . . ." she faltered, chewing on her lip. "I know I've already caused you trouble."

Uncle Joe grabbed her hand and held it, looking her directly in the eye. "You were not responsible for my heart attack, Rosie," he said. "It wasn't your fault. You didn't clog my arteries with years of Oto's chicken fried steak."

She let out a little laugh. "If Oto is responsible, half the town should have their hearts checked," she said. "But if you want to retire, I won't make it more difficult for you."

"Retire," Joe spat out. "And sit around all day and night like I've been doing for the last few weeks? No. That's not what I want."

"What do you want?" Rosie asked the both of them. Realizing that until now, until this very second, she'd never asked them. She felt shamed and selfish.

There was a beat of silence, and then Mary said quietly, "We want to keep the Cove. We just aren't sure that's possible anymore."

"Do you think we could save it?" Joe asked. His voice was nearly as quiet as Mary's. "Do you think there's a chance?"

"I don't know," Rosie answered honestly.

Her aunt looked down at the magazine. "We've spent a lot of years avoiding the truth, avoiding the inevitable."

"We can try," Rosie said. Deep down, she knew this was a long shot. She knew that they had mere days to send in the information, the pictures, the essay, and she also knew that the money might not save them. The money might be enough to fix the problem in the short term, but who knew what the future held . . . whether they won *or* lost.

Still, there was hope, and no matter how small the kernel, Rosie would take it.

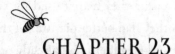

CHAPTER 23

Rosie

It was decided. There would be a Thanksgiving dinner, provided by Oto, at the Cove, and afterward, they could get to work on the Cove. Actually, it had been Oto's idea. Rosie suggested the Friday after, and Oto reminded her that the Friday after Thanksgiving was Black Friday. Nobody would want to come to the Cove to clean it up and get it ready for a photo shoot when they were all standing in line waiting for cheap television sets and discount stocking stuffers. No, he'd told her. It would be far better to do Thanksgiving Day, cook up a gigantic meal, and entice everyone with his famous mashed potatoes.

Even more surprising was the way Everett had reacted when Rosie told him about the plan. She assumed that he'd tell her she was making a mistake, making her aunt's and uncle's lives harder by giving them false hope. Instead, he'd simply said, "What time should I be there?"

Rosie spent most of the day before Thanksgiving working to dust off the ancient website they hadn't used for years, as well as the email. As soon as they had better pictures of the Cove, they'd add those, too. Justin and Elizabeth had already promised to help get social media accounts set up in the meantime.

"What good will this do?" Mary asked, leaning over Rosie's shoulder as Rosie typed furiously into the "about" section of the website. "We have less than two months before we have to make a decision."

Rosie shrugged. "Maybe no good," she admitted. "But what could it possibly hurt?"

"Nothing, I guess."

Rosie turned around to face her aunt and took note of the deepened crease on the older woman's forehead.

"I just don't know what we'll do," Mary said. "If . . . if we really lose this place."

"Maybe that won't happen." She knew she needed to be as realistic as possible, but it just hurt to see her aunt like this.

"At first," Mary continued, "your uncle and I thought this was a good idea, to at least *explore* the option. But with his heart, with him in such a state, I'm worried about what being forced to move will do to him."

"I know," Rosie said.

"He loves this place more than he loves anything else, Rosie." Mary clasped her hands together until her knuckles turned white. "Even me."

Rosie reached out and unclasped her aunt's hands, taking them both in hers. "That's not true," she said. "And if you have to move, if *we* have to move, we'll get through it together."

Mary tried to smile, but it didn't quite reach her eyes. "Thank you," she said. "I don't know when you became the adult and we became the children, but thank you for taking care of us."

There was a ding, and Rosie turned back to the computer. "Hey!" she said. "We've got a reservation for Thanksgiving night."

"Really?" Mary peered into the screen as if she might be able to jump right into it. "How? We didn't get a phone call."

"The website," Rosie said. "I asked Elizabeth to add the link to our Facebook."

"We have a Facebook?" Mary asked.

"We do now," Rosie replied. "We also have an Instagram, Snapchat, and TikTok."

"What's a TikTok?" Her aunt was beginning to panic again. The line between her eyebrows was a crater.

"You don't want to know. But I hear Bonnie and Clyde are becoming quite popular."

"Don't tell Marty," Mary said, a wry grin on her face. "He thinks the internet is controlled by aliens."

"I'm not convinced Bonnie and Clyde aren't controlled by aliens," Rosie joked, exiting out of the screen.

"Wait." Mary reached for the computer. "Who made the reservation?"

"I didn't look," Rosie said. "I'll check later. We'll make sure to give them the best room in the house."

"Do we have a best room in the house?" Joe asked, limping

up to them, his shirt damp with sweat. "I guess we do have that room with the nice toilet. You know, the one we had to replace when Irene's grandson flushed a plastic hamburger a couple of years ago."

The women both nodded. "That's the one," Rosie said. "That's the one."

CHAPTER 24

Everett

Everett couldn't believe he was nervous about Thanksgiving dinner at Corgi Cove. He'd been warmly invited by both Mary and Joe, even though he knew that they probably weren't thrilled about his being there. Southerners were so . . . *polite*. Before he'd left New York, one of his colleagues took him aside and gave him some advice about traveling to the South.

"They're nice," his colleague Joshua had said. "But don't you be fooled by it."

"So, they're not nice?" Everett had asked. He'd just come from a meeting with the higher-ups who'd absolutely chewed him up and spit him out, so his head was already pounding.

"No, they are," Joshua replied. "But if they ever say anything like 'Bless your heart,' be careful. Some phrases aren't as nice as they sound."

"Okay," Everett said. "What else should I know?"

"Tea is always sweet unless you ask for it not to be," Joshua continued. "But," he said, pointing his finger at Everett's chest, "don't ever ask for unsweet tea."

Everett was confused, but he nodded, anyway.

"The world shuts down if it snows," Joshua said. "Everything is fried, Saturdays are for college football, oh, and where are you going again? Texas, right?"

"Right," Everett replied. "Close to Austin, I think?"

"The barbecue is spicy, not sweet. That's a Carolina thing."

Everett left the conversation more confused than before it began, but he held this information close to his vest just in case he needed it. He figured a Thanksgiving dinner with a bunch of Southerners was precisely the place where he was going to need these pearls of wisdom.

He rifled through his clothes trying to find something appropriate to wear and finally settled on a pair of khaki shorts and a blue button-up that he'd brought on a whim, thinking that he might have a casual dinner somewhere one night. He guessed this was as close as he was going to get.

"Tea is always sweet tea," he muttered to himself as he got dressed. "I can do this."

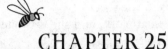

CHAPTER 25

Rosie

Thanksgiving Day was colder than usual, and although it wasn't raining, there was a chance. Rosie knew about that, not only because the sky looked as if it might begin pouring at any second, but also because Irene sent out a mass text message to nearly everyone in town that read, in all caps: *CHANCE OF RAIN.*

Irene had become the town's own personal weatherwoman since she'd upgraded to a smartphone two years ago and downloaded a weather app. For some reason, she thought she was the only one who had access to this pertinent information.

Rosie didn't like bad weather. Well, she supposed nobody truly did, but more than that, she didn't like any weather that wasn't sunny with a sky full of fluffy clouds. She'd been scared of storms ever since the summer she was seven, and she'd had to hide in the concrete concession stand at the pool with the rest of the kids in her neighborhood during a tornado drill.

Her mother had been at work, and she was one of the last kids picked up that day, and by that time, Rosie had gotten herself good and worked up. So much so, that she'd been scared of rain for nearly a year. Even now, a dark sky made her feel like she couldn't breathe.

She tried to push those thoughts from her mind as she got dressed for the day. There were things to be excited about, especially Oto's famous deep-fried turkey. She rummaged through the back of her closet to find a sweater. She didn't have many, but she did have a blue-and-cream-colored knit sweater her mother sent her for Christmas a couple of winters ago. Since moving farther north, it was as if her mother forgot what clothing was and was not appropriate in Texas.

Today, however, Rosie was glad for it.

Outside, a throng of people walked toward the Cove, most of them laughing and enjoying the relatively cooler weather. Oto was inside the huge kitchen, lumbering around and shouting orders as if he were at his restaurant.

Uncle Joe was standing alongside Mary on the front porch, welcoming everyone, leaning heavily on a cane for support. He was pale, but he looked happy, and Rosie approached him, arms outstretched to embrace him.

"Good morning, kid," Joe said. "That's a nice sweater."

"Your mother sent that to you, didn't she?" Mary said before she could thank her uncle. "It looks like her."

"She did," Rosie replied. She heard the disdain in her aunt's voice, but she decided to ignore it. "Are you sure you should be out, Uncle Joe? It's pretty chilly."

"Just yesterday, you told me not to be out in the heat. Which is it?" He gave her a weak grin.

"We'd both prefer it if you'd just stay inside forever," Mary quipped. "But we both know what a disaster *that* would be."

He laughed, the sound like the crunching of gravel. "I reckon it'd be just as bad as when we tried to keep Clyde in that cone after you two insisted we remove his balls."

"Keep it up," Mary muttered. "You may be next."

Rosie took her aunt aside and whispered, "Mom called me. She wanted to know if she should come down."

Mary's mouth set into a hard line before she said, "You told her no, didn't you?"

"Of course," Rosie said. "But she did seem really concerned."

"She's always really concerned," Aunt Mary replied. "She's texted me ten times this morning."

Rosie hated getting into the middle of whatever it was that caused the tension between her mother and aunt. No matter what she did, she felt guilty. She didn't think her mother ever believed that Rosie would choose to stay in Turtle Lake, on purpose, and not come back to her eventually. That alone was a source of contention between all three of them.

"You know we could ask her for help," she said, hesitant. "She would help us."

"Absolutely not." Mary shook her head furiously. "I will not be indebted to her."

Rosie didn't mention that what her aunt had done for her

mother, for her, put Katherine in *her* debt, and that perhaps her mother had been looking for a way to repay it. It wouldn't do any good. "Okay," she said. "I get it. I just had to ask."

"I know you did, sweetheart," Mary said, reaching out to hug her. "And I love you for it."

Susannah approached them, followed in quick succession by Tommy, both of them laden with boxes.

"What's all this?" Mary asked.

"Christmas decorations for the Cove," Susannah said, walking past them and pushing open the Cove's front door with her behind. "Irene and Connie have more in the trunk of Irene's car."

"We already have decorations," Mary replied. "We thought we'd decorate tonight after dinner."

"That's right," Rosie said, smiling at her aunt. Mary had a hard time letting anyone take control. Rosie knew it was going to be hard for her having so many people inside after Thanksgiving dinner, rummaging around and making decisions she might or might not approve of.

Susannah looked at Rosie, gave her a wink, and said, "These are just extra. We don't have to use them."

This answer seemed to satisfy Mary, and she walked away with Joe, helping him move from the front porch and on into the house.

"That was close," Tommy said, setting his load of boxes down. "I thought Ms. Mary was going to make us haul it all away, and I did not want to be doing that. Mama said none of this shit was supposed to come back."

"Don't call it shit," Susannah said. "It's nice stuff!"

"You're only saying that because you don't want Mama to dump it off on you!" Tommy replied, a sly smile playing at his lips.

"I hope it's not all shit," Rosie said, returning his smile. "You were supposed to bring stuff to make the Cove look amazing for the pictures."

"And it *will*," Susannah said with so much conviction that Rosie believed her. "I promise, it will."

"What are you three whispering about?" came a voice from behind them.

They all three turned around to see Everett standing there, his hands shoved down into the pockets of his shorts.

Susannah and Tommy both looked over to Rosie, who was at that moment trying to decide if she was annoyed or happy to see him. Maybe, she realized with surprise, it was a little bit of both.

"We're just talking about decorating the Cove for Christmas," Rosie answered, stepping away from the group so that Everett could stand between them.

"Does he know?" Susannah mouthed to her.

"He knows," Rosie said aloud. And then she said, "Everett, I'd like you to meet my friends Susannah and Tommy. Guys, this is Everett St. Claire."

"No insult in that introduction?" Everett asked, his hand outstretched to take Tommy's. "I'm impressed."

"I'm saving it for later," Rosie replied. "Since it's a holiday, I'll try to only insult you once."

"Lucky me."

"Well, it's nice to meet you," Susannah said, smiling at him.

He smiled back, and Rosie felt a little rise of jealousy in her belly, even though she knew it was completely ridiculous. She was about to suggest that they go find Susannah's husband, Cole, when Susannah pointed at someone coming up the drive, carrying something huge.

"What is that?" Susannah asked.

"Who is that?" Rosie replied.

"Looks like Irene is hauling a giant tequila sign," Tommy said, pointing excitedly. "I call dibs!"

CHAPTER 26

Rosie

After a brief discussion with Irene about why the Cove couldn't advertise Tito's Tequila in the same room they offered the continental breakfast, Rosie began to feel like everything was coming together. Oto was nearly ready to serve lunch, and then once they were all fed and happy, the few of them who knew about the contest would get to work.

Everett looked around at the boxes in the corner over by the stairway and then jabbed his thumb out toward the porch where the rest of the Christmas decorations sat. "I thought we weren't getting started until later."

"We?" Rosie asked.

"You're not going to help?" he asked, a smile cracking his face. "I thought this whole thing was your idea."

"You're hilarious," she replied, rolling

her eyes. "I mean, what are you doing here? I can't believe you really showed up."

"I told you I was coming."

"And you're actually here to help?" she asked. "Or are you just here for Oto's food?"

"Can't it be both?" Everett asked, grinning. "Besides, I over-heard Irene talking about Tito's for the continental breakfast, and now I'm intrigued."

"Only guests get complimentary tequila," Rosie quipped.

"Good thing I'm a guest, then."

Rosie stared at him. No, it couldn't be. She'd forgotten to go back and look at the reservation from the day before. In fact, she'd forgotten about it entirely. Maybe she should work on that. It wasn't a good look not to know about the guests before they arrived.

"So," Rosie said slowly. "You're the guest?"

"The guest?" Everett asked. "Am I the only one?"

Rosie narrowed her eyes at him. "Have you *ever* seen a guest at any point while you've been here?"

"Everett!" Mary said, bounding up to them. "Rosie told me you might come." She looked slightly nervous and maybe a little bit wary. "Welcome."

"I'm not here to talk business," Everett said, his hands up in surrender. "I'm just here to lend a hand."

Rosie studied him. He seemed sincere. For one, he was wear-ing the same casual-style clothes she'd seen on him when he'd come to the farmers' market, and Rosie could tell that for him, this was strictly "day off" attire. For two, his face wasn't doing that calculating thing that it did when he wanted to talk about the fate of the Cove.

"So . . ." Everett said, trailing off. "Can I check in?"

"No," Rosie said quickly, realizing she hadn't gotten up early and made sure the room was ready. "Check-in isn't until three P.M."

"She's kidding," Mary said, jabbing Rosie in the ribs just hard enough for it to hurt. "I got your room all freshened up this morning."

"Lead the way," Everett said, turning around as he followed Mary and stuck his tongue out at Rosie.

A gesture that was so surprising that Rosie couldn't help but laugh out loud.

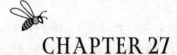

CHAPTER 27

Everett

Rosie led Everett over to the desk at the front of the Cove to check him in. It seemed to Everett that she enjoyed running his credit card a little too much, and he made a mental note to check his statement online just to be sure she hadn't maxed his card.

"Are all of the rooms upstairs?" Everett asked as Rosie walked him past the desk and toward the staircase. He could tell it would be beautiful once decorated with garland for Christmas, and he felt the first sense of guilt for what he knew was inevitable.

"Yes," she replied. "The only bedroom downstairs is my aunt and uncle's."

Everett turned his attention toward the wall, which was adorned with photos, a few of them of Mary, Joe, and Rosie, but the majority were black-and-white pictures of people he'd never seen. "Who are all these people?" he asked.

"Mostly former owners," Rosie replied, stopping to look at a yellowed picture of a girl in braids and saddle shoes standing next to a scruffy dog. "Some of them are relatives of owners or people who once lived here, like this girl, who was sent here when it was a school."

"And you didn't take them down?"

Rosie shook her head. "We felt like, you know, they're part of this place, too. Just because they don't live here anymore doesn't make them less a part of Corgi Cove."

"That's really amazing," he said, meaning it.

Rosie smiled at him. "Yeah, I think so, too."

They looked at each other. He thought for just a moment, Rosie was really seeing him, not for the vulture she acted like he was, but for the person he was standing in front of her and admiring the beauty of this place, the beauty of her. The thought alone was enough to cause him to take one step up the stairs, farther away from her.

"Anxious to get to your room so you can plot our demise?" she asked.

"Today is a holiday," Everett replied with a wink. "No plotting on holidays."

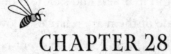

CHAPTER 28

Rosie

The delicious smell of the food permeated the whole house, and there were several people milling about whom she'd never seen at one of their Thanksgiving feasts, many coming by to wish her uncle Joe good health. Rosie knew Oto would serve anyone who came by, and that thought made Rosie smile. She liked the way he took care of everybody.

"Rosie!" Oto called.

She walked around from the dining room and into the kitchen. "What's up?"

"Can you help?" He waved a ladle full of gravy that was precariously close to spilling over. "I send him for extra turkey. I think that damn boy is lost."

Rosie knew *that damn boy* was his nephew, Lloyd. Lloyd had a tendency to wander off. He wasn't the most reliable person in town, but glancing over at Irene and Connie whispering at one end of the dining room, Rosie could guarantee he wasn't the least, either.

"Sure," Rosie said, heading toward the back door. A *whoosh* of hot air hit her in the face. "What can I do for you?"

"Plates," Oto said, pointing again with the ladle. "Line them up for me."

Rosie nodded and got to work.

"Do not sample the food," Oto told her, twenty minutes later, as she snuck a piece of turkey into her mouth.

"But I'm starving," Rosie whined.

"No," he said, but he was smiling. "You are a very bad child."

"I'm not a bad child," Rosie said, her mouth full.

Oto made a noise that was halfway between a growl and a laugh. "Feed people," he said. "Not feed your face."

"Can I help?" Everett asked.

"You," Oto said, pointing his ladle at him.

She held her breath. There was a good chance Oto would tell him to get out of "his" kitchen. He'd done that with Tommy last year and even Uncle Joe the year before.

"Help Rosie," Oto finished.

"Great!" Everett clapped his hands together, and she laughed out loud at his enthusiasm.

"Do I need a hairnet?" he whispered to Rosie.

"Don't say that word around Oto," she whispered back. "He's very sensitive about being bald."

"Do you really do this every year?" Everett asked, taking the plate Rosie handed him and spooning out mashed potatoes.

Rosie nodded, nearly dropping a precious piece of turkey.

"Watch it," Oto barked.

"I don't know how he saw that," Rosie muttered. "And yes, we do this every year. We don't usually have quite this many people, but I think there are a few here who just came out to see Uncle Joe."

"I've never been to a Thanksgiving dinner this large," Everett admitted. "It was usually just me, my sister, and my dad. Once my dad married my stepmom, we sometimes met with her family if my dad was deployed."

"Do you see them on holidays now?" Rosie asked.

"No," he replied. "I'm usually working."

"On Thanksgiving?"

He laughed. "The Lake Queen never sleeps."

"Even Christmas?" Her tone was incredulous now. "You can't tell me you work on Christmas."

"I have," Everett said. "I mean, I don't always, but I usually need to be back in my office on the day after, so there's just no point in trying to get to Connecticut."

"What do you do on Christmas Day, then?"

Everett shrugged. "Usually, I just order Chinese takeout and watch old movies in my apartment."

"I have never heard anything quite so sad."

"I don't mind being alone," Everett said with a shrug.

"Neither do I," Rosie agreed. "But days like today remind me why people are important."

"This is nice, too." He handed Marty a plate.

Rosie looked over at him. If she didn't know who he was and why he was really there, Rosie might have sworn that he was telling her the truth. More than that, she might have sworn he was having a good time.

Everett caught her staring, but he didn't look away from her. Instead, he held her gaze for so long, she thought she might collapse beneath the weight of it. It felt like he'd locked her eyes with his, and after what felt like forever, he repeated, "This is nice, too."

"Excuse me?" Marty said, staring down at his Styrofoam plate with dismay and jerking Rosie and Everett out of . . . well, whatever that had been. "Don't you have a food receptacle with fewer carcinogens in it?"

"What is *carcinogen*?" Oto asked.

Rosie stared down at Marty. "It's one meal," she said to him. "It won't kill you."

"Says the probably lizard person," Marty muttered.

"That's *Miss* Lizard Person to you," she replied. "Now, stop complaining and go eat your turkey."

"Fine."

Oto raised his eyebrow. "Good," he said to her. "You are very good child."

Rosie beamed.

Just then, there was a shriek from out back, and Rosie gasped when the blurry images in the window came into view.

It was Lloyd, waving his hands in the air and screaming, "Stop them! Stop them!"

And it was Bonnie and Clyde, several feet ahead of him. In Bonnie's mouth: what was left of an entire Thanksgiving turkey.

"Oh my God," Rosie said. "Oh my God!"

"They stole the turkey!" Lloyd continued, tripping over the

back steps and flailing in the air until he regained his balance inside the kitchen. "They! They!"

Rosie rushed out of the back door and tried to head Bonnie off at the pass, but she dropped the turkey just in time for Clyde to grab it, veering away from Rosie and scurrying off down the gravel road away from the Cove.

"Clyde!" Rosie yelled. "Get back here!"

From the corner of Rosie's eye, she saw her aunt, clearly mortified, and her uncle next to her, chuckling as he popped a piece of roll into his mouth.

"You go left," Everett said, appearing next to her. "I'll go right."

Rosie nodded. "They're not usually this fast," she said.

"Don't you remember the Jell-O incident?" he asked, just as he lunged for Bonnie and missed.

"Vaguely," Rosie lied. She remembered it in perfect detail and really wished she didn't.

Clyde, sensing the game, dropped the turkey, his tongue lolling out one side of his mouth, only for Bonnie to pick it back up again.

"They're heathens," Everett breathed, catching Clyde around his middle. He handed him off to Rosie. "Take this one. I'll get the other."

Around them, people had come outside and were placing bets on Everett and Bonnie, and Rosie didn't have the heart to tell Everett that even if he caught Bonnie, the turkey would be too disgusting to eat. Besides, it was pretty comedic watching him chasing her around, cursing under his breath every time he missed catching her by an inch.

"You're in trouble," Rosie whispered to Clyde. "So. Much. Trouble."

Fifteen minutes later, a sweating and cursing Everett caught up with Bonnie and what was left of the turkey carcass.

"I don't think this is edible," Everett said. He had a wiggling Bonnie under one arm, and he extended the turkey with the other.

"My turkey!" Oto said, his voice filling with despair.

"I'm sorry, man," Everett replied, dropping what was left of the turkey into the cook's outstretched hands. "She was too fast for me."

"It's not your fault," Rosie said, motioning for him to put Bonnie down. She stared at the dog. "You know better."

Bonnie gave a little bark and trotted off to find Clyde, who'd taken to hiding underneath Joe's legs.

"I'm so sorry," Rosie said, echoing Everett's sentiment. But when she looked over at him, his lips were twitching. He caught her eye, and they both burst into fits of laughter.

Even Oto, after he'd gotten over his shock, began to laugh, and soon, everyone around them was roaring.

"Bad dogs," Oto said once he caught his breath. "I should have fried you!"

That only served to make everyone laugh a little bit harder.

CHAPTER 29

Everett

After lunch was over, Everett excused himself to his room. He'd gotten approximately five feet from the stairway before he was stopped by Connie, Marty, and Irene.

"We know who you are," Marty said, pointing at him. "You're the fella trying to buy the Cove."

Everett repressed a weary sigh and said, "I'm Everett. It's nice to meet you."

"I'm Irene," a short woman with a pixie cut said. "This is Connie, and don't mind Marty. He's grumpy."

"I had to eat off of a Styrofoam plate," Marty grumbled.

"I didn't choose the plates," Everett said, his hands up in submission.

"Humph" was all Marty said.

"You're a tall drink of water," Connie said, moving closer to him. "How tall are you?"

"Six-three," Everett replied, taking a step back.

"You can't flirt with the enemy," Marty attempted to whisper.

"I'm not the enemy," Everett interjected. "And even though I won't discuss business with anyone other than Mary and Joe, I'm not here to do any harm to them. I'm not even here to talk business today."

"Then why are you here?" Irene wanted to know. She had dark, drawn-on eyebrows that made her look perpetually irritated.

"I came here to eat," Everett replied smoothly. "Same as you."

"You didn't even get any turkey," Irene countered.

"And I will regret that for the rest of my life," Everett said. "Rosie took me to Oto's diner a few days ago, and it was one of the best meals I've ever had."

"She's a good girl, our Rosie," Marty replied.

Everett decided not to mention that Marty, less than an hour ago, had suggested Rosie might be a lizard person, whatever that was. Instead, he said, "She is."

Irene eyed him. "Are you staying to decorate for Christmas?"

"I am," he nodded. "I just need to run up to my room and change my shirt. I have turkey all over me from earlier."

"You're staying here tonight?" Connie asked.

"I thought I might be here too late to drive back to Austin," Everett said, which was true. The road back to the city was a narrow two-lane highway. He had no interest in hitting a deer or possum or whatever else was out after dark in his rental.

"We'll be watching you," Connie said, and it would have sounded ominous if she hadn't been winking at him as she said it.

Everett shut the door to his room and leaned against it, finally heaving that sigh he'd been holding in. He thought maybe today would prove some point he'd been trying to make, even though he didn't know what it was. It was obvious, however, that nobody trusted him, and he realized that they absolutely shouldn't. He wasn't just here out of the goodness of his heart. Any goodwill he managed to gain, he planned to leverage for signatures, for a sale. Still, there had been a moment in the kitchen with Rosie, hadn't there?

For just a few seconds, he'd forgotten all about his goals, about his life in New York, about everything but her. Now, alone, he realized just how dangerous that was. He shouldn't be staring at her, and he for sure shouldn't be thinking about her as anything but an obstacle, because that was exactly what she was. There was no doubt in his mind that if not for her, he would have already made the sale. Now he had to go along with this plan that wouldn't do anything but prolong his time in Turtle Lake.

He went to his overnight bag and pulled out a plain white undershirt and put it on. Then he sat down on the bed and observed his surroundings. He wasn't exactly sure what the personality of the Cove was, if not eclectic. When he'd been shown to his room earlier, he'd immediately been hit with the distinct feeling of being in his grandmother's floral apartment as a child. When he'd asked Mary, as politely as he could, if all of the rooms were decorated that way, she'd shrugged and said, "More or less."

He looked down at his phone. By now, his family would probably be done with their dinner as well. He usually waited until the evenings to call on holidays, but he pressed his finger on his father's name and allowed the phone to ring.

"Everett, my boy!" his father said, answering on the first ring. "I didn't expect to hear from you until later."

"Am I interrupting?" he asked.

"Not at all," his father said with a chuckle. "We just finished up. Now we're setting up the card table for a little gin rummy with our pumpkin pie."

"And I assume you'll be cheating, as always."

"Don't you blow my cover now," his father said. "What are you up to on this fine day? How's New York? I always miss it this time of year."

"Well," Everett began. "I'm not actually in New York at the moment. I'm in Texas on business."

"Texas?" his father asked, unable to hide his surprise. "What are you doing down there, Son?"

"It's a sale for the Lake Queen," he replied, hoping his father wouldn't ask too many questions about why he was the one in Texas attempting to make the sale. "There's an old bed-and-breakfast down south of Austin, and we're trying to acquire it."

"On Thanksgiving?"

"No," he laughed. "Not today. But I am down here at the bed-and-breakfast. The family who owns the place invited me to lunch."

"That was nice of them," his dad said. "I guess they must be pretty thankful that you're looking to buy."

"You'd think that," Everett grumbled.

"They're not?"

He rubbed one hand across his face and said, "It's complicated, Dad."

"How so?"

"They're in a tight spot," he explained. "They don't really want to sell, but they're going to lose the place if they don't."

"And they still invited you to lunch?"

"I guess it's Southern hospitality or something," Everett said. "I don't know. I'm a little bit out of my element here."

His father had been career military, which sometimes led him to be more black-and-white than most people. It was a trait Everett himself had inherited. But after his father had married Everett's stepmother, her influence over him had been palpable. She'd done what Everett's mother never seemed to be able to do—mellow him. Now his father tried to consider every side in most situations. Most of the time, it made Everett impatient, but today, he really needed his father's advice.

"Well, Son," his dad began. "You must be doing something right if you got yourself invited to lunch, Southern hospitality or not."

"The thing is, I like them. I like the family. If this weren't business, they're people I might be able to call friends."

"You can't do both?"

"Could you when you were at work?" Everett asked.

"I could have done more of it," his father admitted. "It doesn't always have to be one or the other."

"I think it might have to be this time," Everett said. "I have to make this sale. If I don't, it could be the end of my career."

"I know your career is important to you," his father said. "It was important to me, too. But you want to know something I realized?"

"What was that?" Everett asked.

"I realized at some point that I let my career dictate my entire life. I missed out on so much with you kids, with your mother. And now when I'm with my grandbabies, I spend a lot of time wishing I could have had this time with you and Celine."

Everett sucked in a breath. He'd never heard his father say anything like that. At least, not to him. "I don't have a family, Dad," he replied. "I mean, I have you and Celine and the kids, but it's not the same."

"You don't have that yet," his father corrected him. "That doesn't mean you won't someday, and don't let an opportunity pass you by because you were so worried about your career that you were blind to it."

"Thanks, Dad," Everett said.

In the background, he heard his eight-year-old niece, Maddie, yelling for her papa, followed by the irritated shrieks of his three-year-old nephew, Cameron.

"It sounds like you've got your hands full over there," Everett continued. "I won't keep you. Have a good Thanksgiving. Give everyone my love."

"Will do," his father replied. "And, Son, think about what I said."

"I will."

Everett set his phone down on the bed and stood up. He'd been up in the room long enough. And he knew that he should get downstairs and help with the Christmas decorations before someone, probably Rosie, came looking for him. Even if making friends, or anything more than that with her, was out of his reach, the least he could do was enjoy what was right in front of him in the moment. It was just one night. There was no harm in that.

CHAPTER 30

Rosie

It had already begun raining by the time Everett came downstairs to where everybody else was separating the Christmas decorations into piles on the table. Rosie saw him from the corner of her eye, standing in the entryway of the dining room. Beyond them, in the large living room, there was a fire crackling in the fireplace.

Rosie couldn't remember the last time it had been cool enough to have a fire, and seeing it burning there, next to her aunt and uncle as they unboxed the artificial tree, made her heart sing. She forgot about her apprehension over the contest and let the warmth wash over her.

"It's really raining out there," Everett said to her as she approached him.

"It is," Rosie agreed. She knelt down to give Clyde's head a scratch.

"I'm impressed your fireplace works," Everett continued. "I doubt you get much use out of it down here."

"We light it a few times a year," she replied. "Uncle Joe loves to pretend like we're some snowy bed-and-breakfast in Vermont when it gets chilly like this."

"It's more than chilly," Susannah said, carrying a box in from the front porch. "I forgot these were out here." She set the box down in front of them. "I think these came from Irene. I'm afraid to see what's in here after that Tito's sign."

"It's just nutcrackers," Irene called from in front of the fireplace. "They were Bill's."

"Who's Bill?" Everett asked. He bent down to peer into the box.

"He was Irene's husband," Rosie explained. "He died last year. He collected them."

"I thought you could put them on the mantel," Irene said. "Don't you think they'll look nice up there?"

"I do," Rosie said, reaching out to hug Irene. "Thank you so much for letting us borrow them."

"Oh, honey, it's nothing," she replied. "He'd have wanted you to have them."

Rosie picked out a few of the nutcrackers and walked over to the mantel above the fireplace. "I think we could put several up here and maybe one or two in the bedrooms."

"I like this one," Everett said. He held out an ornately decorated Santa Claus nutcracker. "He's pretty big. Maybe we could put him in the middle?"

Rosie searched for something sarcastic to say. She was still uncomfortable having him here, especially in this intimate setting, but she couldn't come up with anything. He looked genuinely excited by the nutcracker, so she stepped aside and made space for him to place it on the mantel.

"That looks nice," she said.

"My mother collected nutcrackers," he said, still staring at the Santa Claus. "She put them up every year the day after Halloween."

"We used to decorate that early." Rosie reached up and wiped a fleck of dust from the nutcracker's beard. "But we haven't had any guests besides you since summer, and it just didn't seem like it would matter to make a big show for just us."

"I decorate my apartment just for me," he said, finally turning to her.

"You do?"

"Yeah," he said. "I love Christmas. Have you ever seen Christmas in New York? It's amazing."

"But you said you work on Christmas!" she said.

"I like the decorations." Everett shrugged. "I like the way everything looks when it's all lit up. I like the snow and the food and everything about it."

Rosie smiled. She liked this little piece of information that didn't fit. She never would have guessed that he cared at all about the holidays. He certainly didn't look like the kind of person who would care. Granted, she'd never really known anyone like Everett. But she'd seen enough cheesy romance movies to know that the Big City Guy in suits and fancy shoes was almost always a Grinch.

Joe called them over to the tree, garland wrapped around his shoulders like a boa. "Can you two put this garland up around the staircase?" he asked.

Rosie took the garland. "Sure," she said, inclining her head toward Everett. "Come on."

All around them people laughed and talked while they decorated the house, and Rosie saw Elizabeth, Justin's daughter, taking pictures of the scene with her phone. "Will you send some of those to me?" she asked her.

"Already done," Elizabeth replied. "Dad says we have to get home pretty soon because there are a few houses around town without power, and he wants to make sure our fish tank doesn't get too cold."

"Is it the storm causing the power to go out?" Rosie asked her. "Have you heard?"

"I guess," Elizabeth said. "My friend Emily said that they're getting sleet in Austin."

"Sleet?" Everett asked.

The girl shrugged. "That's just what Emily said, but she lives here in Turtle Lake, so I don't know how she'd know anything about it."

"It's probably a good idea to go home just in case," Rosie said.

"Dad cares more about those fish than me," Elizabeth muttered.

"They listen better than you do," Justin said from the doorway. "Let's go. It looks like it's slacking off a little bit out there. Maybe we can miss the next downpour."

Elizabeth waved her goodbyes as Everett and Rosie walked to the top of the staircase to start on the garland.

They worked for a while, adding the garland and making sure that there were no loose scraps lying around on the floor that someone (primarily Uncle Joe) might trip on. Outside, the rain continued falling, and Rosie felt herself feeling more and more chilly. They might actually have to turn on the heat if the temperature kept dropping. She didn't think that her bees were in any danger. There were often short cold snaps in Texas, and she'd never had to worry before, but she made a mental note to check for damage to the hives after the rain stopped.

"I think the staircase looks really good," she said once they were done.

Everett nodded his agreement. "Hey. Why don't we get a picture of you, Mary, and Joe on the stairs. You could submit that, too."

"I guess we could." Rosie thought about it. "Do you think the stairs are the best place for it?"

"I do," he replied. "I'll take the picture if you'll go get your aunt and uncle."

Rosie hesitated.

"I'm not going to ruin the picture," Everett said with a laugh. "I promise. I told you today isn't about business. Hell, I gave you my credit card and haven't even checked to see how much you charged."

"Maybe you should have."

"Trust me, I will first thing tomorrow morning."

Rosie grinned and motioned for Aunt Mary and Uncle Joe to join them. "Come over here for a minute," she said. "Everett is going to get a picture of us on the staircase to send in to the contest."

Mary cast a confused glance between Rosie and Everett. "Does he know about the contest?"

"He does," she replied. "I told him about it before I told the two of you."

Now Joe looked confused. "And you're helping us?"

To Everett's credit, he had the wherewithal to look embarrassed. "Look," he began. "I'm not rooting for you to fail. If this is something that might help you keep the Cove, I'm not going to stand in your way."

"It seems a little bit like you've actually been helping us," Mary said. "The stairs look great. Joe messes it up every year."

"Well, that was uncalled for," Joe mumbled.

"How are you feeling?" Rosie asked him. "I know it's been a long day for you."

"I'm fine," Joe said. "This has been the best day I've had in months, thanks to you and everybody else here. Now, help me find Bonnie and Clyde for the photo."

"Do we need them in the picture?" Mary asked. "After the havoc they wreaked today?"

"Honestly, woman," Joe said, turning to her. "It's like I don't even know you anymore. First you insult my decorating abilities, and then you want to keep the Cove's mascots out of the picture."

"To be fair," Rosie interrupted, "you just put the garland in a straight line down the stairs. It was pretty bad."

Joe looked to Everett for help, but he was already laughing. "You can't take their side," Joe said. "We men have to stick together."

"I think sticking together might be dangerous for both of us," Everett replied, stepping closer to Rosie.

She went rigid when his hand brushed hers. He didn't seem to notice, or at least it didn't bother him, because his hand lingered there, his pinky nearly wrapped around her own. After what felt like forever, he moved away from her and said, "Okay, you three head up the stairs, and I'll find the dogs."

By the time the evening was winding down, they had the Cove nearly decorated. The tree was up, the mantel was complete, and they'd laid out the Christmas rugs, wreaths, and spread the holly tablecloth across the table.

"It looks fantastic," Mary said, beaming.

"Now all we've got to do is put the lights on the outside," Rosie replied. "We can do that as soon as the rain stops tomorrow."

"I can't believe it's still coming down," her aunt said. "I expected it to be done by now."

"I guess I should head back over to the cottage," Rosie said. "It's pretty late. I meant to have Irene and Connie give me a ride, but I forgot to ask before they left."

"Oh, stay." Mary linked her arm with Rosie's. "We've got plenty of room, and none of us will have to get wet in the process."

"I don't know," she replied. "I didn't bring any clothes or anything, and I hate leaving Toulouse all night."

"You know just as well as I do that fat cat is asleep on your bed and doesn't care a fig about where you are right now," Mary said. "Not as long as you left food out for him."

"I did," Rosie said, thoughtful. "I knew I was going to be gone all day."

"Come on, then," Aunt Mary said, leading her up the stairs. "I'll get a room ready for you. It'll be just like old times."

"We already gave Everett the best room," she complained, only half kidding. His was the biggest—it was at the end of the hallway with a beautiful view of the lake. Of course, with the rain coming down as hard as it was right now, and the fact that it was dark, it didn't really matter.

"I'll switch with you," Everett offered.

"No," Rosie said. "I'm just giving Aunt Mary a hard time."

For a moment, she thought he was going to say something else, but he didn't, and she allowed her aunt to lead her up the stairs and toward the comfort of the waiting bedroom.

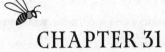

CHAPTER 31

Everett

Everett had to admit—he was proud of himself for making a reservation at the Cove. He was exhausted from the day, and the room was nice and cozy. It had its own small gas fireplace, and he lit it after his shower and sat down in the overstuffed chair in front of it. If he hadn't been so tired, he might've wished for a book. He could understand the appeal of a place like this over the Lake Queen, if he were being honest with himself, which he guessed had been the theme of the day. He'd put his business expectations behind him and had more fun than he thought he would.

Now, as he sat in front of the fire, he felt relaxed, but in the back of his mind, he was thinking about Rosie. He hadn't missed the way their fingers had touched just before the picture on the staircase, and he hadn't missed the fact that she hadn't moved away from him. It was a surprise.

He knew it probably didn't mean anything, at least he hoped it didn't. There was no way anything could happen between the two of them, not when he knew the inevitable was coming. Still, it had been nice. His last relationship—if he could even call it that—had been fun, but it hadn't meant anything, not to either of them. That was why he'd been so angry at himself for letting it mess up his standing at the corporate office. It had been stupid, and he didn't want to make the same mistake again.

In the hallway, he heard voices, and he slipped out of his chair to take a peek. It was Rosie and her aunt, standing in front of the doorway to another room. Mary was handing Rosie a hairbrush, and they were laughing about something. Rosie's hair was wet and up in a bun, and she was clearly wearing a pair of her aunt's too-big pajamas. They had little corgis wearing Christmas hats all over them. He wanted to slip out and go over to them, to her, and say something, anything, to make her stay and talk to him.

His door creaked, and Rosie turned around and caught his eyes. Everett shut the door as quickly as he could, turning off both the fireplace and the lamp beside his bed, just in case either Rosie or Mary had the inkling to come and talk to him. He couldn't trust himself right now not to say or do something stupid that would mess everything up for all of them.

Tomorrow it was back to work, back to the plan, and hopefully, very soon, back to New York.

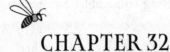

CHAPTER 32

Rosie

Rosie slid in between the cool sheets of the bed and sighed. The mattress was better, even though it was older than the one she had at the cottage, which was a castoff from the last time the Cove upgraded. She'd forgotten why she stopped spending the night here. She used to do it all the time after moving out. They'd done Friday night movies or board games with the guests, and even after the guests stopped coming, she'd still spend the night sometimes, just for fun.

Listless, she scrolled through her phone and looked at the pictures she'd taken throughout the day. The ones Elizabeth sent her were cute, and she created a folder to add photos and the video she wanted to use for the contest. She'd written the essay the night before. She wanted to have her aunt and uncle look over it, but she was nervous about letting anyone see it. She felt like she bared her soul within the pages, and she didn't like feeling vulnerable, especially not with Everett around.

She flexed where their fingers had touched. She'd seen him looking at her through the crack in his door while she stood in the hallway talking with her aunt. They'd actually been discussing him, and she wondered if he'd heard. Mary never missed anything, and she thought that maybe Rosie and Everett were "mending fences," as she put it. Rosie wasn't sure if it was that so much as they were two planets that had mistakenly entered each other's orbit and were about to crash and burn.

Rosie didn't like confusing situations. That's why she'd liked Tommy. He was uncomplicated. He was easygoing and kind, and that's what she thought she wanted for a long time. But she didn't love him. He'd wanted to marry her, but she knew that deep down even Tommy knew it wasn't going to work. After they broke up, she figured it was easier to close herself off from relationships. She concentrated on her bees, her family, and her life at the Cove. Now all of that was up in the air, and she couldn't tell if the jumble of feelings she had right now was influencing her ability to keep Everett at a distance. No matter what she did, he always seemed to be there, and it was starting to feel as if it was more than just because he wanted the Cove.

As she drifted off to sleep, she tried not to think about the man settling in for the night just a few doors down.

It was the crack of thunder that woke Rosie.

The noise was so loud that she shot right out of bed and nearly tumbled to the floor. She sat there for a few seconds, stunned. She couldn't remember where she was, but the lightning that illuminated the room reminded her.

The Cove. She was at the Cove. Everything was fine. It was just a storm.

She got up and turned on the light, padding over to the window to look outside. The rain was still coming down in solid sheets. Behind her, the light flickered once, twice, and then went out. In the hallway, she heard voices.

"Rosie!"

She felt her way to the door and opened it.

Her aunt stood holding a flashlight. "I think the lightning must have struck something, because the power went out."

Everett's door opened, and he hurried out, buttoning up his shorts. "Is everyone okay?"

"Where's Uncle Joe?" Rosie asked.

"I told him to stay in bed, but I doubt he will," Mary replied.

Rosie opened her mouth to answer, but the noise coming from above them was deafening.

"That can't just be rain," Everett yelled.

"Hail!" came Joe's booming voice from downstairs. "It's hail!"

"My bees!" Rosie shot down the stairs to where her uncle stood clad in a checkered robe, leaning on his cane. "I have to go and make sure they're okay."

"Not in this," Joe said, struggling to be heard above the racket.

Rosie didn't wait to hear any more. She ran to the front door and sprinted out into the storm in her bare feet.

The hail pelted her head, arms, and back, but she kept pace, heading for her cottage. Rosie couldn't believe she hadn't taken precautions earlier in the day. That had been so stupid. Now her bees were in danger, and she didn't know if the hail had already damaged them before she had time to get there.

She didn't hear Everett the first few times he called her name. It wasn't until he caught up with her and grabbed her shoulder that she stopped just a few feet away from the cottage.

"What in the hell are you doing?" he yelled at her. "Are you insane?"

Rosie, exhausted and freezing, pointed at the hives.

"What can you do now?" Everett said, pulling her toward the porch of the cottage.

"I just need to check." Her words came out in pained huffs. "I just need to check."

"Tell me what to look for." He jumped up onto the porch.

"Check to see if they're blown over," Rosie replied, trying to ignore the stinging in her feet. "I can't tell from this far away."

Everett nodded and went back out into the storm while she went inside the house to find the bungees she kept in her closet. She kept them there to secure the hives during the springtime, when the storms usually came with gusts of raging wind. "I should have thought about this," she said out loud, grabbing whatever she could find.

"They look okay," Everett said, meeting her at the door. "I don't see any damage."

"Help me with these," Rosie said, handing him half of the bungees.

She hurried over to the hives, giving them a cursory glance, and was relieved to see that his assessment had been correct.

"What do I do?" Everett asked.

"Put it over the top," she instructed, showing him. "Hook it to the bottom. You get the half on the right. I'll take the half on the left."

They worked silently while the hail assaulted them. By the time they were finished, Rosie felt like her hands and feet might fall off.

"Come on." Everett took her hand. "There isn't anything else we can do tonight."

Rosie nodded, allowing him to lead her back up toward the Cove. "Ow," she said, as the adrenaline left her body and she began to feel the rocks scraping the bottoms of her feet.

Everett looked down at her and then, in one swoop, picked her up despite her cries of protestation, and carried her the rest of the way.

CHAPTER 33

Everett

Everett set Rosie down on the front steps of the Cove, but he didn't let her go right away. From inside the house, candles had been lit.

"What were you thinking running out there without any shoes on in the middle of a storm?" he asked her.

She didn't move away from him, either, but her eyes were burning as bright as the candles inside. "I didn't ask you to pick me up and carry me," she said. "I didn't ask you for your help."

"You'd still be out there if it wasn't for me," he replied, unable to hide his irritation. "You needed my help."

"I don't understand why you keep saying that!" Rosie said, her voice nearly as loud as the rain. "I don't need your help! I don't *need* anything from you!"

"You don't know what you need," Everett nearly growled. He pulled her closer to him until their bodies, both soaking to the bone, were touching.

To Everett's surprise, Rosie didn't push him away from her. Instead, she stayed right where she was, looking up at him, daring him to do something.

He leaned down and brought his mouth down to her level. He hovered there, hesitating, and they both pulled away from each other when the front door opened and Mary shot out, every wrinkle on her face turned down with worry.

"What are you two doing out here?" she asked, rushing them back inside. "Come back in!"

Rosie pushed herself away from Everett and stopped inside, not looking back at him. Mary, however, gave him a long, knowing look before closing the door and leaving the storm behind them.

CHAPTER 34

Rosie

None of them knew the extent of the damage until the next morning, when it was finally light enough to go outside and take a look around. The power was back on, but there were limbs down all over; the largest limb had come down right square on the roof of the Cove.

"You're missin' some tiles!" Tommy said from his position on the roof. He stood up and waved at Mary, Joe, and Rosie, who were standing on the ground below him. "There's some damage up here, I'm not gonna lie."

"Great," Rosie muttered.

"It's all right, honey," Mary said, wrapping one arm around her.

Rosie didn't answer. Nothing felt right to her at the moment, absolutely nothing. Luckily, there hadn't been any damage to the cottage or to the beehives. Toulouse was angry, but fine, and she was grateful for that, but it didn't fix the confusion she felt inside over what happened the night before.

She'd nearly kissed Everett.

Rather, he'd nearly kissed her, but it was hard to see it that way when she just stood there, *wanting him to kiss her.*

Now she was staring up at the roof and wishing she could just go back to bed.

But Rosie couldn't do that. She had things she had to do today, including submitting the photos of the Cove to the contest. She'd also promised Susannah she'd help at the salon at their Black Friday event, working at the front counter at noon after her regular receptionist went home.

Even though she knew that the chances they'd make the finals were slim, she worried that damage to the Cove could cause them to lose it all if they couldn't get it fixed.

"What are we going to do?" Rosie asked her uncle Joe.

"You're late," Susannah said when Rosie arrived at the salon at 12:03 P.M.

"Are you kidding me?" Rosie set her bag down behind the counter and waved goodbye to Susannah's receptionist, Kayla.

"I'm double-booked today because of the discount," Susannah said. "I literally have ten minutes before my next client arrives."

"Well, that's not my fault," she replied.

"I know," Susannah sighed. "I'm just starving and regretting my life choices."

"Hard same," Rosie agreed. "You heard about the damage to the Cove, right?"

"What?" her friend asked, surprised. "No! What happened?"

"I figured Tommy would have told you. A huge branch fell on the roof, and we've got some damage. I don't know how much, but any damage at all is bad news."

"I'm so sorry," Susannah said. "I'm sure Tommy called me, but I haven't had time to check my phone all day."

"I don't know what we're going to do," she continued. "There's no way we can afford to repair anything."

"Shit," Susannah said under her breath. "You're still submitting to the contest, right?"

Rosie nodded. "As soon as I get home tonight."

The door jangled, and a woman Rosie vaguely recognized as the local Baptist pastor's wife walked in.

"Oh, Rosie!" she said, her eyes lighting up. "I'm so glad you're here."

"She can't be converted, Miss Wanda," Susannah said. "Trust me, my mama has been trying for at least a decade."

"It's not that," Wanda, whose hair was clearly dyed at home a fire engine red, replied. "Although we sure would love to see you at Sunday school."

Rosie leaned against the counter. "Thank you."

"Now listen, I saw your beeswax lotion on the television this morning, and I want to buy some. I know Susannah carries it here, and that's why I came by."

Rosie shot a confused glance at Susannah. "You saw my lotion on the TV?"

Wanda nodded. "Sure did."

"Are you sure it wasn't another brand?" Rosie asked. "Burt's Bees maybe?"

"No, sugar, it was you!" Wanda reached out and patted her arm. "I saw it on *Breezy's Big Black Friday Blowout* special on the public access."

"Wait," Susannah said. "Breezy Cole was talking about Rosie's products on her television show?"

Wanda, who by this time seemed to be a tad exasperated, said, "Yes, girls! She said your products were so exclusive that you didn't even have a website where we could order, but she has twenty pots, and she's giving five of them away. I thought since I know you, I could go around her and just buy one direct."

"We've got one left," Susannah said, pointing to the little table off to the side of the desk.

"Do you have any more?" Wanda asked Rosie.

"Not until spring," Rosie replied. "Breezy bought me out the last time I was at the farmers' market."

"I guess I'll just take the one, then," Wanda said, a disappointed sigh escaping through her lips. "I wanted to give them as Christmas presents."

"I'll look when I get home to see if I have any extra," Rosie offered, still in shock that Breezy Cole, of all people, would be giving her, of all people, free publicity on television.

"That would be amazing! Thank you!" The woman reached across the counter and hugged Rosie, nearly suffocating her.

"No problem," she mumbled.

"I can't believe Breezy Cole mentioned you on air!" Susannah said once Wanda had gone. "You didn't tell me you met her!"

"I forgot. She bought all of my body butter, but that was the day Everett showed up at the farmers' market and my truck wouldn't start, and we had to have it towed back to town. Tommy's still got it down at the shop."

"Speaking of Everett," Susannah said, nodding to the client who walked in. "Be right with ya, girl. Go have a seat at my station." She turned her attention back to Rosie. "I heard he spent the night at the Cove last night."

"He did," Rosie admitted. "As a paying guest."

Her friend looked disappointed. "So it wasn't a spur-of-the-moment-type deal?"

"No," Rosie said, rolling her eyes. "Do you think that if I wanted to spend the night with Everett I'd do it at the Cove? Wouldn't I take him to my own house?"

Susannah seemed to ponder this. "Yeah, I guess. Dang, I'd been looking forward to asking you about that all day."

Rosie tried to decide if she wanted to tell Susannah about the "almost kiss" she'd shared with Everett. Part of her was *dying* to tell someone, but she wasn't even sure how she would explain it. First they were fighting and then they were just . . . almost kissing? That didn't even make any sense to her. She'd wanted to slap him right across the face, and then he pulled her to him, and all she could think about was what his mouth would taste like on hers.

"Why are you making that weird face?" Susannah said, pulling her out of her thoughts. "Oh my *God*, you *did* do something with him!"

Luckily, she was saved from having to answer that remark by Susannah's next client, a woman in her mideighties excited about her discounted perm.

Rosie spent the rest of the afternoon helping out as she could, trying not to think about Everett or the Cove or anything else until she could have some alone time to do it. Most of the people who came into the salon were in great moods, looking for beauty products as Christmas gifts or buying gift certificates or taking advantage of the salon discount on eyebrow waxing and other services. Rosie couldn't be sure, but she thought Susannah probably made more money on Black Friday than she did the rest of the year.

When she finally left Susannah, making promises to fill her in on everything soon, all Rosie wanted to do was go home and go to bed. Instead, she fed Toulouse and sat down at her laptop to submit all the pictures she'd taken from the day before. Maybe it was just because she was tired, or maybe it was because she'd seen what the Cove looked like that morning, or maybe it was because all she'd eaten that day was a piece of toast and honey, but everything felt completely hopeless.

Toulouse jumped up onto the kitchen table and rubbed the top of his head under her chin. He wasn't normally an affectionate cat, but he had an uncanny ability to take notice when Rosie was upset.

She petted him along the length of his body and said, "I'm afraid we may have to move soon."

Toulouse stretched himself out and flopped over.

"I know we'll be fine no matter where we go, but I don't want to leave this place," she continued.

Once in a while, she wondered what it might be like to live closer to her mother. Her mother had always been the one to push her—to insist on good grades and after-school activities, to remind her that it was important to have a group of friends. At the time, Rosie figured it was because her mother hadn't had the best childhood growing up. It was part of the reason her relationship with Mary was so strained. Katherine certainly got the short end of the stick when it came to parents between the two of them. But Rosie, who assumed that she was much more like the father she'd never gotten the chance to know, chafed against these demands. She was introverted by nature. She didn't like cheerleading and Girl Scouts. She didn't like math club. She just wanted to go home after school, eat a snack, and watch TV.

When she'd arrived in Turtle Lake, her aunt and uncle hadn't pushed her to do anything except go to school. Their only demands were that she try to make friends and get decent grades, and they sometimes asked her to help out at the Cove. That had been back when they were busy during every season and employed a full-time housekeeper and receptionist. Without that push from her mother, Rosie was allowed to move at her own pace for the first time in her life.

It was something Rosie was proud of—her own life, her own pace. But now, faced with the possibility of losing everything she thought was important, she wondered if it was possible that she was still just that scared fifteen-year-old girl.

She stood up from the table, and Toulouse meowed his disagreement before settling himself on the couch. "I've got to go to sleep," she said to him. "I swear, if anybody ever overheard me talking to you, they'd think I've lost my mind. I'd appreciate it if you wouldn't tell anyone about this."

Toulouse gave her a noncommittal yawn.

She guessed it didn't matter where she lived—some things, some cats, would always be the same.

CHAPTER 35

Rosie

The next morning, Rosie woke up feeling a little better. Aunt Mary always said that everything seemed better in the morning, and over the years, Rosie had come to agree. Whenever she was feeling anxious or upset in the evening, she tried to lie down and sleep. Most of the time, it worked.

What she needed to do, she thought to herself as she ate a bowl of cereal for breakfast, was work on the essay to submit to the contest. She'd been too tired to do it the night before, and there were only a few days left before the submission deadline. But when she sat down at her computer to type, nothing came.

She was just about to start typing gibberish when she heard two separate yips at the front door. It was Bonnie and Clyde, come to check on her. Toulouse, sensing danger, ran into the bedroom as the two dogs bounded into the cottage, tongues flopping.

"Good morning," she said to them, reaching down to give their heads a pat.

Bonnie set to sniffing Toulouse's empty food bowl while Clyde stayed put, soaking up the attention. Rosie figured after they'd been forced to stay with her while Uncle Joe was in the hospital that they might not be itching to come back, but it was part of their routine, and they were both smart enough to know that a visit to Rosie in the morning nearly always meant a treat.

Rosie obliged and then gave one final look at her laptop before pushing it closed and promising herself she'd figure it out later. For now, she was going to get herself decent and head up to the Cove to see if there was anything she could do to help out. Maybe they could come up with a plan to fix whatever damage had been done to the roof—at least good enough not to scare off any potential guests (who was she kidding?) or the people in charge of the contest (again, who was she kidding??).

Rosie walked with the dogs a few steps ahead of her. The cooler weather brought on by the storm hadn't lasted, and now she felt sticky. But as the Cove came into view, Rosie wasn't sure if what she was seeing was a figment of her imagination or maybe some kind of heat mirage.

There were people everywhere.

She could see her uncle on the porch, sitting on a rocking chair that used to be in one of the guest rooms. The dogs ran right up to him and he grinned, leaning down to pet them. He reached into his pocket and pulled out a piece of beef jerky, tore it in half, and fed it to them. When Joe looked up and saw Rosie coming, he smiled and put a finger to his lips.

She grinned. He wasn't supposed to be feeding beef jerky to the dogs, and he knew it. Mary scolded him about it all the time. She thought beef jerky was far too expensive to give to the dogs.

Rosie approached the porch, waving to a few familiar faces. "What's going on?" she asked her uncle. "What are all these people doing here?"

He shrugged. "Your aunt says they're here to fix the roof and clean up the yard."

She scanned the yard for her aunt, but she couldn't see her. She jumped off the porch and looked up at the roof. She nearly tripped when she saw a familiar face squatting down next to another man, pointing at one of the tiles.

It was Everett.

The man next to him looked down, saw Rosie, and gave Everett a nudge. Everett waved at her and then walked over to the other side of the roof, out of her view.

A couple of minutes later, he came jogging up to her, drenched in sweat.

"Hey!" he said. "I wondered when you'd show up."

"How," she said, trailing off. "Why . . . What are you doing here?"

CHAPTER 36

Everett

Honestly, Everett wasn't entirely sure what he was doing there. Well, he knew *what*. He'd been helping out on the roof for nearly an hour. The other question, why, was another answer entirely.

"It looked pretty rough out here when I left yesterday," he said.

"Well, yeah," Rosie replied. "The storm was terrible."

"It looked like you could use some help."

He thought for a minute that she might roll her eyes or make some kind of a snarky comment as she usually did when he mentioned helping her or her family with anything, but she didn't. Instead, she smiled.

"Who are the guys up on the roof?" she asked.

"They work for the Lake Queen," Everett admitted. "It's their day off."

"Wait, what?" Rosie asked, surprise written all over her face. "What are they doing *here*?"

Everett gave his best nonchalant shrug, but in actuality, he was praying that word about this never got back to anybody in New York. He'd paid them double their usual pay to work today and made them promise not to say anything to anyone, but he couldn't be positive that word wouldn't get out. Then he'd really be up a creek.

"They're good guys," he replied. "I told them about what happened, and they offered to help. They're all from around here. I think two of them live in Turtle Lake."

Rosie squinted up at the roof. "Oh yeah," she said. "I think I see Tommy's cousin, Rocky."

"He's up there," Everett said. "He called Tommy about helping out, and by the time we got here, half the town turned up to work on the yard."

Her bottom lip quivered, and he thought for a second that she might cry. He resisted the urge to pull her into him and hug her, the memory of two nights ago on the porch still seared into his memory.

He didn't know what would have happened if Mary hadn't come outside when she did. Her interruption had both irritated and relieved him. He'd wanted to kiss her so *badly*. He'd wanted to pick her up again and carry her, the way he had in the rain, right upstairs to his bedroom, tear through her soaking clothes, and lay her right down on the bed. Although he doubted that it would have gone quite that far, it certainly would have gone further than an almost kiss.

"Thank you," she said at last.

Everett wondered if she was thinking about the same thing he was, but before he could ask, Susannah bounded up to them.

"Hey, sleepyhead!" she said to Rosie. "I wondered when you'd show up."

"It's not that late!" Rosie protested.

"It's nearly eleven A.M.," Susannah replied. "I thought you were gonna sleep the whole day away."

"I was up earlier," she said, crossing her arms over her chest. "But I was trying to work on the essay for the contest."

"How's it coming?" Susannah wanted to know.

"It's not," Rosie admitted. "I've been trying to write it for days, but I just can't seem to make it work."

"You better get a move on it," Susannah said. "Isn't it due soon?"

"In less than a week. Don't worry; I'll get it done."

"I know you will," her friend said, taking her arm.

"COME AND GET IT!"

They all three turned to the house, where Mary was now standing next to Joe, holding a metal pot and wooden spoon, clanging them against each other.

"TIME TO EAT!"

Instantly, the work stopped, and everyone clambered up toward the porch, happy to get out of the sun and into the cool of the house where the smell of food was wafting out through the open door.

Everett followed along behind Susannah and Rosie as they

talked. He'd never seen Rosie look so happy. She was smiling, a genuine smile, and laughing about something Susannah said that he hadn't heard.

Inside, Mary looked just as happy as Rosie. She was humming as she shuffled everyone into the kitchen to fill their plates with a brunch that included biscuits and gravy, bacon, grits, pancakes, and toast. Everett couldn't remember the last time he'd eaten so well before he'd come to Turtle Lake. Most of his meals consisted of takeout, whatever he could easily scrounge up in his apartment, or some kind of protein shake on the go. He'd nearly forgotten what it was like to sit down with people and eat.

"Is this something you-all do a lot?" Everett asked Mary as he took a plate from her.

"Do what, sugar?" Mary asked.

"Feed people," he replied.

"Oh, I love to feed people," she said. "It's one of the reasons Joe and I decided to open the Cove. I couldn't see myself working in a restaurant all day, but right here in my own kitchen? Now, that's where I shine."

"My stepmother likes to cook," Everett said. "I don't get home too much anymore, but I know she cooks a big meal every night for my dad and usually my sister's family, too."

"Well, you tell her I'm taking good care of you," Mary said, grinning at him.

He nodded. "Yes, ma'am."

He took his plate of food and circled back around into the dining room. There were no places left at the table, so he went out onto the front porch and sat down on the steps, the expansive lake set out before him. It truly was beautiful.

"What are you doing out here?" Rosie asked from behind him.

"The dining room was full," Everett replied, patting the porch space next to him.

She sat down, her plate loaded with food. "God, I love pancakes."

"I don't like the way the syrup sticks to my teeth," he said, crinkling his nose.

"My mom never let me have pancakes as a kid," Rosie explained, stabbing her fork into a hunk of pancake. "She said the syrup would coat my teeth and I would get cavities."

"Clearly, that's not a concern for you now," Everett said, grinning.

"Nope." She folded the mass into her mouth. "So good."

They sat in silence for a few minutes as they ate. Most of the time, Everett would be looking for something to say to fill the air. It was just who he was. Talking was at the heart of his career. He talked to people all day, every day. There was always someone to talk to about *something*. It usually made him uncomfortable to sit silently next to someone he knew. What were they thinking about that they didn't want to share with him?

But sitting next to Rosie, it was different. He didn't worry about any of that. He was comfortable sitting with her in silence.

He knew this comfort was dangerous, just like he knew the way hiring workers away from the Lake Queen was dangerous. Everett knew that what he should have done was encourage the family to sell, right then and there, so that they wouldn't be responsible for any repairs. It *should* have been an opportunity for a sale. Instead, all he could think about was Rosie and her aunt and uncle and literally everyone in the town and how they would react when they realized their beloved Corgi Cove was damaged.

All he wanted to do was *help*, and not in the way he'd said he wanted to help before. That was a line he used, and this was the truth. Maybe Rosie knew the difference this time, and that was why she hadn't rolled her eyes at him. Maybe there was something obvious about the way he'd said it or his body language that tipped her off.

He didn't know. All he really knew was that the only thing he'd felt good about the entire time he'd been in Texas was what he'd done today. Well, that and the food. The food made him feel very good.

"I guess we should get back to work," Rosie said, finishing the last piece of bacon on her plate and standing up.

"We?" he asked, following suit.

"Well, I'm going to help now that I know what's going on," she said. "It's not my fault nobody told me."

"I thought about calling you," he said. "But I wasn't sure if you wanted me to."

Rosie looked at him, studied him, for what felt to Everett like forever. Finally, she said, "I wouldn't have minded."

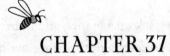

CHAPTER 37

Rosie

Rosie's hands were blistered by the time she was done picking up sticks from the yard a few hours later. Everett resumed his perch on the roof, helping Tommy's cousin, and Rosie and Susannah and even Aunt Mary worked in the yard flinging sticks into a huge dumpster the workers from the Lake Queen brought over.

"Do you think they'll take this trash back to their hotel?" Susannah asked, throwing a pile of trash she'd collected into the dumpster. "Is that even legal?"

Rosie shrugged. "I don't know, but I don't mind thinking about how the Lake Queen might be the receiver of our trash."

Susannah laughed. "I don't, either. They're the worst."

"The worst," Rosie echoed.

"But you know who isn't the worst?" her friend continued. "Everett."

Rosie bent down to pick up a branch and didn't say anything.

"Oh, come on!" Susannah said, throwing her hands up in the air. "He did all of this today. He got the Lake Queen guys here, and you and I both know they wouldn't have come out here, on a SATURDAY, for free. Don't pretend like you don't know that, Rosie."

"Fine!" she said, trying to keep her voice down and failing. "He's not the worst! He's not! In fact, he's so not the worst that I almost kissed him the other night! Is that what you want to hear?"

Susannah stared at Rosie, openmouthed. "You what?"

Rosie sighed and looked up at the sky. It was still so hot, even at three o'clock in the afternoon. "I almost kissed him," she said at last. "Or maybe he almost kissed me and I almost let him. I don't know. We almost kissed each other."

"When?" Susannah demanded.

"Thanksgiving night," she said. "During the storm. He helped me secure the hives and then he . . ." She trailed off, embarrassed. "He sort of carried me back to the Cove because I was barefoot."

"Oh my God, and you didn't tell me?"

"I wanted to tell you yesterday at the salon!" Rosie said. "But people kept coming in, and we were never alone."

"You've heard of a phone, right?"

"I said I was sorry."

Susannah considered this. "Okay, fine, I'll forgive you."

"Thanks," Rosie said.

"If, and only if, you call me *as soon as* he kisses you for real," Susannah finished.

"He's not going to kiss me for real," she replied, hurting her own feelings as she said it.

"Why not?" Susannah wanted to know. "Why wouldn't he kiss you for real?"

"Because nothing can happen!" Rosie said, exasperated. "Nothing can happen because technically he's the enemy."

"He's not the enemy. He's just a guy who's trying to do his job."

Rosie looked over at her friend. "And his job is to buy the Cove."

Susannah took her arm and herded her over to a dry spot in the grass. "Sit down," she said. "I have something groundbreaking to tell you."

Sensing Susannah's sarcasm, Rosie rolled her eyes but did as she was told. "What?"

"Just because he's here to buy the Cove doesn't mean he's a bad guy," Susannah said. "You're holding this thing against him because you don't want to give up, but if it weren't him, it would just be someone else."

"I know," Rosie said. And she did know, but she was trying to sort through those complicated and unexpected feelings.

"Look at this stick I found!"

They stood up as Marty marched toward them, holding out a moss-covered stick and jogging in their direction.

"Careful there, old man," Susannah warned. "You don't want to trip and have that stick go straight up your nose."

"Look at it!" Marty repeated, holding it out to them. "What do you think is going on with this thing?"

Rosie and Susannah shared a look.

"Well?" he asked.

"It looks like a moss-covered stick, Marty," Susannah said. She reached out for it but Marty snatched it away.

"I think I'll take it home for research purposes," he said. "Do you think Mary and Joe will mind, or will they want first dibs?"

Rosie resisted the urge to laugh. "No," she said. "You're welcome to any stick you can find."

"Hot damn," Marty replied.

"Marty, I gotta ask," Susannah began. "What do you think is special about this stick? Is it part lizard?"

Marty gave Susannah a look like she was insane and replied, "Of course not."

"Oh," she said.

"Why would you think this has anything to do with lizards?" he asked.

Susannah's cheeks turned pink. "Sorry, I just thought . . ."

Marty put the stick into his back pocket. "It's aliens, obviously."

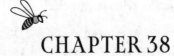

CHAPTER 38

Everett

So far, Francesca had called three times that day, and Everett had ignored her every single time. She'd been waiting on an update since before Thanksgiving, and he wasn't entirely sure what to tell her besides a few short texts that read, *I'm working on it* and *I'm making progress*, neither of which were entirely true.

His phone dinged.

I'd just like to remind you that you cannot avoid me forever, the text from Francesca read. *We need to talk.*

Everett shoved the phone back down into his pocket when he saw Rosie just up ahead, looking at him.

"Hey," he said, walking toward her. "Things are looking pretty good around here."

"They are," Rosie agreed. "Most everybody has gone. I think Uncle Joe and Aunt Mary are about spent."

"So am I," he said. "I haven't worked this hard since the summer I worked construction with my uncle."

Rosie laughed.

"What?" Everett asked.

"I'm just trying to picture you working construction."

"It wasn't the career for me," he agreed. "I have to say, though, the heat was never quite as bad as it is here."

"Oh, you haven't seen anything yet," Rosie replied. "In the summer, it's much, much worse."

"I'm sweating like a . . . what is it I heard Irene say earlier today?" Everett asked. "Like a whore in church?"

"That sounds like Irene."

He nodded. "She's very eloquent."

Rosie looked around where they stood and then grinned at him conspiratorially. "So, do you want to cool off?"

"Connie already offered me an ice bath back at her place," he said, returning her grin.

"Come on," she said, motioning to him with her hand. "I'm about to show you my favorite place at the Cove."

Everett followed after her, intrigued. He knew he should say his goodbyes, get in his car, and call Francesca back with a made-up apology, but he just didn't want to. What he wanted to do, right that moment, was go wherever Rosie was leading him.

CHAPTER 39

Rosie

Rosie couldn't remember the last time she went to the little piece of shoreline just past the cottage. It was secluded from view, a place where no tourists and very few locals ever went. Technically, it was part of the public beach, but Rosie always considered it hers. As a teenager, she'd gone nearly every day to sit and read, swim, or just think. She'd never even shown Tommy or Susannah.

"Wow," Everett said when they got there, just as the sun was setting and the sky was beginning to fade orange and purple. "This is beautiful."

"I know," she said, beaming. "I love it."

"I can see why," he replied.

She pulled her shoes off and dug her toes into the soft earth, and pretty soon, Everett was doing the same.

"I'm still sweating," he said after a few minutes.

"Well," Rosie said. "Get in."

"You first."

She shrugged. "Fine."

Later, she would tell herself that it was the heat and the exhaustion from the day that made her strip down to her bra and panties and wade out into Turtle Lake right there in front of Everett St. Claire.

She turned around once she was waist-deep. "Are you coming?"

Everett's mouth hung open, and it made him look like a teenager on prom night, but he wasted no time in undressing and following in after her.

"This feels great," he said at last. "I don't know why, but for some reason, I thought the water would be cold."

"It's colder than it is in the summer," Rosie explained. "But it's been so warm today that the sun heats up the temperature of the water."

"Thanks, Bill Nye the Science Guy," Everett joked.

She splashed him, stumbling back and nearly going under when he returned the favor.

"Are you all right?" he asked, wading over to where Rosie bobbed in the water.

She dunked all the way under the water as he approached and grabbed at his ankles, pulling him down. When she came back up, the look on Everett's face was one of such surprise that she burst out laughing.

"That was mean," Everett sputtered, wiping water from his face.

"Aw, did you get wet?" she said, sticking out her bottom lip. "I hate that for you."

"You better swim away right now," he replied, lunging for her and barely missing.

Rosie dove under the water again and then paddled away from him as he gave chase. She couldn't remember the last time she'd had fun like this, the last time she felt so *free*. All that mattered right now was right this moment, and any thoughts or stress she'd been feeling melted away into the water, sinking beneath the surface and down to the murky bottom of the lake.

When Everett finally caught up to her, he grabbed her around the waist, and she let him, pushing herself into him so that they both fell back down into the water. They were both laughing until he turned her around to face him, and they were inches away from each other just like they had been the night of the storm.

Everett reached out and tucked a wet strand of Rosie's hair behind her ear, and when she didn't pull away from him, he whispered, "I won't kiss you unless you want me to."

Every part of her body wanted him to. It was getting dark, and it was no longer nearly as warm as it had been when they'd first arrived. Still, she wasn't cold. She wasn't shivering. It felt like her body was on fire and the heat was warming the water around them.

"I want you to," Rosie said at last.

He leaned further into her.

"But I think we both know it's a bad idea," she finished.

He pulled away and studied her, a mix of longing and confusion written all over his face.

"You know it is," Rosie persisted. "This cannot end well. Even if you don't buy the Cove, you're going back to New York the first chance you get, and no matter what happens, I'm staying here, in Turtle Lake."

"How can you be so certain that you know what you'll do?" Everett asked. "How can you be so certain about anything?"

"I'm not," she said simply. "I don't know what's going to happen today or the next, but I told you—this is my home. This place, and even if I have to move away, that isn't going to change."

Everett seemed to consider this. "You're right," he said at last. "I'm sorry. I never should have pressured you."

"You didn't. I want to kiss you. I want to be here with you, but what happens tomorrow when we wake up after these last few days and realize that it was a mistake?"

"I could never consider you a mistake," he replied.

"You might feel differently when my aunt and uncle sign those papers and I hate you again," she said, only half joking.

"They might not sign them," he said, shrugging.

"You and I both know that the contest is a one in a million shot," Rosie said, answering her own fears out loud. "It's a dream. I know it's not real."

Everett closed the distance between them once again. "If it's not real, and Joe and Mary sell the Cove, you can hate me then, okay? But not a day sooner."

Rosie nodded. "Okay."

"And it doesn't matter if you hate me," he continued. "I'm not going to hate you."

She couldn't help it. She laced her fingers with his and said,

"Maybe if we just kissed right now, just this once, and get it out of our systems, it would be all right."

Everett swallowed. "Are you sure?"

"Yes," Rosie said. "I'm sure."

He unfurled his fingers from hers and reached up to lift her chin, licking his lips slightly as he leaned down toward her.

Rosie held her breath, willing herself not to close her eyes, so she could see him in the dark as he got nearer to her, and his lips, slightly parted, brushed her own. She leaned into him and moaned slightly when his tongue slipped inside her mouth.

His kiss was soft and urgent. He wasn't rushing anything, but there was a longing that she recognized, partly because it matched her own. It was the release of a buildup deep within the depths of her soul, and she had to work not to cry out in protest when he finally pulled away from her.

"Thank you for showing this place to me," Everett said as she led him back toward the shore.

"Thank you for today," she replied.

She busied herself pulling on her pants and T-shirt, trying her best not to watch as Everett did the same. Even in the dark, from a couple of feet away, she could see him, and it was hard not to ask him to kiss her again. That kiss hadn't done anything to squash the feelings that were building up inside of her, and she knew right then and there that she was in deeper than she ever could have realized.

CHAPTER 40

Rosie

Rosie stared at the SUBMIT button on the contest website. She had everything added—pictures of the Cove, the video she'd compiled, the signed consent form from her aunt and uncle, and the essay she'd finished up the night before coming home from the lake with Everett.

This was it. This was the moment of truth.

She closed her eyes and clicked the button.

She sat there for a few minutes praying to whichever god might be listening that the Cove had a chance. Then she let out a sigh and clicked over to her email to check to see if there was a confirmation from the website for the submission.

To her surprise, she had nearly a thousand emails in her inbox. She hadn't checked her email for the last few days, since before Thanksgiving, but she'd never had this many emails before, not even in her spam folder. She clicked on the first one.

> Dear Ms. Reynolds, I am writing to inquire about your beeswax products shown on Breezy's Beauty Buzz through Austin Public Television. I would like to place a future order . . .

Nearly every email she clicked read the same way. By the time she was done, Rosie figured she had enough orders to last her through several seasons. It was becoming increasingly clear to her that she was going to need more bees.

Rosie shut her laptop. There was plenty of room at the cottage to add more hives if she wanted to. Maybe she would be able to find a place for her bees if she had to move. There were places in Turtle Lake with land. If she could find it, she could make enough money to support herself and maybe even her aunt and uncle with orders like this coming in regularly. She briefly thought about driving to Austin, finding Breezy, and hugging her.

Toulouse jumped up onto the table, something shiny in his mouth. "What do you have?" Rosie asked him, but Toulouse scurried off and into the bedroom. She followed him and found that he'd managed to weasel his way into the closet and into the box of Christmas decorations she'd pulled out of storage at the Cove.

She leaned down and retrieved the silver bell Toulouse was batting around like a mouse and looked at it. It had been a present from her mother the Christmas she turned twelve. It was engraved with her name. Her mother had always been good at Christmas.

She'd decorated every single year, and later, when they'd had more money after her mother married her stepfather, she'd paid someone to decorate. Rosie loved waking up in a Christmas wonderland every day during the month of December.

"Do you think we should decorate?" she asked Toulouse.

The cat meowed at her, pawing at the bell. Rosie grabbed the box and two more. She brought them out into the living room and set them down on the couch. Carefully, she unpacked everything and laid it out. Most years, she didn't decorate the cottage. It was enough just to see the Cove lit up, but this year, she thought she might go ahead and decorate at least a little, especially since it might be her last year.

Surprisingly, the thought didn't make her want to cry as she busied herself hanging up the wreath Susannah made her their senior year in high school and the little gnome figurines her uncle Joe had carved for her.

All of these things could go with her if she left. Toulouse could go. The bees could go. Bonnie and Clyde, those devils, could go. Everything that made her home a home could go—all except for the land. She'd been holding on to this place for so long that she'd never been able to separate herself from it. She was afraid that if she had to leave, she'd go back to being that scared fifteen-year-old who didn't know who she was.

But that wasn't true, not anymore.

Rosie grabbed her phone and opened the camera. She took a picture of the silver bell and sent it to her mother with the caption, *Remember this?*

A few minutes later, as Rosie was once again fishing the bell out of Toulouse's mouth, her phone dinged.

That was a wonderful Christmas.

Rosie smiled. It had been a wonderful Christmas, clear up to the point that Rosie tried to smoke a cigarette in the bathroom on Christmas Eve and set the smoke alarms off, and her stepfather, in a panic, thought the Christmas tree was on fire.

He'd completely destroyed the tree with the fire extinguisher foam before she found the courage to run out and confess what she'd done.

I'm still sorry about the tree, Rosie typed back.

Are you decorating for Christmas with Joe and Mary? her mother asked.

No, Rosie typed. *Just me at the cottage.*

Three little bubbles appeared, and then her mother replied, *Send me a picture when you're done. Would love to see what it looks like. Miss you.*

Rosie wished her relationship with her mother was as easy as it appeared to be through text. She knew her mother missed her, truly she did, especially around this time of year. Christmastime was for families, after all, wasn't it?

I miss you, too, Rosie wrote. She took a deep breath. *Maybe you should come for Christmas.*

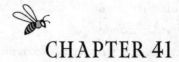

CHAPTER 41

Everett

"So far, you've given me no explanation for ignoring me for the last two days," Francesca was saying. "I'm starting to think you've decided to stay in Texas and become a farmer."

"I told you I was busy yesterday," Everett replied. "You asked me to convince the family to sell, and that's what I've been doing."

"Once they realize they aren't going to win that silly little contest, you mean," Francesca said.

"Right," he agreed. "Once that's all said and done, I'll push a little bit harder, but I think it's a mistake to do it before then."

"I'm not there, so I can't say you're wrong," Francesca said. "But I can send you some help if you think you need it."

"I don't need any help," Everett said. "What I need is for you to give me a little bit of credit."

"Credit?" his boss asked smoothly. "Credit for a man who's made no sales . . . ever?"

"You know just as well as I do that I want to be done here as quickly as possible," he said. "Nobody you could send will get it done faster than I will."

"You've got until the first of the year," Francesca said. "After that, I tell your boss, and I'll send someone else to close the deal."

"Understood."

Everett stared down at his phone. He was absolutely fucked, and he knew it.

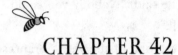

CHAPTER 42

Rosie

Rosie couldn't believe it was already December. Everything in Turtle Lake was decorated, and the kids in town were skipping around singing Christmas carols and giggling to each other about what they hoped Santa would bring them. She overheard one little girl telling her friend she'd asked for a pony, and Rosie smiled to herself, wondering if every seven-year-old girl wanted a pony at some point in their lives. She knew she had.

But Rosie's absolute favorite part of the season was the Christmas play put on by the First Methodist Church. Every year, it was *A Christmas Carol,* and every year, it was a complete and utter disaster. Of course, why wouldn't it be with Irene as the director? She brought a case of Miller Lite with her to every single practice, regardless of the protestations of the minister.

"You were supposed to bring the dogs,"

Irene said to her from the steps of the church. "They need to be fitted for their costumes."

"The only reason you need to fit them for costumes is because they ate their costumes last year," Rosie replied. "Maybe it's time to retire the dogs as part of the play."

"They're the best part!" Irene scoffed. "Everybody loves them as Bob and Emily Cratchit!"

"Tommy and Susannah have to read the lines offstage," Rosie protested. "It sounds ridiculous."

"Please just go get them for their fitting," Irene said, crossing her arms over her chest.

"Aunt Mary is bringing them," she said. "She's also bringing the extra fabric she found in the attic."

"I'm sure Connie will appreciate that. I assume we'll have to replace your uncle as Jacob Marley."

"You'll do no such thing," came a voice from behind Rosie.

Aunt Mary and Uncle Joe stood there with Bonnie and Clyde; both dogs were unhappily leashed.

Bonnie gave a little yip of protestation, almost as if she knew what she was about to endure, and Rosie did her best to stifle a laugh.

"Are you sure you're feeling up to it, Joe?" Irene asked. "Marty said he'd be perfectly willing to take your place."

"That old coot?" Joe replied.

"He knows all the lines," Irene said.

"He's been tryin' to take my role for years now," he said. "Tell him to go back to the Ghost of Christmas Present where he belongs."

"This is a community play," Mary said, turning to her husband. "Neither one of you two are going to be vying for an Academy Award."

"Stranger things have happened," Joe said.

"Yeah, like two corgis playing the Cratchits," Rosie muttered.

"I reckon I can let him have my part," Joe conceded. "He doesn't have much to live for, after all."

Rosie snorted, unable to help herself. It was such an *Uncle Joe* response.

"Come on," Irene said, motioning to Joe and the dogs. "The beer is getting warm."

CHAPTER 43

Texas Southern Living *Headquarters*
Dallas, Texas

"Have you sorted through those entries yet?" Sissy Collins, editor in chief, asked her intern, leaning over the computer to peer at the screen. "Anything good?"

"There are a hundred entries," the intern said dryly.

"And?"

"And it's going to take me more than twenty minutes to get through them all."

Sissy sighed, rolling her neck. Print subscriptions were down, and they were working like hell to get the online copy going. They needed this contest for their big launch. If any of them wanted to survive without losing their jobs, they needed this.

"Most of these places are boring,"

the intern continued. "Nothing new or exciting or . . . wait, hold on."

"What is it?" she asked, leaning back over her intern. "What did you find?"

"Look at this place." He hovered the mouse over one entry.

Sissy squinted, gave up, and went to her desk to retrieve her reading glasses. "Let me see," she said, finally. "Where is Turtle Lake, Texas?"

The intern shrugged. "Maybe over close to Austin?"

"Maybe," she said. She tapped her chin with her stiletto nail. "I think it's a resort town. We'll have to check, but a resort town would be a great location to film."

"We have to pick five finalists," he replied. "We've got to go to all of them."

"Well, at least one of them should be interesting," Sissy said. "Then we can let the readers choose."

"It's called Corgi Cove," he said. "That's kind of a cute name."

"Oh, look at the corgis in the picture!" Sissy exclaimed. "I suppose it's named after them?"

The intern scrolled down past the pictures and clicked on the essay portion, scanning through it. "It is. Well, named after their first pair of corgis, apparently."

"Put them on the list," Sissy said.

"We have to convene the committee," the intern replied. "We can't just . . ."

"Put them on the list," Sissy repeated. "The committee can pick four. I want this one."

"Fine," the intern said. "Corgi Cove is in our top five."

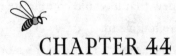

CHAPTER 44

Rosie

Rosie felt the first week of December melt away, and she was more than grateful for the cooler weather the new month brought with it. Everett made himself scarce since their kiss in the lake, and she wondered if it was because he thought it was a mistake. If it had been, it sure hadn't felt like it.

She'd never had a kiss like that before. Truthfully, she hadn't kissed many men in her life. There had been her boyfriend back in Houston, and Tommy, of course, and then a couple of drunken kisses in Austin when she'd gone to bars with Susannah, but overall, the kiss with Everett had been something different entirely.

It was supposed to satisfy her, satisfy them both, and although she couldn't speak for Everett, all she wanted to do was to kiss him again. That would be a desire she would put in the back of her mind, since they'd agreed it wouldn't happen again, and she knew that it would complicate everything that much more if she were to give in.

"That sure is a serious face for so early in the morning," Joe said, peering at her from across the table in the kitchen. "You don't like your aunt Mary's sausage?"

Rosie looked up from her plate. She'd come over early that morning to help her aunt change bed linens and get two of the rooms ready for guests, a couple of Irene's relatives coming in for the play that evening. Rosie brought over some of her personal stash of beeswax soap and lotion for the bathrooms, which delighted Mary.

"I'm fine," Rosie said finally. "Just thinking, that's all."

"It's too early for all that," Joe replied with a wink. "Especially today, since we're all going to be forced to watch that terrible play."

"It's not so bad," Rosie lied. "Besides, the dogs are in it."

"That's why it's terrible," Mary muttered from her position at the sink where she was rinsing plates.

"You could always say no," Rosie offered.

"It's too much fun to say no," Joe laughed, nearly choking on his toast.

"Watch yourself," Mary said without turning around. "I won't have you recovering from a heart attack only to have you choke to death at the breakfast table."

"What time will the guests be here?" Rosie asked, taking the piece of leftover toast from her uncle's plate.

"They're not guests," Joe said. "They're Irene's cousins."

"They're paying," Mary replied. "That makes them guests."

Joe grunted.

"You like them," Rosie said to her uncle. "You've always liked them. They're nice people, and they don't have to stay with us, you know. They could stay with Irene free of charge."

"Would you stay over with Irene?" he asked her, cocking his head to the side.

She thought about it. "Maybe if I were getting free beer."

Joe laughed. "You and me both."

"They'll be here before lunch," Rosie said, standing up. "I meant to bring some honey with the other things I brought to have at the table. I'll run home and get it before Susannah and I leave to go Christmas shopping."

"Thanks, sweetheart," Mary replied. "They'll like that."

"I have no idea what I'm gonna get my mom," Susannah said as they walked around town. "I swear, she hates everything."

"She does not," Rosie replied.

"Last year I spent two hundred dollars on this beautiful hand-crafted leather bag from this leatherworker in Austin. She saw it in a store window and had been talking about it for months. And do you know what she told me when she opened it on Christmas morning?" Susannah asked.

"What?"

"I thought this came in black."

Rosie burst out laughing. "Well, she knows what she wants."

"I hate you both," Susannah said. "Oh, hey, let's go into this shop right here."

"It's the Christmas On the Square shop," Rosie replied. "We never go in there. You always say it's too cheesy."

"Oh, come on," Susannah said, taking Rosie's arm. "Maybe I'll buy my mom a cute angel ornament."

"But she hates that stuff."

Susannah grinned. "I know."

Rosie couldn't remember the last time she'd been inside the pop-up shop. It was owned by a little couple who retired from teaching years ago. Now they opened up the shop the first day of November and stayed open until New Year's. It was cute, with over-the-top decorations and cheery staff all dressed like some variation of Mrs. Claus.

"Welcome to the North Pole!" a round woman wearing a red velvet dress said when Rosie and Susannah entered. "What can we help you find on this fine day?"

"I'm looking for a present for my mother," Susannah said. "Something she'll hate."

The woman took a step back from Susannah, her mouth forming a little O in surprise.

"She's kidding," Rosie replied, shooting Susannah a glance.

"So funny," the woman said, not meaning it in the slightest. "Have a look around and let me know if I can help."

"You can't say that stuff to these people," Rosie whispered to her friend. "You'll short-circuit them."

"Are you suggesting they're robots?" Susannah asked. "Because if so, Marty needs to hear about it ASAP."

Rosie had done most of her shopping already. She'd gotten a new pair of overalls for her uncle and a set of plates for her aunt that matched her favorite set at the Cove. There were several that were missing or chipped, and she'd ordered them months ago. Really, the only people left for her to shop for were her mother, stepfather, and Susannah.

She looked at the ornaments on the tinsel-covered trees. She looked at the snow globes on the lace tablecloths. Everything was lovely, overpriced, and Susannah had been right—cheesy. And then her eye caught on a ceramic village on a table near the back of the shop. There was a school and a church with a steeple, and houses that, when you pressed a button, had smoke come out of the chimneys. She picked up a miniature child wearing a red hat and gloves, and that's when she saw it. A cottage that looked just like hers. It was nothing short of perfect, and for some reason, it made her think of Everett. She hadn't planned on getting him a present, but something told her that he would love it, that he would appreciate it as much as she did.

"What'd you find?" Susannah asked, appearing next to her. "That's pretty! It looks just like your house!"

"It does," Rosie murmured.

"You should get it."

Rosie couldn't bring herself to put it down. "I think I might."

"Great," Susannah replied. "You buy that, and I'll buy this for my mom." She held up an ornament with a fat, rosy-cheeked cherub on it.

"You aren't serious," Rosie said.

"Why not?" Susannah asked innocently. "It'll go perfectly on the tree."

"Your mother does a specific Christmas theme every year," Rosie pointed out. "Never, in the ten years I've known her, has she ever had a cherub theme."

"There's no time like the present," Susannah said. "There's no time like the present."

CHAPTER 45

Rosie

Bonnie and Clyde followed Rosie down the road to the cottage after her shopping excursion, intermittently running in front of her and lingering behind her, and Rosie wondered if they were trying to escape their fate for the evening.

"I wouldn't want to dress up if I were you two, either," Rosie said to them as she walked. "I think you're wearing one of Aunt Mary's old tablecloths this year."

She stopped walking when she saw a tall figure leaning against the porch, staring at her.

"I wondered when you'd be back," Everett said, smiling.

"I was Christmas shopping with Susannah," she replied, trying to hide her pleasure at seeing him.

"I didn't mind waiting," he said. "I like the view."

"So," Rosie said, leaning up against the porch next to him. "What are you doing here so early?"

"What did you get me?" Everett asked, eyeing the shopping bags.

She thought of the ceramic cottage. Embarrassed, she hid the bags behind her back. "Nothing," she said.

"You've got three bags there," he replied. "It doesn't seem like nothing."

"Seriously," Rosie said. "What are you doing here?"

"Okay, so when I was driving back to Austin the other night, I noticed they were setting up for some sort of Christmas carnival a few towns over." Everett bent down to give the dogs a scratch behind their ears. "It looked interesting, and I thought I might see if you wanted to go."

"You want to go to Christmas Candyland in Bellevue?" Rosie asked, a laugh escaping from her throat. "Seriously?"

He shrugged. "Why not?"

"It's for children!" she exclaimed, but she couldn't hide the delighted smile. She hadn't been to Christmas Candyland in years.

"So, you don't want to go?"

"I didn't say that," Rosie replied.

"Great!" Everett said, clapping his hands together. "Let's go, then."

"There's a lot going on today. There are two guests at the Cove, and I need to get inside and get these presents put away, and then tonight there's a thing . . ."

"I can wait," he replied. "I already said I don't mind to wait."

"Are you sure?" Rosie asked. "Aren't you terribly busy and important?"

He laughed. "I am," he said. "And today, I want to spend my terribly busy and important time with you."

She didn't have to think twice about it. "Okay," she said. "But I have to be back by four o'clock to see the state of Texas's worst play, ever."

CHAPTER 46

Everett

Everett didn't think it would be so easy to convince Rosie to go to the carnival. He'd prepared himself for her to refuse entirely, but she hadn't. Instead, she'd been happy to go. Now he was wondering if he'd made a mistake in taking her on the outing. She'd mentioned to him more than once that he was *in for a fun time*.

"Park over there," Rosie said, pointing to what appeared to be a dirt pasture of some kind. "It's closer."

"Are you sure?" he asked, peering over the steering wheel. "It looks like a mud slide."

"It's fine," she said. "See?" She gestured to the cars in front of them. "They're all parking here."

Everett did as he was told, and they got out and walked toward the Bellevue Fairgrounds. All around them, families moved toward the sound of Christmas music and the smell of candied apples and cotton candy floating through the air.

"Everybody here has kids," he said as they walked.

"I told you this was for kids," Rosie replied. "Susannah and I used to take the kids we babysat for in high school."

"Well," Everett said, shrugging. "At least there's food."

Rosie's eyes lit up. "The food is great. And you can sit on Santa's lap if you want to!"

"I'll pass," he said dryly.

"Don't be like that," Rosie said, taking his arm. "You're already on his naughty list, I'm sure. You don't want to offend him by refusing to sit on his lap."

"I think if I sat on Santa's lap at a children's carnival, I might be on more than a naughty list."

She laughed and gripped his arm a bit tighter.

Everett paid their five-dollar-apiece entry fee into the carnival, and they were given red-and-green-swirled wristbands to wear to prove they'd paid. It also, according to the elf he'd paid, guaranteed that they could ride any ride they wanted. Shortly after that, he confirmed to them that the rides were mostly for children weighing less than fifty pounds.

"So, what do you want to do first?" Everett asked Rosie.

She glanced around. "I'm starving."

"Your wish is my command." Everett motioned to a food truck a few feet away. He walked closer and squinted at the menu. "What's a 'fried Oreo'?"

"It's exactly what it sounds like," Rosie replied. She held up two fingers to the woman in the truck and reached into her back pocket to retrieve some cash.

"So, it's . . ."

"Dipped in batter and fried," Rosie said to him.

"Here ya are, sugar," the woman in the truck said. She handed Rosie two fried Oreos. "Watch out, they're hot."

"Thank you," Rosie said, handing over the money. She gave one of the Oreos to Everett. "This will be the entirety of your daily caloric intake, but it's worth it. Besides, it's a requirement to eat at least five thousand calories at Christmas Candyland."

He took a bite. "It's hot!" he said, opening and closing his mouth.

"I told ya!" the food truck woman called to them.

"It's pretty good," Everett said, finally, after they'd walked away. "The roof of my mouth has third-degree burns, but it's good."

"They don't have fried Oreos in New York?" Rosie asked him.

"I'm sure they do," he replied, taking another bite. "But I've never had one."

"Fair food is the best food," Rosie said. "Well, fair food and gas station food."

"Gas station food?" he asked.

"Yeah, like corn dogs and catfish," she said. "Those always taste better coming from a gas station."

"I don't even know how to respond to that."

"Well," Rosie said slowly, licking at her bottom lip to grab a stray piece of fried Oreo, "that's because you're a Yankee."

"You still have a little . . . Oreo . . . on your mouth," he said, reaching out to wipe the crumb.

They stared at each other for a long moment, Everett's gaze dipping from Rosie's eyes to her mouth, and for a heartbeat, he thought about kissing her, like he'd wanted to do all damn day, since the moment he saw her coming around the corner to her cottage.

But then he thought about his phone call with Francesca and the job he was there to do and all the reasons why he shouldn't, all the reasons why in a few days, once the contest was over and she and her family were out of options, Rosie would hate him again.

"Rosie," he began.

"Oh, look!" she exclaimed, cutting him off. "Face painting! Come on!"

Rosie pulled him toward a yellow tent where several families were crammed inside, looking at pictures of painted faces hung up on the posts holding up the tent. There were butterflies and dragons and tigers, and the children leaving the tents giggled and pointed at one another in all their painted glory.

"You're not serious," Everett said to Rosie.

"Why not?" she asked. "I haven't had my face painted since I was in kindergarten."

"I think there's a reason for that."

"Look." Rosie pushed her finger into his chest. "You invited me here. The least you could do is pretend to enjoy it."

He raised his hands up in surrender. "Okay, okay. Face painting it is."

She grinned. "What are you going to get?"

"I don't know," he replied, peering at the pictures. "Maybe a lion?"

"I think I'm going to get a bee," Rosie said.

"Of course you are."

A man with a snake coiling over his face beckoned to them to come forward, and Rosie sat down on the stool in front of him. "I'd like a bee," she said to him.

"Perfect," he said, reaching for his brushes. "And for your boyfriend?"

She said, "Oh, he's not my boyfriend . . ."

At the same time Everett said, "I'm not her boyfriend."

The snake man looked at them both, first embarrassed and then amused. "All right. Whatever you two say."

CHAPTER 47

Rosie

Rosie spent the rest of the afternoon leading Everett around and subjecting him to the delights of Christmas Candyland, which included a fun house, a guessing game where Everett won two goldfish, a Christmas ornament craft fair, and foot-long hot dogs for lunch.

It was nearly three before they walked back to Everett's car, tired, full, and faces cracking from the face paint.

"That was fun," she said as they drove. "Thanks for inviting me."

"It was," Everett replied. "Thanks for going."

"You did me a favor, really," Rosie admitted.

He looked over at her. "How so?"

"A couple of Irene's cousins stay at the Cove every year on the night of the Christmas play in town," she said. "They're nice,

but I always end up spending the whole day entertaining them. It's exhausting. Last year, they asked me if I'd go to the Piggly Wiggly three towns over for the potato salad they like."

Everett laughed. "That's an odd request."

"You don't know the half of it," she grumbled.

"I'd think you'd be glad for guests," Everett replied. "Even if they are annoying."

Rosie shifted in her seat. "My uncle says they're not really guests, but I think that's because my aunt gives them such a big discount."

"Why does she do that?" he asked.

Rosie shrugged. "They're Irene's family."

"Not a very good way to run a business," Everett said.

"You think two guests in December are going to make a difference?"

"Probably not," he agreed. "When will you hear about the contest?"

"Sometime this week, supposedly," she said, feeling a familiar anxiety set in. She thought by now they probably weren't going to hear anything at all, but she didn't want to tell Everett that. She wanted to hold on to hope just a little bit longer.

He didn't say anything else on the drive back to Turtle Lake, and Rosie looked out the window at the countryside whizzing by them. They'd had a good day, a fun day. She hadn't thought about anything except what was right in front of them, and more than once, she'd reached out for his hand, only to find him reaching out for hers, too.

She didn't want to think about anything past today. She didn't have to. It wasn't a requirement to worry over things all the time and stress about what might happen. Rosie thought that she could have one day to enjoy herself, one day to think about Everett and the way things could be if circumstances were different.

"You all right?" Everett asked her.

"What?" she asked. She hadn't realized they were back at the Cove. "Yeah, sorry. I guess I'm just tired."

"Well, you can go take a nap now," Everett replied. "I've tortured you enough for one day."

"You didn't torture me," Rosie said. "I had a great time. Besides," she continued, "I can't take a nap. I have to attend the world's worst play, remember?"

He laughed. "Oh, that's right."

She looked over at him. "Do you want to go with me?"

"Where?" he asked. "To the world's worst play?"

Rosie nodded. "It's going to be, well, the worst, but it's the most anticipated event in Turtle Lake all year."

"Well, then," Everett said, cutting the engine. "How could I miss it?"

CHAPTER 48

Rosie

"I really should start paying you for feeding me," Everett said to Mary, scooping mashed potatoes from his plate.

"Don't insult me, boy," she replied good-naturedly. "Besides, you're going to need your strength for this evening."

"Rosie told me," Everett said. "I have to admit, I'm a little afraid."

"Ignore them," Joe said, reaching for the mashed potatoes, only to have Mary slide the dish away from him. "It's not as bad as all that. Bonnie and Clyde are in it."

"They are?" Everett asked, shooting a confused glance at Rosie.

"Just wait," she replied. "No explanation could do it justice."

Joe's phone rang, and he pulled it from his pocket and looked down at it, scowling.

"Who is it?" Rosie asked.

"Some number from Dallas," Joe replied. "It's been calling me all day. I don't know anybody in Dallas. Damn scammers."

"Did they leave a voicemail?" Rosie asked.

"Don't have it set up," Joe grunted. "Nobody I know would leave me a voicemail, anyway."

"You can block the number," Everett offered.

Joe slid the phone back into his pocket. "You can show me how to do that after the play. Finish up. Bonnie and Clyde can't be late."

They decided to walk to the church. It was less than a mile to the center of town, and Joe said he thought he could use the fresh air. Rosie was happy he suggested it—she liked walking into town at night with the Christmas lights glowing.

The lights were old. Many of the decorations were from the 1950s and 1960s. They'd been found in storage several years ago when the town council cleaned out city hall. Instead of throwing them away, they'd all voted to restore them and use them every year. Rosie thought they made Turtle Lake look lovely.

A steady stream of people walked toward the church, and Rosie waved at the people she knew, and she and Everett waited while her aunt and uncle stopped to talk.

"Is the whole town coming out?" Everett whispered to her.

"Just about," she said. "Why? Are you worried about getting a good seat?"

"A little," Everett replied with a sly smile. "I don't want to miss Bonnie and Clyde."

"Come on then," Rosie said, grabbing his arm. "Aunt Mary and Uncle Joe will stay out here talking until right before it starts. We can save them seats."

She found them seats on the end toward the middle of the fellowship hall, right next to Connie, who seemed delighted to see Everett.

"Well, hello," she said to him, smiling. "What are you doing here?"

"Rosie said this was the best Christmas play in the state," he replied. "I wouldn't want to miss it."

"Now, Irene's my best friend, so all I'm going to say is that I think Rosie might be pulling your leg," Connie said. She reached down into her purse and pulled out a small silver flask. "Here, better drink this for courage."

"Connie!" Rosie exclaimed.

"What?" Connie asked, her voice dripping with innocence. "I've seen this play thirty-two times. I deserve a little nip or two."

Rosie took the flask from Everett and unscrewed the top, sniffing it. "Good Lord, what's in here?"

"Irene's whisky," Connie replied. Then she leaned closer and whispered, "The kind she keeps under the counter."

"What does that mean?" Everett asked Rosie.

"It means it's her own recipe and totally illegal," she explained. She tipped the flask back and then coughed.

"Shhh!" Connie hissed. "If anybody else sees, they'll make me share!"

"Sorry." Rosie tried to keep her eyes from watering. "Here." She handed the flask to Everett. "Your turn."

He looked between Connie and Rosie, sighed, and then said, "Here goes nothing."

They were three or maybe four swigs into the whisky by the time the play started. Everett couldn't remember. It was the strongest drink he'd ever had in his entire life, and that was saying something.

He nearly fell out of his chair when he saw Clyde, in all his corgi glory, sitting in a chair, panting, wearing a Bob Cratchit costume, complete with little wire-framed glasses. It didn't get any easier when he heard a man's voice come from the side of the stage, speaking as Clyde.

"Shhh!" Rosie whispered, bringing her finger to her lips.

Everett did his best to stifle his laughter, but he wasn't the only one in the crowd who was amused, and it didn't take long for Clyde to jump out of his chair and run to Bonnie when she trotted out in her costume, the back end of the dress so long it trailed behind her, which caused her to spin around in circles trying to catch it.

"I think you've had too many nips from the old flask," Rosie said.

"I think this is the most fun I've ever had," Everett replied, practically crying. "This is the best day of my life."

"It gets better," Joe said, leaning over Rosie to reply to Everett. "There's a part with a chicken."

Just as Tiny Tim pranced onto the stage to proclaim, "God bless us, every one!" Joe's phone began to ring. It echoed through the fellowship hall, and Irene came out from the side of the stage to glare at him.

"You're in trouble now," Rosie said to him. "Give me that." She snatched it out of his hand and hurried out into the hallway.

She looked down at the number. It was a Dallas area code and a number she didn't recognize. The phone stopped ringing, but before Rosie could find the button to silence calls, it started ringing again.

Frustrated, she answered. "Hello? What? Do you know it's after business hours?"

There was a short silence, and then a hesitant female voice said, "Hello? I'm sorry, I'm trying to reach Mr. Joseph Roberts of Corgi Cove in Turtle Lake, Texas."

Shit.

"I'm so sorry," Rosie said. "Were you hoping to make a reservation? We don't usually take them anywhere else but our business phone. Wait, how did you get this number?"

"No," the woman said. "No, it's not about a reservation."

There was some mumbling on the other line, and then a noise almost as if the phone had been dropped.

"Hello?" Rosie asked. "Hello?"

"So sorry!" another voice said into the phone. "That was my intern."

"Um, okay." Rosie knitted her eyebrows together. "May I ask who *this* is?"

"This is Sissy Collins from *Texas Southern Living* magazine."

Rosie nearly dropped the phone.

"Are you there?" Sissy asked.

"Yes," she said after a heartbeat. "Yes, I'm so sorry."

"We're looking for Joseph Roberts," Sissy continued. "You don't sound much like a Joseph, no offense."

"He's my uncle," Rosie replied. "Is this about the contest?" Her words were coming out in a rush, and she felt like her heart might just beat out of her chest.

"I'm sorry, but I do need to speak with him," Sissy said.

"I'll go get him," Rosie said, already heading for the fellowship hall. "I'll go get him right now."

CHAPTER 49

Rosie

Rosie paced in the foyer while her uncle spoke with the Sissy woman on the phone. She couldn't imagine they'd call people to tell them they hadn't been selected for the contest, but she was too afraid to hope.

"Yes, ma'am, I understand," Joe was saying. "Yes, I look forward to it. Yes, thank you very much. Goodbye now."

"So?" Rosie asked just as Mary and Everett and the rest of Turtle Lake came out of the fellowship hall.

"You didn't tell me there would be an encore where the kindergarten Sunday school class tap-danced to 'Mary Did You Know,'" Everett said to Rosie. "I really could have used another shot from Connie's flask."

"Shhh!" Rosie said, waving him off. "Uncle Joe! What did she *say*?"

"Who was it, Joe?" Mary asked, her forehead creasing. "Is everything okay?"

"Let me think!" he said, staring down at his phone.

Rosie stepped closer to her uncle. "What did they want, Uncle Joe?"

"They want to come here next week," Joe said, his voice bewildered. "That woman said we, uh, Corgi Cove, is in the top five finalists for that contest you entered, Rosie."

"We made it?" she shrieked. "We made it?"

Mary took Joe's phone from his hand and stared down at it, as if Sissy Collins might still be there, waiting to say something else. "Are you sure, Joe?" she asked.

Joe nodded. "I asked her twice. She said five finalists had been picked, and we were one of them. They want to come next week and take video and pictures for their website so people can vote for the winner."

Rosie reached out and wrapped her uncle in a hug. "I can't believe it!"

"We may have life left," he said, hugging her back. "We may just have a little life left."

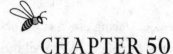

CHAPTER 50

Everett

Everett stood on the sidelines watching Rosie and her aunt and uncle celebrate. He was happy for them. He didn't think he would be, when he'd allowed himself to think that the impossible might happen, but he was. It complicated everything, and he wasn't thrilled about having to tell Francesca, and still, he couldn't help but be happy for them.

Rosie was so excited, she looked like she might burst. When she turned around to smile at him, he grinned and gave her a thumbs-up, and her smile faltered for a half second, as if she were remembering, for the first time that day, just exactly who he was and why he was there.

He was an outsider, an interloper, and he knew it. He'd been pretending for weeks that he could fit in here, be friends with them, but deep down they all knew why he was there, and it wasn't to be their friend.

Everett went outside and sat down on the steps of the church, trying to remember the way back to the Cove. If he left now, he could be back at his apartment at a reasonable time, call Francesca, and they could strategize. Although it wasn't the best news, a finalist in a contest wasn't a winner in a contest, and Everett thought the chances that they'd win were still pretty low. At least, that's what he'd tell her.

"What are you doing out here?" Rosie asked, stepping up behind him.

"Waiting for you," he said because he didn't know what else to say. "I guess congratulations are in order."

"They are," Rosie said, sitting down next to him. "Although I guess you probably aren't thrilled about it."

He looked over at her. "I'm happy for you," he said.

"But you don't think we'll win," she replied.

"I don't know if you'll win," Everett answered honestly. "But I do know that you won't be signing any papers anytime soon, and for that, I know you're thrilled."

"But it's not good for you," Rosie said. "I know that."

Everett looked over at her. "It doesn't matter what's good for me," he found himself saying. "This is good for you, and that's what's important."

"Maybe," she said. "Or maybe it's just prolonging the inevitable."

He stood. "It's probably time for me to head home," he said.

"Where?" Rosie asked. "To New York?"

Everett smiled. "No. To Austin."

"How many drinks from Connie's flask did you have?"

He shrugged. "A few."

"You're not driving back," she replied.

"You gonna get me a room at Corgi Cove?" Everett asked, smiling. "I heard it's expensive now that it's famous."

"No," Rosie said, reaching out her hand to him. "I have a better idea."

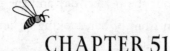

CHAPTER 51

Rosie

Rosie had no idea what she was doing. She'd made a split-second decision to invite Everett back to her cottage. Now that they were nearing her front door, she didn't know what she would do with him.

Well, she had a couple of ideas.

"You know I'm not drunk, right?" Everett asked her as she slid the key into the lock on the front door.

"Fine," she said, shrugging. "Go home."

He lingered outside on the porch for a few seconds before stepping inside. "I didn't say I wanted to go home."

Rosie smiled. "What do you want, then?"

She felt a little rush go through her as she said the words. She couldn't stop being happy. She couldn't stop feeling like she was on top of the world, knowing there was hope for the Cove, a one in five chance actually. She couldn't stop herself from thinking about the perfect day and the perfect ending standing right there in front of her, looking at her as if he were about to devour her.

Everett closed the gap between them and kissed her. It was every bit as hungry as it had been last time, but it wasn't rushed now. He took his time with it, his tongue inching inside her mouth and then tracing along her jaw and neckline.

Rosie leaned into it, moaning.

"If you keep making noises like that," he breathed into her hair, "this is going to lead straight to your bedroom."

Rosie pulled herself away from him and said, "I'll lead the way."

Before her aunt and uncle had given her the cottage to live in, they'd occasionally used it to rent out to guests who wanted some privacy, and her room, despite the clutter, looked very much like one of the rooms at the Cove. The walls were a soft pink, and her bedspread was the signature floral pattern.

Everett looked around and smiled. "This looks familiar," he said.

She shooed Toulouse out of the room and shut the door. She had no idea what she was doing, standing there in her room with Everett, but she hoped that while obvious, it wasn't too desperate. Before she could say anything, he closed the gap between them.

"That night of the storm," he said to her between kisses. "I wanted to come to your room. I thought about it all night. About what . . . about what I wanted to do to you and about what we could do together."

Rosie watched as if outside her own body, as her fingers moved to the collar of Everett's shirt and began to unbutton it.

"I thought about it, too," she said. "But I didn't think this could ever happen."

Everett gripped her hands in his as she began to pull his shirt from his shoulders and said, "I want this, but I need to make sure that you want this, too. I want to make sure you understand that this will be something neither one of us can ever take back."

She looked him in his eyes. "I understand," she said. "And I want this. Right now, this is all I want."

That was all the invitation Everett needed. He pushed her back toward the bed, one hand on her waist and one on her ass, until her back legs were flush against the mattress. He pulled her T-shirt over her head and worked the button and zipper of her jeans, pushing them down so that she stood before him in nothing but her bra and panties.

"My turn," Rosie said, finally pulling at his shirt. She ran her hands down the length of his chest and he shuddered. He bent down to put one of her peaked nipples into his mouth, his tongue pressing against the fabric of her bra.

Rosie grabbed him, desperate to feel his weight on top of her.

"I want to see you," he said to her. He pulled at his belt. "I want to see all of you."

She lay herself back onto the bed and slid off her panties, the slickness between her thighs unbearable. She flung the wet garment to the floor with one of her feet and then reached behind to unclasp her bra, not taking her eyes off him for a second.

She was rewarded when he finally sprang free from his boxers, and they were left staring at each other, completely naked.

"Merry Christmas to me," Everett said, his voice full of awe.

She couldn't help but laugh.

"Are you laughing at me?" he asked, quirking an eyebrow.

"No!" Rosie replied, nearly choking. "No, just at what you said."

Everett grinned and climbed onto the bed, positioning himself on top of her. He put his hands on her thighs and pushed them back so he could settle himself there while he got to work kissing her, from her eyelids to her neck to her nipples and then down her stomach, and even further still.

She gasped when he began to lick and suck her most intimate parts, and she squirmed beneath him.

"Shhhh," he whispered. "Be patient."

"No," she breathed, pulling him back up to her so she could kiss him. "I've been patient long enough."

Everett growled into her mouth when she wrapped her legs around him, and he slid himself into her, slowly at first, deliciously, and then with more force until she was crying out, begging him not to stop.

That night, Rosie fell asleep, for the first time in a long time, utterly and completely happy.

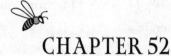

CHAPTER 52

Everett

Everett awoke the next morning to four paws on his chest and a wet nose against his cheek. Toulouse crouched there staring at him, his little, furry head cocked to the side. Everett made to pet him, but the cat jumped down, meowing all the way to the crack in the doorway.

"Mmphlomp," came Rosie's muffled reply.

Everett looked over at her. He thought she might wake up, but she didn't. She simply rolled over, and he watched her face, her deep breathing in and out, and the way her nose scrunched when the pillowcase touched it.

Silently, he got out of bed, pulled on his pants, and followed Toulouse into the kitchen, where he found the cat's food and filled his bowl. In his pocket, his phone buzzed. He pulled it out and looked down at it.

It was Francesca.

As quietly as he could, he opened the front door and stepped out onto the cottage porch.

"Hello?"

"Were you asleep?" Francesca demanded. "It's after nine A.M."

"No," he replied. "I'm awake."

"You don't sound like it," she said. "You sound like shit."

"Thanks," he said. "Is there a reason why you called?"

"Did you have something you wanted to tell me?"

Everett glanced around the yard, half expecting Francesca to pop out of a bush. "I don't know what you're talking about," he said at last. "Nothing has changed since the last time we spoke."

"Hasn't it?" she wanted to know. "Didn't your little bed-and-breakfast just become a finalist in that hillbilly magazine?"

Everett pulled his phone away from his ear and stared at it. How did she already know?

"I've been keeping up with the contest," Francesca continued. "They posted it on their website this morning. When were you going to tell me?"

"Like you said, it's only nine A.M. I've barely had time to have breakfast."

"You said they wouldn't win," Francesca replied. "You said they didn't stand a chance of winning."

"They *won't* win," he said, a little louder than he meant. "They made top five. That doesn't mean they've won the contest."

"I don't know if you believe that," she said.

Everett wanted to tell her that he didn't know what he believed anymore, especially after last night. He'd never woken up in the morning next to a woman and felt like all he wanted to do was stay there with her until she woke up. He'd never intended for that to happen. He'd never intended for a lot of things to happen. He was caught somewhere between wanting what he knew he shouldn't and wanting to do his job.

Instead, what he said was, "I do believe it, and so should you. We'll close on the deal by the first of the year at the latest. You'll have your sale, and I'll be headed first class back to the city."

It was the only thing he could say to get her off his back, to make her believe he was still on her side, even though every instinct in his body was telling him that he was saying precisely the wrong thing.

"I hope you're right," Francesca replied. "For both our sakes."

Everett pressed END CALL and shoved his phone back down into his pocket, cursing to himself. It wasn't until he'd turned back around to go inside that he saw her standing there, tears streaming, her features taut with a mix of rage and heartbreak. Before he could say anything at all, something to fix what he'd just done, Rosie slammed the door shut right in his face.

CHAPTER 53

Rosie

Everett banged on the door. He shouted her name and then he banged on the door some more. He was so loud that Toulouse began to meow, but Rosie ignored them both.

She'd overheard the whole thing. At least, she'd overheard the parts that mattered. When she'd woken to find him gone from her bed, Rosie got up to find him, hoping that he hadn't left. She'd had so many things she wanted to say to him. The previous night had been everything she'd been longing for, for weeks, but before she could join him on the porch, she'd heard him talking to someone and soon realized that it had to be one of his colleagues from New York.

At first, she'd been confused, then hurt, then so angry that it took all of her self-control not to go out there and slap him right across the face.

She went into her bedroom and shut the

door and flopped back down on her bed. How could she have been so stupid? So completely and utterly stupid? She couldn't believe she'd allowed herself to think that he cared about her, that anything could be anything other than what it was. He was here to buy the Cove.

Nothing more.

She sat up when the knocking and calling out her name stopped and at last there was silence. Then she heard the squeal of tires as they peeled out of the driveway, and Rosie knew for certain that he was gone. She ran through everything that happened the night before, trying to find some crack that she'd missed, some telltale sign that he'd been lying the whole time, but she couldn't think of anything.

He'd said to her that they couldn't take it back. What had he meant by that? She thought he meant that something would change. She thought he meant that they had changed, but right now it felt like she'd been standing still the whole time while he ran circles around her.

Stupid. Stupid. Stupid.

Rosie had nearly drifted off into a fitful sleep when she heard knocking on her front door again, this time accompanied by barks. She sat up, rubbed her eyes, and tried to decide if she wanted to answer. It could be Everett again, back to try to talk.

Slowly, she crept into the living room and pulled back the curtain behind the couch. To her relief, it was Susannah standing there, looking irritated, and Bonnie and Clyde scratching at the door.

"What took you so long . . ." Susannah trailed off when she saw Rosie standing before her. "Wow, you look like shit."

"Thanks a lot," Rosie said, stepping back to let her friend inside. "I didn't sleep very well."

"I bet not," Susannah said with a wink. "Don't think half the town didn't see you walking off with Everett last night after the play."

"Great," she replied, heaving a sigh and sitting down on the couch.

Susannah's eyebrows knit together and she sat down next to Rosie. "I thought you'd be a little smugger about it, to be honest."

Rosie tried, but everything she'd been holding in for so long came pouring out, and she told her friend everything—about the day at Christmas Candyland, about bringing Everett back to her cottage and everything they'd done, and finally, what she'd overheard this morning while he was on the phone.

When she was finished, Susannah reached out to hug her, holding her close and wiping away her tears. "Oh, Rosie, I'm so sorry," she said. "What an asshole."

"I didn't think he was an asshole," she said, sniffing. "I mean, I thought he was at first, but then . . . I don't know. I'm stupid."

"You're not stupid. *He's stupid.*"

"No, he's smart," Rosie replied. "He knew exactly what to say and exactly what to do so that I'd trust him."

"Is it possible you heard the conversation wrong?" Susannah asked. "Is it possible you took it out of context?"

She shook her head. "No," she said. "There is no way."

"Okay, then." Susannah stood up. "Then forget about him.

We've got other things to worry about, which is why I'm here in the first place."

"Like what?" Rosie asked, leaning back onto the couch.

"Get your ass up," Susannah demanded. "We've got a fucking contest to win."

CHAPTER 54

Rosie

The entire town was aflutter with the news that Corgi Cove was in the top five for the contest. The news, like all good gossip, spread fast, and nearly everyone was waiting on pins and needles to see the fancy magazine people arrive in Turtle Lake.

"How does it look?" Mary asked Rosie the morning of Sissy Collins's arrival. Connie brought the fresh flowers this morning, and Irene, God love her, brought her best wine. Even Marty came by with some of his 3D printings of . . . Mary held out a small green figure. "What is this?"

"I think that's a lizard," Rosie said with a slight wince.

"Put it behind one of the nutcrackers," Mary said.

Rosie obliged and then said, "It looks great. Everything looks great."

"I'm so nervous," her aunt continued. "I didn't think I could ever be nervous again after your uncle's heart attack. I thought it scared the nervous right out of me, but here I am, a bellyful of butterflies."

"There's no reason to be nervous," Rosie said, even though she felt exactly the same way. "They're not here to judge us. They're just here to get pictures and video for the website."

"And then people are going to vote!" Aunt Mary said, raising her hands up to the heavens. "What if nobody votes for us?"

"I'm going to vote for us," Rosie replied with a grin. "So that's at least one vote."

"Where's Joe?" Mary asked, suddenly turning around where she stood. "He said half an hour ago he was going to sweep the porch."

"I didn't see him out there when I got here," Rosie said. "Maybe he's out on the back porch?"

Her aunt set her mouth in a grim line. "Out there with Irene and Connie," she said.

Rosie knew exactly what that meant, and she followed her aunt out onto the back porch to find all three of them sitting in rocking chairs, eating the pumpkin bread Mary made fresh the night before.

"You!" Mary said, wagging a finger at them. "What did I tell you about that pumpkin bread?"

Connie, at least, managed to look guilty. "It's just one piece," she said. "It's so good, Mary, you can't expect us to leave it all to some people from Dallas."

"Those *people* are our *guests*," Mary pointed out, snatching what was left of the bread from Connie.

"You've got two more loaves inside!" Joe protested.

"And you're not supposed to be eating it, anyway!" Mary scolded him. "Remember what Dr. Noth said?"

"Then why did you make it?" he asked, standing up to follow her inside. "You know it's my favorite!"

"For the guests!" Mary said, this time, unable to hide the hint of a smile. "I swear it, old man, you're going to be the death of me."

Rosie grinned. She loved listening to their playful arguments. It sometimes amazed her to think about how her aunt and uncle had been married longer than she'd been alive. What kind of dedication it must take to be with another person for all those years? Her own parents hadn't even been able to make it past Rosie's first year of life, but it wasn't something she was angry about. That was just the way it was.

She felt her chest tighten, though, when she thought about what it might be like for her years from now. Would she be married? Would she have a family? Would she, one day, be having a silly argument in her kitchen with her husband about pumpkin bread?

Rosie didn't really know what she wanted, but she would be lying to herself if she hadn't allowed herself to fantasize about what it might be like to know Everett well enough to at least think about these kinds of things. Now, when she thought about him, all she wanted to do was crawl into bed and get under the covers.

"What are you thinking about, sweetheart?" her aunt said, coming up behind her. "You look so melancholy."

"Nothing," Rosie said quickly. "I'm just nervous about today, that's all."

"Didn't you just tell me that everything was going to be great?" Mary asked. "Or was I talking to your body double?"

"Shhh! Marty will hear you."

Mary took her hand and led her over to the couch in the living room. "Is this about Everett St. Claire?"

"What?" she asked, feeling her cheeks flush. "Why would you ask me that?"

"He hasn't been by since the night of the play," Aunt Mary said. She looked Rosie in the eye. "I know that car of his was parked at your house all night. And if I hadn't known, Connie and Irene would have told me."

She sighed. "Why does everyone in this town insist on knowing everybody else's business?"

"That's our way," Mary replied. "How else would I have known that you and Susannah were smoking behind the gym in eleventh grade?"

"Or that I failed my Spanish test my senior year?" Rosie asked, trying to smile.

"Now, I only found out about that because Connie pulled it out of the trash."

"I never should have thrown it away in front of the flower shop."

Mary patted Rosie's hand. "Did something happen? With Everett?"

Rosie bit at her bottom lip. "He just wasn't the person I thought he was," was all she said.

"And who did you think he was?" Mary asked.

"I don't know," she said with a shrug. "But I hope we win this contest so that I never have to see him again."

As if on cue, there was a little knock at the front door, and it opened a crack. A woman pushed her head through and looked around. "Hello?" she said in a thick Southern accent. "Anybody home?"

"Yes!" Mary said, jumping up. "Please, come on in!"

CHAPTER 55

Everett

Everett sat on his couch, scrolling through movies on his iPad. He couldn't find anything he wanted to watch. Rather, he didn't really want to watch anything. He didn't want to be in this apartment, and he didn't want to be in Texas. For days, he'd contemplated ways he could apologize to Rosie, ways he could say something, anything, to make her understand that she'd heard his conversation with Francesca all wrong.

Of course, she hadn't heard it wrong. She'd heard it completely right, and that was the problem. He'd sounded like an asshole. He knew it. She knew it, and now she would probably never speak to him again.

And he wouldn't blame her a bit.

Twice, he'd gotten in his car and driven halfway to Turtle Lake only to turn back around and drive home to Austin, where

he pulled over and sat at the city limits sign, trying to decide if he was pathetic or stupid. This seemed to be his pattern lately—mess up his entire life completely and then have absolutely no idea how to fix it. How had this happened?

All his life, he'd wanted to work in the city, in a huge office, make money, and be the guy, THAT guy that everyone went to, to fix things. And for so long, he had been. When he'd been sent to Texas, he thought he was going to the end of the earth. He'd dreaded the trip, and somehow, for a little while, he'd enjoyed himself. He started to think about a different kind of life, with different people, as a different version of himself.

Then he'd fucked it all up.

He had a decision to make, and he had to make it fast.

CHAPTER 56

Rosie

Sissy Collins was a spitfire. For such a tiny woman, she sure did take up a lot of room. She buzzed about from room to room, directing her cameraman and assistant like it might be everyone's last day on earth.

"I love these decorations!" Sissy cooed. "They're so vintage."

Rosie wasn't entirely sure that was a compliment, but she replied, "If you like these, you should see the ones around town."

"Oh, could we?" Sissy asked, clapping her hands together. "We could get more footage of this *charming town*."

"Sure," she said. "Anything that you think might help."

Sissy snapped at her entourage. "Load up," she said. "We're going out."

Rosie directed Sissy's driver to park in front of the flower shop, which was the most central location in town. Everyone already knew they were coming today, so Rosie was prepared for people to stare. What she hadn't prepared for was half the town dropping what they were doing to come over and see what all the fuss was about.

For once in her life, she was thankful for Connie, who opened the door to the flower shop and hustled them all inside.

"Thanks," she said. "I thought we were about to be eaten alive."

"Irene and I started a phone tree last night to call everyone and tell them not to show up at the Cove this morning. Apparently, a few people had the idea that they could 'help' by being there to cheer your aunt and uncle on."

"Thank you," Rosie said again, hugging Connie.

"What a *charming place*," Sissy said. "Mind if we take a few shots?"

"Be my guest," Connie said, smiling broadly.

"That's the second time she's said *charming* in the last hour," Rosie whispered to Connie.

"City folks," she replied.

Rosie spent the rest of the afternoon showing Sissy and her people all around the town, introducing them to people and posing for pictures outside some of the more picturesque shops.

"Before we go back to the Cove, would you like to see my cottage?" Rosie asked Sissy as they headed back.

She thought about it. "Is it part of the property?" she asked.

Rosie nodded. "Yes. I live there now, but before that, my aunt and uncle used it as a rental."

"Sure," Sissy replied. "We could get a few more pictures before we turn in for the night."

Rosie led them down the path to the cottage after they parked their rental cars at the Cove. It was a mild night, and it thrilled Rosie that the weather was so lovely for Sissy and her team. It really had seemed like Sissy was impressed with the place, and even though she knew that the magazine didn't have control over who won and who lost, it was nice to feel like she and her aunt and uncle were making a good impression.

"Oh, how cute!" Sissy breathed when they reached the cottage. "Wait, are those *beehives*?"

"Yes!" Rosie said. "I make beeswax products and sell honey when it's in season. Right now, they're pretty much done for the winter."

"Do you have one of those . . ." Sissy trailed off, thinking. "Oh, what are they called?"

"A beekeeper suit?" her intern offered.

"Yes!" Sissy said. "One of those? We could get a few pictures of you wearing it in front of your hives. That would be so charming!"

Rosie resisted the urge to giggle and went inside to put on the outfit. She'd left her phone on her nightstand all day, wanting to give the team from the magazine all of her attention while also conveniently ignoring any inquiring calls from townspeople. But when it buzzed as she was getting dressed, she went over to check.

There were three messages from Everett and several missed calls.

Can we talk?

I'd really like to sit down and explain some things.

Please, Rosie.

Rosie set the phone down and backed away, feeling sick to her stomach. She'd been telling herself that they were going to win the contest and that she'd never have to see Everett again, however unrealistic it was.

"Everything okay in there?" Sissy called from the porch.

"Yes!" Rosie answered. "I'm coming."

She felt silly standing in front of her beehives posing for photos, especially in her suit. She didn't think that she'd ever had her picture taken like this before.

"Okay, now put your hand on your hip," the photographer said. "Just like that. Great! Great!"

As she posed, she heard tires on gravel, and through her mask, she saw Everett's sleek BMW drive down the path.

"I'm sorry," she said, taking off her mask. "Could you-all give me just a few minutes?"

"Sure," Sissy replied, raising her eyebrows at the car. "We'll walk down toward the lake and take a few pictures down there."

"Thanks," Rosie replied, giving her a grateful smile.

She walked toward the car, taking as many deep breaths as she could as she watched Everett get out and wave at her. He looked as nervous as she felt. She hated that he had the audacity to look that way at her when *he* was the one who'd ruined everything.

"What do you want?" she asked him. "I'm busy."

"You look it," he replied.

Rosie rolled her eyes. "Go back to Austin," she said, turning around.

"No, Rosie, wait," he said, catching her by the arm. "Can we please talk?"

"What else is there to talk about?" she asked him, feeling her face warm at the memory of overhearing his conversation. "I think I heard all that I need to, don't you?"

"No," Everett said. "You don't understand."

"Then why don't you explain it?" she asked, crossing her arms over her chest. "Because I heard you tell someone that you know that we aren't going to win the contest and that you'll be buying the Cove. That's what I heard."

"I know," he said, looking sheepish. "But that's not the whole story."

"Do you or do you not think we're going to lose this contest?" she asked. "Because as you can see, the people from the magazine are here, and they seem pretty confident we have a chance."

"I think you have a chance," he replied. "But I couldn't say that to my boss."

"Why not?"

Everett sighed. "Because I don't want to lose my job. I can't go back to New York without a sale. Surely, you understand that."

"So you're hoping we lose?"

"No," he said. "No, that's not what I said."

"It sure seems like that's what you're saying."

"I'm saying I'm between a rock and a hard place," Everett said. "I don't know what to do here."

"I don't know what you're doing here, either," Rosie replied. "Honestly, I don't. It seems like you've made yourself clear—you need us to lose so that you can win."

"I don't want anyone to lose," he said. "That's what I'm trying to tell you."

"Well, somebody has to lose," she replied. "If we lose, then you win. You get the Cove. If we win, you lose, and you go back to work empty-handed."

He looked at her. "Do you want me to go back to New York?"

"What?" Rosie asked, taken aback by the question. Of course she didn't want him to go back. All she wanted was for him to say he was sorry, give up his job, and stay here with her forever. But of course she couldn't say that. She couldn't even think it without wanting to throw up.

"Do you want me to go back to New York?" Everett repeated.

"You'll have to. Either way, you'll have to."

"That's not what I asked." He took a step closer to her.

Rosie backed up. She couldn't trust him. She knew she couldn't. He'd proven it, hadn't he? "I think," she said. "I think it's best for both of us if you do."

CHAPTER 57

Rosie

The way the Cove lit up at night was enough to make her feel a little better. She'd always loved the way the Cove looked after the outside was decorated with Christmas lights. The night before Sissy and her crew arrived, they'd gotten the outside of the Cove decorated with lights. They looked pretty good for being mostly purchased on a budget from Dollar General. After they'd realized most of their old lights were burned out, Rosie had tapped into her beeswax savings to buy more. She really needed to send a thank-you email to Breezy for buying all of her lotion at the last farmers' market.

When she got inside, she found several of Sissy's crew at the dining room table eating sweet potato casserole and her aunt, smiling up a storm, serving them.

"Where's Uncle Joe?" she asked.

"He's out on the back porch with a couple of those camera boys and some of Irene's moonshine."

"Where's Sissy?" Rosie asked. She glanced around. "Did she already go back up to her room for the night?"

"No, she's in the living room in front of the fire," Mary replied.

Rosie wandered into the kitchen and grabbed a bottle of wine off the wine rack and opened it. She poured two glasses and went into the living room. Truly, in front of the fire was the most glorious place to be.

"Hi," Rosie said to Sissy. "Here. I brought you some wine."

"Oh, aren't you the sweetest," she said. "Thank you."

"I don't know if it'll be as nice as what you're used to," Rosie said, apologetic. "We just have one liquor store here."

Sissy smiled. "What do you think I'm used to?"

"I don't know," she said, laughing. "It just seemed like the thing to say."

"Honey, I'm from a town smaller than this in Kentucky. Good wine is not something I need in my life to be happy."

"I never would have guessed," Rosie replied. "You don't look it."

"You remember that movie with Reese Witherspoon?" Sissy asked. "Oh, what's it called? *Sweet Home Alabama*?"

She nodded. "I love that movie."

"Well, it's like that for me, except I'm far more beautiful than Mrs. Witherspoon," Sissy said with a wink. "And, of course, I've never gone back."

"Before I lived here, I lived in Houston," Rosie admitted. "I hated Turtle Lake at first."

Sissy took a sip of her wine. "How come?"

She shrugged. "I was fifteen. I was angry. I hated my mother."

"I can identify with all of that," Sissy replied, taking another sip.

"But I've come to love it. I can't imagine living anywhere else."

"If I lived at Corgi Cove, I might feel the same way," Sissy said. "I shouldn't be telling you this, but when I saw this place, I made the executive decision to put you on the list."

"Really?" Rosie asked, turning to her. "How come? And please don't say that it's charming."

Sissy laughed. "Well, it is," she replied. "But it's not just that. This place has got personality. So many of the other places we saw were just fine, but they didn't speak to me like Corgi Cove did." She looked around. "Although, I have to admit, it could use a few coats of paint."

Rosie debated for a few seconds what she said next, but she decided that it didn't really matter. It wasn't a secret. "Well, if I'm being honest," she began, "we're about to lose this place. We can't afford it anymore. That's the reason why it looks the way it does."

Now it was Sissy who turned to Rosie. "Oh no," she said. "How is that possible?"

"Did you see that huge hotel on your way into town?"

Sissy nodded.

"That's the Lake Queen," Rosie said. Then she took a long drink from her wineglass. "I guess that place isn't entirely the reason. My aunt and uncle aren't particularly good at promoting themselves, but the Lake Queen came in a few years ago, and now most people who come to Turtle Lake stay there."

"And now you're going to lose this wonderful place?" Sissy asked.

"We might if we don't win the contest," she said. "I'm only telling you this because I know you don't have any control over who wins. I'm not asking for sympathy."

Sissy finished her glass of wine. "You should have brought the whole bottle for this conversation," she said. "And don't worry, your secret is safe with me."

"Thank you," Rosie said. "Maybe if we win, we can get a few coats of paint."

"I think you'll be able to do more than that," Sissy replied. "You know, we've got something in common, you and I."

"We do?"

"We do," Sissy said. "As editor in chief, I wouldn't normally come out here with a team to photograph a place. I'd just wait for the team to come back and put it all together and make it look nice."

"Oh, really?"

"Yes," the woman continued. "But the magazine, much like this place, needs help. Nobody is buying magazines anymore. This contest is supposed to be a much-needed boon to the launch of our website. We need to do well, or I'm afraid I'll be out of a job before the next year is over."

"I have to admit I hadn't read your magazine before my best friend Susannah told me about the contest," Rosie said. "But she has a subscription for her clients at her hair salon."

"That's about all we're good for anymore," Sissy said. "Hair salons and doctor's offices."

"And you think the website will help?"

"I hope so," Sissy said. "Just like I hope you'll win. I mean that. I truly do."

Without thinking, Rosie reached out and hugged her, and Sissy let out a little gasp of surprise. "I hope we both win," Rosie said. "We can both get a new coat of paint."

CHAPTER 58

Everett

Everett watched New York come into view from his window seat on the airplane. He'd called Francesca the day before to let her know that he was coming home; she'd have to send someone else to Texas. She hadn't been thrilled, but truthfully, he hadn't cared.

He knew he might lose his job once he got to the office, but the best thing he could do was tell them that he'd had a personality conflict with the potential clients and that the company would be best served by sending a more experienced person into the field. Maybe he'd still be able to keep his old job.

Maybe.

For now, Everett just needed the plane to land as far away from Texas as he could possibly get. LaGuardia seemed like a good start.

CHAPTER 59

Rosie

It was nearly Christmas. Rosie knew this because everyone she met on the street seemed to be reminding her. Besides that, it was as if the great state of Texas knew it, too, because the weather had shifted from mild to nippy, and Rosie was reveling in it.

She hadn't heard another word from Everett, and neither had her aunt and uncle, a fact that Mary had lamented more than once. No, she didn't want to sell the Cove to Everett, but she'd come to like him, and his absence with no word why was starting to upset her, especially after a few of her calls to him went unanswered.

"Do you think he's ill?" she asked Rosie. "He was here all the time; we couldn't get rid of him, and then POOF!"

"I don't think he's sick, Aunt Mary. I'm sure he's just busy."

"Busy with what?" Mary asked. "We're the only reason he's in the state."

Rosie searched for any kind of excuse that would placate her aunt. "Well, I'm sure we'll hear from him sooner or later," she said. "Unless we win of course."

Mary fixed her with a stare. "Did something happen between you two?"

"What?" she asked. "No, what are you talking about?"

"I'm smarter than I look."

Rosie was about to reply when her aunt's cell phone beeped from inside her apron pocket. She took it out and stared at it, put it back in her apron pocket, and then took it out and stared at it again.

"Rosie?" Mary asked.

"Yeah?"

"Why is your mother asking me if the twenty-third would be a good day to arrive at the house for Christmas?"

Shit. In all of the chaos of the last couple of weeks, Rosie had completely forgotten that she'd invited her mother to come for Christmas. She hadn't thought she'd really come, anyway. They hadn't talked about it again. She figured her mother would at least call to discuss it with her first.

"I'm so sorry," Rosie said. "I sort of . . . asked her if she wanted to come for Christmas."

"You did what?" Mary asked, still staring at her phone. "Rosie, why would you do that without talking to me first?"

"I didn't think she'd come," she said. "It was a spur-of-the-moment thing. She hasn't come in so long, and I just didn't think . . ."

Aunt Mary held up her hands. "I don't want to talk about it right now." She walked away without saying another word.

Rosie stood in the kitchen staring after her.

"What was that all about?" Joe asked, coming in off the back porch. He was getting along so much better lately. It was hard for her to remember that he'd even had a heart attack. "Your aunt looks like she's seen a ghost."

"Yeah, the Ghost of Sisters Past," she muttered.

"Who, Katherine?" Uncle Joe replied. "What's going on with your mother?"

"She's coming for Christmas," Rosie said.

"Your aunt invited your mother to Christmas?" he asked, his tone surprised. "Well, I'll be damned. I never thought I'd live to see the day."

"No. I did, and then I forgot to tell Aunt Mary that I'd done it."

Joe let out a low whistle under his breath. "You're in trouble now."

"I know," Rosie said. "You don't have to remind me." She sat down at the kitchen table. "It's just that with everything going on lately, I forgot."

"You havin' trouble with that Everett?" he asked, sitting down across from her.

"Why does everybody keep asking me that?" she said.

Her uncle laughed. "You think we're blind, kiddo?"

"There is nothing going on between me and Everett," Rosie replied. "At least, not anymore."

"Do you want to talk about it?"

She shrugged. "No. Maybe. I don't know. It's stupid to be upset over Everett when we have the contest coming up. There are a lot more important things to worry about."

"I don't know about that."

"I do. He was here to buy the Cove. That's it."

"Was?" Joe asked. "Where did he go?"

"I don't know," she said. "He said he might go back to New York."

"Did he, now?"

"Well, he asked me if I thought he should," Rosie admitted.

Uncle Joe rested his hands on the table. "And what did you tell him?"

She sighed. "I told him I thought he should."

"Why was he asking you that in the first place?" he wanted to know. "If he's just here to buy the Cove and nothing else?"

The tightness in her chest threatened to suffocate her, and before she realized it, tears were sliding down her cheeks.

Joe scooted his chair over to where she sat and embraced her. "Shhh," he said. "It's all right. It's going to be all right."

"I know," Rosie said, straightening. "I'm sorry."

"There's no need to apologize," her uncle replied. "You know, I think maybe your aunt and I put too much pressure on you. All of this nonsense about saving the Cove. It's been a lot to deal with."

"It's not nonsense. This is our home."

"No," Joe said, taking her hand. "My home is with you and Mary. And if you don't mind an old man giving you his two cents, that Everett St. Claire is an idiot if he doesn't come back."

CHAPTER 60

Everett

Christmas in New York just didn't feel the same. Everett hoped he'd feel better once he walked into his building, but all he felt was nervous. He'd already told Francesca, but now he had a meeting with his "big" boss, his real boss, Jared. Jared was the whole reason he ended up in Texas in the first place. Everett hoped that when he left for the day, he wouldn't be leaving with a box of his things as well.

"Everett!"

He looked up from his phone to see one of his work buddies, Patrick, standing in front of him. "Hey, man, what's up?"

"Long time no see!" Patrick said, clapping him on the back. "I heard a rumor you were down South."

"I was," Everett admitted.

"Damn, Jared is vindictive, huh?"

He nodded. "Yeah, well, it wasn't all bad."

"I've never been any farther south than Pennsylvania," Patrick said.

"I don't think that counts," he replied, grinning.

"No, probably not," Patrick said, a bit deflated. "So, you're here to see the big guy?"

Everett waved when Jared's receptionist motioned to him. "Yeah, I gotta go," he said. "Hopefully, not to my death."

"Good luck, man."

Everett took a deep breath and headed into Jared's office.

Jared stood up and reached out to take his hand. "How are ya, Everett?"

"I'm good," he said. "Glad to be back."

"Are you?" Jared asked.

"I am," he replied, bracing himself. "If I still have a job, that is."

"Why wouldn't you?" Jared asked, sitting back down behind his desk.

"Well," he began. "We did have a major disagreement, and then you sent me to Texas to buy a bed-and-breakfast that I ultimately failed to buy. I assumed that you wouldn't be pleased."

"I'm never pleased. Can you remember the last time you saw me pleased?"

He thought about it. "Last Christmas," he said. "When your former assistant got drunk and puked on that guy you hate from Accounting. What's his name?"

"Mike," Jared said, a hint of a smile on his face. "I hate that guy."

"Everybody does."

"Look," his boss said, getting down to business. "I'm not going to fire you. At least not today. Sending you to Texas was a mistake. I was angry, and I shouldn't have done it."

"I appreciate that," Everett replied. "But you weren't the only one who was wrong. We both said some things we regret."

Jared waved him off. "So, assuming you're not forever scarred from your time in the Lone Star State, are you ready to get back to work?"

Everett thought about it. Just minutes ago, he'd been praying he wasn't fired. He'd been wondering if there was anything he could do or say to save his job, and now, looking around the office, seeing Patrick and Jared and everyone else he thought he missed . . . well, he wasn't sure.

What was left for him here, really?

"Well?" Jared asked. "What are you waiting for?"

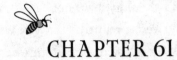

CHAPTER 61

Rosie

It was December 19. Voting on the website was in full swing, and Rosie and Susannah were making their way around town asking everyone to make sure they voted.

"Marty, you have to vote," Susannah was saying. "It's for the Cove!"

"I don't use the internet," he replied, crossing his arms over his chest. "You know that. It's the same reason I don't own a cell phone. I'm not going to explode when 5G takes over."

Susannah rolled her eyes. "I know your wife has a laptop," she said. "She uses it to give one star reviews to every restaurant that has a tip option on their credit card machines."

"I also know," Rosie stepped in, "that you use her laptop to order GMO pineapples from Costa Rica."

"How did you know about that?" Marty whispered, his face horrified. "Who told you?"

"It doesn't matter how I know," she said. "All that matters is that your secret is safe with us if you vote."

"Fine," Marty replied. "I'll go home and vote, but if you tell anybody . . ."

"We won't!" Susannah and Rosie said in unison.

"Do you think this will be enough?" Rosie asked Susannah once Marty had walked away mumbling to himself about 5G. "I mean, I know we need more than the town to vote for us, but do you think this will even help?"

"How could it hurt?" Susannah asked.

"I don't know. I'm nervous."

"Don't be," Susannah said. "It'll either work out or it won't."

"That's very comforting," Rosie said.

"I'm serious. You can't control everything. It's going to be what it's going to be."

"I know that." Rosie picked at an imaginary piece of lint on her shirt.

"Do you?" Susannah asked. "Because everything, even people, are unpredictable."

"Are we still talking about the Cove?" Rosie asked. "Because it feels like you're talking about something else."

Susannah waved at Connie, who was helping an older woman into her car with a bouquet of roses. "What happened with you and Everett, Rosie?"

"Nothing," she replied. "Nothing good, anyway."

"Let me guess," Susannah said. "He didn't turn out to be the person you thought he was."

"Yep."

"And because he wasn't the person you thought he was," her friend continued, "you decided you were done with him."

"It's not like that."

"Tell me what it's like, then."

"I overheard him telling someone that he thought we were going to lose and that he was going to buy the Cove," Rosie said.

"Oh, shit."

"Yeah."

"I'm sorry," Susannah said. "I really thought he was a good guy."

"Me, too," she replied. "And then there's that whole thing with my aunt."

"What thing?" Susannah asked.

"I invited my mother for Christmas, and she'll be here this afternoon."

"You did what?" Susannah stopped so abruptly that two people behind them nearly knocked into her.

"I invited my mom," Rosie explained. "And I didn't think about asking Aunt Mary first, and she's mad about it, and she's mad at me for not discussing it with her, and everything is a mess right now, and I know it's only ten A.M., but I could really use a big old drink."

Rosie wasn't sure if she was truly seeing the hustle and bustle going on at Corgi Cove or if the two margaritas she and Susannah had over lunch were making her hallucinate.

"Uncle Joe," Rosie said, "what's going *on*?"

He gave her a broad grin. "We're booked up, that's what," he said. "Booked up through Christmas."

"Really?" Rosie asked. "How is that possible?"

"It's that contest," Joe replied. "It's on the internet, I reckon. People have been talking about it all day. Most of these folks are city folks from Austin who saw the Cove and wanted to get away for the holidays."

"Are we prepared for that?" she asked.

"Not in the slightest," Aunt Mary said, hurrying over to where she and Joe stood. "Joe, I sent you out ten minutes ago to sweep that front porch!"

"I'm infirmed, Mary," he said, clutching his heart. "I move slower these days."

"Nonsense. You've been talking to the guests."

"That sounds like me," he agreed, ambling off with his broom.

"Can I help with anything?" Rosie asked her aunt. "Why didn't you call me when things started getting busy?"

She looked at Rosie. Things had been icy with them since Mary found out that she had invited Katherine for Christmas, and now, with the Cove completely full, Rosie was sure that it made the situation a hundred times worse.

"You can take these towels up to room three," Mary said finally. "And, Rosie?"

"Yeah?"

"Your mother and stepfather are going to have to stay with you in the cottage," she said. "I'm sorry, but we just don't have the room."

Rosie had known the moment that her uncle told her they were booked that this was going to happen, and she supposed she deserved it for inviting her mother unannounced. Still, her cottage was an absolute wreck. There was no way, after helping here this afternoon, she'd have time to clean it.

"Sure," she said, finally, giving her aunt a weak smile. "Of course."

"Scoot," Mary said, waving her off. "We've got a lot to do today!"

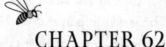

CHAPTER 62

Rosie

They were having a cocktail hour. There hadn't been a cocktail hour at the Cove in at least three years, and Rosie, despite the general tenor of the day, couldn't help but grin at all the people milling about the Cove, talking to each other, and enjoying Mary's signature hot toddy.

"This is so good," an elderly woman in a green dress with cats printed on it said to Mary. "There's something in here that I can't quite put my finger on. What is it?"

"That's my secret ingredient," Mary said, pouring the woman another. "I could tell you, but I'd have to kill you."

"Oh!" the woman said, laughing. "Aren't you a card!"

Joe, for his part, was having a very in-depth conversation with the cat woman's husband about yodeling. Rosie could tell that Joe wanted any excuse to leave the conversation and kept subtly gesturing to her for help, but they both knew that Mary would kill them if they staged an escape. Entertaining the guests during cocktail hour was important.

Rosie was just about to go over and at least suggest a new topic when the front door opened and Katherine stood there, followed closely by Rosie's stepfather, Rick.

Katherine looked around the room, clearly surprised to see so many people there. Although Rosie hadn't told her much over the years about the Cove's trouble, her mother was a smart woman. She knew what was going on.

Mary's lips went into a tight smile when she saw the duo, and she walked over to air-kiss her sister's cheeks, and they exchanged hellos.

Rosie watched, not even realizing that she was holding her breath until Joe came over and whispered, "They'd never draw blood in front of a crowd."

She chucked the rest of her hot toddy and replied, "There's always the privacy of the kitchen."

"Rosie!" Katherine said, rushing over to envelop her in a hug. "I've been trying to call you. We nearly got lost on the drive in from the airport. I haven't been here in so long, I'd forgotten the way!"

"I'm so sorry," Rosie said, somewhat sheepish. "I think I have my ringer on silent."

"It's okay. We found it, didn't we, Rick?"

Rick, ever the strong and silent type, merely nodded.

"Hello, Rick," Rosie said, reaching past her mother to hug her stepfather. "How was the trip?"

"Oh, you know," he said, smiling.

Rosie smiled back. He hated to travel, but he loved her mother, so he endured.

"Can I get either of you a drink?" she asked.

"I'd love to go to our room first," Katherine replied. "We've been in the car forever and on the plane before that."

Rosie and Mary exchanged a glance.

"Well," Rosie said. "We've had a huge influx of guests today. We weren't expecting it, and now the Cove is booked up."

"Okay," Katherine said. "So, where do you expect us to sleep? Out on the porch with the dogs?"

"The dogs don't sleep on the porch," Joe said, coming inside. "They have their own beds."

Rick cleared his throat.

"We thought you two could stay with me at the cabin," Rosie replied.

"Are you sure?" Katherine said. "Isn't there just one bedroom in the cabin?"

"I'll take the couch," Rosie said. "Seriously, it's fine."

"All right, honey," her mother said. She looked over at Mary. "Can we have a drink first?"

Rosie fixed everyone a drink, and they sat down among the throng. Katherine seemed impressed the Cove was so full and hadn't complained at all about being relegated to the cottage with Rosie.

Bonnie and Clyde were making their way around the room, charming everyone they came into contact with. As irritated as she got with them sometimes, they were truly delightful dogs.

They loved everyone, even people . . . well, maybe even most especially people . . . who didn't seem to like them. They were a little bit like cats that way, she supposed.

She reached down absently and scratched Clyde's ear. Her mother and aunt were having a conversation, and Rosie couldn't believe that they were both smiling. She couldn't remember the last time she'd even heard them talk without some sort of an argument taking place.

"Rosie!" her mother called. "Come over here for a second!"

She got up and walked over to where her mother and aunt sat. "Do you two need another drink?"

"What?" Katherine asked. "Oh no, we're fine. Do you remember that Christmas you were five and your aunt Mary and uncle Joe sent you that rocking horse? What was it you called him?"

"Brownie," Rosie said automatically. "And yes, I remember."

"Do you remember that you rode that thing until the springs popped off, and you flew across the living room into the coffee table?" Katherine continued. "We had to take you to the ER on New Year's Eve."

Rosie lifted up her bangs to show a scar just below her hairline. "I'll never forget it," she replied. "You put Brownie in the garage and wouldn't let me ride him anymore, and I was devastated."

"You had to have six stitches!" her mother protested. "It was for your own good!"

Mary burst out laughing. "I can't believe that!" she said. "I cannot believe *you*," she said, pointing at Katherine, "didn't call to tell me how mad you were that I'd sent Rosie a gift that nearly killed her!"

"I wasn't about to tell you that I'd let Rosie get hurt!" Katherine replied, laughing as well. "I was afraid you'd think I was a terrible mother!"

Mary clasped her hand and said, "I would never think that."

Rosie felt herself warm all over. Maybe it was the hot toddy, and maybe it was Christmas cheer, but she couldn't help feeling that everything in that moment was just as it should be.

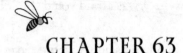

CHAPTER 63

Rosie

The year she'd been sent to Corgi Cove to live with her aunt and uncle, Rosie's mother came for Christmas. Still desperate to get back to Houston, Rosie harbored fantasies that if she could just act angelic enough, her mother would pack her up and take her home.

It didn't happen that way.

In fact, Katherine and Mary spent a good portion of Katherine's trip bickering over one thing or another. Rosie had been too young to really care about the intricacies of the relationship her mother and aunt had, but she HAD cared when their argument was about her. From what she gathered, Katherine *had* wanted to take her home, and Mary hadn't wanted to allow it. She didn't think six months was long enough for Rosie to have a chance to thrive.

Rosie had burst into the kitchen where they were arguing so that she could add in her two cents. That's when she noticed that her aunt was crying, sitting at the table, looking down at her cup of coffee. Her mother, for her part, was standing near the sink, arms crossed over her chest and staring out the window.

Mary had looked up at Rosie, tried to smile, and said, "I understand that you're unhappy here. If you'd like to leave, I'll help you pack your things."

Of course, in the end, Rosie *hadn't* gone home to Houston with her mother. Part of her wanted to. Part of her wanted to so badly, and it hadn't just been her aunt's devastated face that changed her mind. That had been the Christmas break that she went out with Tommy for the first time and became close with Susannah. It had been the Christmas where her uncle revealed to her that she could live in the cottage when she turned eighteen, if she helped him make some improvements. It had also been the Christmas she realized that if she went back to Houston, her aunt and uncle might not want her back a second time. That thought upset her more than she wanted to admit.

As an adult, Rosie knew that Aunt Mary and Uncle Joe would have taken her back as many times as necessary, but at fifteen, she hadn't been sure.

So she'd stayed, and she believed her life had been all the better for it. Still, she was nervous about her mother being at the Cove for Christmas.

"The cottage looks different than the last time I saw it," Katherine said, looking around Rosie's messy house. "It's clear you didn't know we'd be staying with you."

"Sorry," she said, sheepish. "I would have cleaned if I'd known."

"So, all those guests just appeared out of thin air?" her mother asked, handing her bags to Rick. "What's going on that you're so busy?"

"It's the holidays," Rosie said with a shrug.

"Rosie," Katherine replied. "When was the last time Corgi Cove was so busy during the holidays?"

"You can talk to Aunt Mary about it in the morning," she replied.

"Fine, fine." Katherine waved her daughter off. "Last I remembered, the cottage just had one bedroom."

"You and Rick can take it," she said. "Just give me a minute to change the sheets."

"You can't sleep on the couch!" Katherine replied. "That's no more than a glorified futon."

"It's fine." She decided against telling her mother she'd slept there plenty of times, when she and Susannah had too much wine and she'd been too tired to make it to the bedroom.

"Will you show me the hives in the morning?" Rick asked. "I've always wanted to see them."

"Of course," Rosie replied, smiling at her stepfather, grateful for the change in subject. "First thing in the morning."

She went back into the bedroom and cleaned up as much as she could. She changed the sheets and made sure there was a fresh roll of toilet paper in the bathroom. That would absolutely be something her mother would notice. She knew that in her mother's house, there were scores of bathrooms and a maid to keep everything clean. They hadn't had a maid at the Cove in five years, and she'd never had anyone come to the cottage to clean. It felt too weird. Now she was wishing there was someone better than her to keep the place nice for unexpected guests.

When she came back out, she found that Toulouse had found her mother and Rick and had made himself comfortable between them. Then she realized why—Bonnie and Clyde were scratching at the door, begging entrance.

"Didn't you hear the dogs?" Rosie asked.

"I wasn't sure if they were allowed inside," her mother replied, stroking Toulouse.

Rosie glared at both of them, but especially at Toulouse, who was looking particularly pleased with himself to have found an ally.

"Traitor," she whispered to him as she opened the door.

Bonnie and Clyde came bounding in, sniffing around until they noticed Katherine and Rick. Much to Toulouse's and Katherine's dismay, they jumped right up onto the couch and began licking them. Toulouse jumped down and meowed all the way to the bedroom.

"These dogs don't have any manners," Rosie's mother said.

"They're corgis," Rick replied. "I don't think it's in their genetics."

"Uncle Joe would take offense to that," Rosie said, laughing. "But I agree that these corgis in particular don't seem to have any manners."

"I read in a magazine that dogs act like their owners," Katherine said, testing a pet on Clyde's head and deciding she didn't like it.

"And Aunt Mary would take offense to *that*," Rosie said. "Anyway, they come and go as they please. But I promise I won't let them stay with you in the bedroom tonight."

Rick looked a little disappointed.

"What about the cat?" Katherine asked.

"I can't tell him what to do," Rosie replied. "In fact, nobody can."

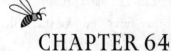

CHAPTER 64

Rosie

The next morning, Rosie awoke to Rick cooking breakfast in her kitchen. The couch hadn't been nearly as comfortable as she remembered, but she'd slept through the night for the most part, and she had to admit it was nice to wake up to the smell of eggs and bacon.

"Where did you get this food?" she asked him, stretching. "I don't have anything in my refrigerator."

"I noticed," Rick replied. "I went up to the big house and your aunt gave me a few things. She offered to cook for us, but with all those people milling about, I figured it would be easier on her if I just brought this back."

"And you got my stove to work?" Rosie marveled. "I can't even remember the last time I used that thing."

"Again, I noticed."

She laughed. "I'm not much good in the kitchen," she said. "I think all the cooking genes got used up with Aunt Mary."

"Don't let your mother hear you say that. She thinks she's a great cook."

"She burns toast."

"Yep."

Rosie wandered away from Rick and into the bathroom by way of the bedroom. She hoped there was still some hot water left.

"Oh, Rosie," her mother said when she saw her. "I was wondering when you'd be up."

"Mom, it's only seven thirty."

"I've been up since five."

Rosie walked over to where her mother was standing in front of the closet. "Why would you get up so early?"

"That's what time I get up every morning," Katherine replied. "I usually go for a run, but I didn't want to get lost, so I just did some yoga."

Rosie wanted to laugh, but she knew her mother wouldn't appreciate it, so instead she said, "What are you doing over here?"

"Trying to make some room for our luggage so that the room doesn't look any *more* cluttered than it already does. But your closet is packed full of junk."

"It's not junk," she said defensively.

"Well, this at least is lovely." Katherine held up the small porcelain cottage Rosie bought at the Christmas shop. "It looks a lot like this place."

"I know," Rosie said, her voice nearly a whisper.

"Why don't you put it out?" Katherine asked, starting for the living room. "It would look great on your coffee table!"

"No!" Rosie said a little too quickly, and her mother turned around to stare at her.

"What's wrong?"

"Nothing," she replied. "It's just that it's a Christmas present." She took the cottage from her mother's hands. "It's not for me."

"Who's it for?" Katherine pressed.

"Just a friend," Rosie said, putting it back into the closet and closing the doors. "Come on, let's go eat breakfast."

After eating and showing Rick the bees, Rosie walked him and her mother up to the Cove. She was having a hard time believing that it was December 20 and that Christmas was less than a week away. More importantly, they'd all know by Christmas Eve who won the contest. Rosie couldn't bring herself to think about it. It seemed both too close and too far away.

Looking at the bustling Cove, Rosie wondered if they could just keep going forever on the business the contest was drumming up, even though she knew that was impossible. It was going to take money, real money, to make the place successful again. Still, she couldn't help smiling when she saw her aunt and uncle. They looked like themselves again.

"Rosie!" Joe said when he saw her. "We sure could have used you an hour ago!"

"She was asleep," Katherine replied, giving him a peck on the cheek.

"I'm sorry," Rosie said. "I should have set an alarm."

"Oh, it's fine," Joe said. "Besides, we've got Irene and Connie coming in later to help us out, free of charge. If you ask me, they just want to be nosy and see what all the hubbub is about."

"I don't blame them," Rosie said. "There's a lot of hubbub going on around here."

"Your aunt's in the kitchen. Cleanin' up breakfast."

"I'll go in and say hello," Katherine said.

"Would you like a tour of the grounds?" Joe said to Rick, clapping him on the back. "Between you and me, I could use some air."

Her stepfather nodded. "Sounds good."

Rosie stayed in the living room. She smiled at a few of the guests lingering by the tree and helped herself to a cup of apple cider and a few gingerbread cookies. When she'd been younger and living at the Cove, her aunt had put cider and cookies outside her door nearly every morning in December. Normally, Aunt Mary wouldn't approve of cookies for breakfast, but Christmastime had different rules. Some mornings, instead of the cookies, she'd wake up to a gift. Once it had been a charm bracelet, and another, a pair of Candie's tennis shoes she'd seen in Austin and begged for.

She smiled at the memory.

She was still lost in thought when she heard elevated voices coming from somewhere in the house. Nearly all of the guests had gone—either to their rooms or somewhere outside, and Rosie stood up and followed the noise.

It didn't take her long to realize that it was coming from the kitchen and that the voices were her mother and aunt.

"I cannot believe you're trying to tell me how to run my business!" Mary was saying.

"Well, I can't believe you don't want me here!" Katherine replied.

"I never said that!"

"You didn't have to," Katherine continued. "I know Rosie invited me, but I thought she'd cleared it with you first, or I never would have come."

"Well, she didn't."

"You never talk to me," her mother replied. "You never tell me anything. I never know what's happening here unless Rosie tells me about it."

"And she told you the Cove was failing?"

"Of course not," Katherine said. She crossed her arms over her chest. "She'd never tell me that. She knows you wouldn't want me to know."

"Then how did you find out?" Aunt Mary wanted to know.

"I'm not an idiot, Mary. Corgi Cove has been in trouble for years. And then, wouldn't you know it? One of my friends from Houston called me to tell me she'd seen *your* bed-and-breakfast on the website of her favorite magazine, trying to win some ridiculous contest."

"It's not ridiculous!" Rosie said, cutting in. "We've made it to the top five. We could *win*!"

Both women turned to stare at her.

"You could have come to me," Katherine said, turning back

around to her sister. "I would have helped. You know I would have."

"We don't need your help," Mary said.

"You do, clearly. I suspected it was bad, but I never realized it was this bad."

"It's fine. We're FINE."

"I've never understood why you never let me help you," Katherine continued. "There is nothing I wouldn't help you with."

"At what cost?" Mary asked. "How long would I have to hear about how you swooped in and saved the day? How long would you make me feel like a failure?"

"Would you two stop it?" Rosie interrupted. "It doesn't have to be this way. I don't understand why you both insist on arguing over everything. There's no reason for it."

"You wouldn't understand," Mary replied. "You don't have a younger sister who tells you what to do every second of every single day."

"No," she said. "You're right. I don't have a sister, but I wish I did. Because if I did have a sister, I wouldn't waste all my time hating her."

"I don't hate your mother," Mary said at the same time Katherine said, "I don't hate your aunt."

"Well, you could have fooled me," Rosie replied. "But the truth is that you need each other. You always have."

Mary let out a long sigh. "I don't want your mother's money."

"Neither do I," Rosie said, nearly laughing.

"What's so funny?" Katherine asked. "What's so funny about wanting to help family?"

"Nothing," Rosie said. "But there are other ways you can help."

"How?"

"Voting, for one thing." Rosie smiled.

Now it was Katherine's turn to let out a sigh.

"And you can help me get started on lunch," Mary said, one side of her mouth ticking up. "Although you never were a very good cook."

"Don't let her near the toast," Rosie said. "Rick says she burns it."

CHAPTER 65

Everett

Everett sat at his desk on December 23, staring at his computer, willing himself to get something done. It was his last day before Christmas, and all he needed to do was finish up a few reports and he'd be out of there for the holidays.

Still, he couldn't make himself work. He'd been trying for days, but nothing felt right. He was walking in a haze, and he told himself that it was because he'd gotten out of the ebb and flow of the city. It was going to take some time to readjust. Life here was faster than he remembered, unforgiving. Nobody had time to do anything except work, and he found himself wishing for the slow pace and easy lifestyle of Texas, although he'd never say it out loud. Everyone here would think he was nuts.

Maybe he was.

He sighed and shut his laptop only to re-open it again and then check his phone for the eighty-seventh time that day. If he could just get finished, he could leave. He could go home, finish packing, and then get on the road to Connecticut to visit his family.

"Mr. St. Claire?"

Everett looked up to see a mailroom boy standing there, his rolling cart filled with letters and packages.

"Hey, Brendan," he said. "What's up?"

"I'm sorry, sir." Brendan held out a small parcel to Everett. "I forgot to give this to you this morning with all your other mail."

"That's okay." He took the package and looked down at the plain brown wrapping. "I wonder who it's from."

Brendan shrugged. "There's no return address."

"Okay, well, thanks," Everett said, lost in his thoughts. "Hey, have a good holiday."

"You, too, sir," Brendan replied, taking his cart and moving on.

Everett sat back down at his desk and pulled out a letter opener from his front drawer. He sliced through the packing tape and opened it to reveal a white Styrofoam box with a lid. He frowned. What had he been sent? Who sent it? He didn't know anyone who would send him a package without a name attached.

He pulled back the lid of the Styrofoam and looked inside. It was breakable, whatever it was. Everett pulled it out and was surprised to find that it was a small ceramic house.

No, it was a cottage.

He looked into the box for a note, but there was none.

Everett inspected the cottage further. It was ornate. And beautiful. And . . . familiar. There was something familiar about it. He'd seen it before or at the very least, seen something like it before.

That's when he realized what it was. It was Rosie's cottage. It was even painted the palest shade of pink just like hers was. He stared at it in awe, realizing that she must have sent it.

He wondered what was happening at Corgi Cove right now. He wondered what Rosie was doing, what her aunt and uncle were doing since he left. He wondered if they felt relieved that nobody from the Lake Queen was intruding on their holiday festivities. He knew for a fact that Francesca hadn't sent anybody back down there after his return, opting to wait until they knew for sure about the contest.

He'd been to the website and voted every single day, even though all it did was make him feel guilty for the way he'd left things there . . . with Rosie. If he had his way, he'd go back and fix it, but he didn't even know what he'd say or what he'd do that could make her believe he was on her side, truly. Right now, at least, in his taller-than-tall building in Manhattan, he guessed he wasn't.

"You about ready to close up?" Jared asked, appearing in Everett's office doorway. "The boss told everybody they could leave, but I offered to stay late and come in tomorrow. I figure that'll earn me some extra brownie points."

"Don't you have plans for the holidays?" Everett asked. He'd known Jared a long time, nearly five years, but he didn't know anything about him. Not really. Their relationship never extended beyond work talk, and, as he'd recently learned, work arguments that got him sent to the Lone Star State.

"My mom lives up in Rochester," Jared said with a shrug.

"And you'd rather be here working than visit?" Everett asked.

Jared laughed. "I'd rather be here than anywhere. My mother knows better than to ask me to come home. Take it from me, Everett, if you want to move up, you've got to show commitment."

"Thanks," he replied. "I'll take that into consideration."

"You do that," Jared said, peeling himself off the doorframe. "It's good advice."

Everett sat there a moment, looking from his laptop to the cottage. Jared was right. If he wanted to get ahead, something he'd always said he wanted, then staying late and coming in on Christmas Eve was the thing to do. Only the company's most dedicated employees would do that.

Or he could go and visit his father in Connecticut.

Or . . .

Everett thought about it. He picked up the cottage, turning it over in his hands. Not everything in his life had to be calculated, did it? He could take a risk. He could make a life that didn't have anything to do with reports and money and dedication to a company that could, would, replace him in a heartbeat.

He stood up, closing his laptop and leaving it on his desk. He took nothing but the cottage on his way out.

CHAPTER 66

Rosie

It was Christmas Eve. She'd gotten up early, even before her mother and Rick, and headed to the Cove to help her aunt for the day. A few of the guests had left the day before, headed to meet family in Austin or another town, but some of the guests had stayed, mostly older couples, excited to be spending Christmas together at the bed-and-breakfast.

"You didn't have to get here this early," Mary said as Rosie set the table for breakfast. "There are just three couples. Your uncle and I could have handled it."

"I wanted to help," she said. "I'm sorry I wasn't here on time yesterday."

"You were dealing with your mother," Mary replied. "That was enough."

Rosie grinned. "Did you two work it out?"

"I don't know if you'd call it that. Your

mother wrote me a check, and I put it down the garbage disposal."

"Aunt Mary!"

"What?" her aunt asked, the picture of innocence. "That's exactly what your mother expected me to do. She knows I'd never take her money."

"She just wants to help."

"I know," Mary said, her voice quiet. "But I need you to understand why I can't accept it."

"What if we don't win the contest?" Rosie asked, setting down a juice glass. "What if . . ."

Mary set down the basket of silverware she had on her arm and walked over to her, gently cupping Rosie's face in her hands. "Then we'll figure it out."

"But she owes you," Rosie continued. "You took me in. You raised me."

"No," Mary said. "We helped raise you. Your mother and me and your uncle Joe, and even Rick, God love him. We did it together. And what a wonderful job we did, too."

Rosie sat down in one of the chairs at the table. "We can do this together, too," she said.

"Rosie," her aunt said, sitting down next to her. "Did you know that your uncle Joe and I always wanted a child?"

Rosie looked over at her aunt. "You did?"

She nodded. "But it wasn't in the cards for us. I was terribly jealous of your mother when she found out she was pregnant with you. Terribly jealous."

"I didn't know that."

"Your mother knew," Mary continued. "She knew, and when she told me about you, I felt like she'd done it on purpose to slight me. To show me that she could do something that I couldn't. I know that's childish, but it's how I felt."

"I'm sorry," Rosie said because she didn't know what else to say.

"No. I'm the one who's sorry. When she brought you here all those years ago, I can't imagine how hard it was for her. She did it because she loved you so much, and I thought that I could help. That I could raise you better, but do you know what I realized?"

"What?"

"I realized that you were amazing, so amazing that I suppose I realized what a fantastic job she'd done, and that only made it worse, how I treated your mother," Mary said. "Rosie, I'm sorry. I'm so sorry."

She reached out and took her aunt's hand. "I am who I am because of you," she said. "Because of my mother. You don't have to be sorry."

"But I am," Mary said. "I owe you both an apology. I've been too proud my whole life."

"I guess that's something we have in common. So will you let my mom help you?"

Mary stood up and gave Rosie a small smile. "Let's just wait and see how this contest goes," she said. "You never know what might happen."

CHAPTER 67

Rosie

It was as if the great state of Texas sensed that it was Christmas Eve, and responded by bringing the temperatures to near freezing. Rosie was glad that her bees were cozy in their hives, and she was glad to be safe inside the Cove with the fire roaring.

"I'm just saying," Marty said, shifting on his feet in front of a guest. "That phone you've got could give you cancer sooner than smoking will."

Rosie walked up to him, touching his arm gently. "Hey, Marty, could you help me bring out another tray of appetizers?"

"Huh?" Marty asked, squinting at her. "Where's your aunt?"

"Are you suggesting that bringing out appetizers is women's work?" Irene called from across the room.

"No," he said, bristling. "Come on, Rosie."

She grinned. "Thanks."

Half of the town was crowded into the Cove to watch the live results of the vote on the magazine website. They were going to be announced at eight P.M., which was more than two hours away. Still, people had been streaming in and out all day, and Rosie wondered what the reviews of the guests would say after spending so much time with the townsfolk.

She wasn't entirely sure that they would be positive.

"I thought it was supposed to be warm in Texas," Rick said, winking at Rosie as she led Marty toward the kitchen. "At least that's the way I remembered it."

"Did you forget to bring a coat?" Rosie joked, taking note of the thick sweater that her uncle Joe had clearly loaned him.

"At least I don't have frostbite," Rick grumbled.

"I told you to pack a jacket!" Katherine called from the kitchen.

He rolled his eyes and continued on into the living room.

"Hey," Rosie said to her aunt and mother. "Do you have any more snacks to take out to the living room? It's getting pretty low out there."

"I just took two plates of those Hawaiian sliders out there," Mary said. Then she saw Marty and said, "Oh, of course. Hang on."

"I see what this is," he said, crossing his arms over his chest. "You think I'm scaring the guests."

"Marty, do you remember a few years ago when you told that man with the psoriasis that his skin looked like lizard scales and you asked to take a sample?" Mary said.

"He did not," Katherine said, trying not to burst out laughing. "You're making that up."

"You didn't see it!" Marty protested. "It wasn't no psoriasis!"

"We had to give the couple their stay for free," Mary continued. She looked pointedly at Marty. "Do you want to be banned for another five years like last time?"

He hung his head. "No, ma'am."

"Then stop scaring the guests." She put a tray of tarts in his hand. "Go on now. Scoot."

Marty went without another word.

"This weather is making everyone antsy," Katherine said. "But I get the impression that Marty is always . . ."

"Batshit?" Rosie offered.

"Well, I wasn't going to say it like that," her mother replied.

"You'd be right to say it like that," Mary said. "But he's our batshit, so we put up with him."

"You've got quite a community here," Katherine continued. "It's wonderful how many people showed up for you today."

"We're all close," Aunt Mary replied. "It's been this way for as long as I can remember. The town looks out for each other."

"I have neighbors I've never even met," Katherine said. "And I don't like the ones I have."

"I doubt they like you, either," Mary replied.

The two women looked at each other and burst out laughing.

Rosie watched them working together. It seemed for the time being that they'd mended fences, and for that she was glad. It was Christmas Eve, after all, and it wouldn't do to have people watching her aunt and mother yelling at each other while drinking cider and listening to Christmas carols.

She left them to it in the kitchen and wandered back out into the thrum of people. Tommy and Susannah had arrived, and they came bearing gifts.

"What's all this?" Rosie asked.

"Oh shut up," Susannah replied. "I know you and Joe and Mary have presents for us under that tree."

Rosie grinned. "Let me help you put them down."

"So," Susannah said once they'd put the presents down and were waiting for Tommy to bring them back something to drink. "Have you heard from Everett?"

"No. Why?"

Susannah shrugged. "I was just curious."

"I don't think I'll be hearing from him again," Rosie replied.

Susannah smiled slyly. "We'll see."

"What's that supposed to mean?"

"It means we'll see," Susannah said. "Let's go check on those drinks. I'm going to need one if I have to deal with Marty on Christmas Eve."

Everyone who'd managed to cram themselves into the Cove had gone quiet. There was less than an hour left before the live announcement of the contest winner, and the tension in the air was so thick, Rosie thought she could probably cut it with a knife.

Mary was buzzing around the room, filling up drinks, and her uncle was sitting in his chair by the fire absently reaching down for one of the corgis. But looking around the room, Rosie noticed that she didn't see Bonnie and Clyde anywhere. In fact, she couldn't remember the last time she'd seen them that evening.

Joe seemed to realize the same thing, and he stood up, scanning the crowd. Rosie squatted down to see if they'd gotten under someone's feet or in the flurry of people had decided they'd had enough and were hiding underneath the furniture.

When she didn't find them, she walked over to her uncle and said, "When was the last time you saw the dogs?"

He shrugged. "I can't remember. They went out with me on the back porch a couple of hours ago, but I haven't seen them since."

"Did they come back inside with you?" she asked.

"I thought they did," he replied, paling. "Rosie, I don't remember."

"You go look out on the porch, just in case," she said. "I'll go check upstairs. Maybe they accidentally got locked in one of the guest rooms."

Her uncle nodded and headed off. Rosie went upstairs to check the guest rooms, but she found nothing. There was no trace of Bonnie or Clyde in any of the rooms. She called to them, but there was no scurrying or barking. She went back downstairs, hoping her uncle had found them.

"It's too dark out," Joe said, his brow furrowed. "I called them, but I couldn't hear them or see them."

"They weren't upstairs," Rosie said.

"What's wrong?" Mary asked. "You both look like you've seen a ghost. Don't worry. I have a good feeling about tonight."

"We can't find Bonnie and Clyde," Rosie said.

"What?" Mary asked. "They've got to be around here somewhere."

"They're going to make the announcement soon!" Susannah said, hurrying up to where the three of them were huddled. "What are you doing in here?"

"We can't find the dogs," Joe said, his voice nearing panic. "Have you seen them?"

"No," Susannah said. "Come to think of it, I haven't."

"I'll go look outside," Rosie offered. "Uncle Joe, get me a flashlight."

"You're going to miss the announcement!" Susannah said.

"I won't," Rosie promised. "But we have to find the dogs. It's cold outside, and they aren't used to it."

"Do you want me to come with you?" Susannah asked.

Rosie shook her head. "No," she said. "Stay in here with Aunt Mary and Uncle Joe. Try to keep him calm. He's worried."

"Okay," Susannah said. "Be careful."

Joe returned with the flashlight, and Rosie put her phone into her pocket and headed outside to see if she could find Bonnie and Clyde.

The cold hit her so hard that it almost took her breath away. Rosie stumbled down the stairs and into the dark, flicking on the flashlight.

"Bonnie!" she called. "Clyde!"

She shone the flashlight around the yard, searching. "Where are you?" she muttered to herself as she walked around. There wasn't any sign of them, and she figured that if they had been outside to begin with, they would have been scratching and whining at the door.

Rosie walked farther down the path toward her cottage. In the distance, she saw headlights. She expected them to turn and take a right to go into town, but instead they continued straight in her direction.

She felt her heart skip a beat. She was alone, in the dark, in the freezing cold, and some random car was heading toward her. She didn't know who it could be. Nearly everyone she knew was up at the Cove, waiting to hear the results of the contest.

When the car stopped just in front of her, she turned on her heel to hurry back up to the Cove, but she stopped when she heard a voice, a familiar voice, call her name.

She turned around to see Everett standing there in the glow of the headlights, just as the first fat snowflakes started to fall to the ground. Rosie stood there staring at him, unsure what to say, and wondering if he'd brought with him, just for her, a Christmas Eve snow all the way from New York City.

CHAPTER 68

Everett

Everett couldn't figure out what Rosie was doing standing out in the freezing cold, looking frazzled and holding a flashlight. At first, he thought he saw a look of happiness pass over her face and she made a move to go to him, but she stopped herself.

"What are you doing here?" she demanded.

"What are *you* doing here?" he asked.

"I live here!" Rosie said, not taking a step closer to him.

Everett sighed and closed the distance between them. "I mean out here in this weather. It's freezing."

Rosie's brow furrowed. "The dogs!" she said, as if remembering. "We can't find them. I've got to find them."

"I'll help you."

"No," she replied. "I don't want your help."

She started off down the path, her flashlight cutting through the darkness. Everett trailed after her, leaving his car running and the headlights glowing.

"Wait!" he said.

She ignored him and kept walking.

He cursed and broke into a jog, catching up to her and grabbing her arm. "Hey!" he said. "Stop!"

"What?" Rosie whipped around. Snowflakes were falling onto her face.

Everett opened his mouth to respond, to tell her why he was there, to explain everything, but instead he just said, "Let me help you."

"I don't know where they are," she said, her voice panicked. "I can't hear them, and it's so cold."

"I'm sure they're okay," he replied. "They're smart dogs. Where would they go if they accidentally got locked out of the Cove?"

She shrugged. "I don't know." Then she grabbed his arm. "Maybe they went to the cottage!"

"Let's go," Everett said, pulling her along down the path.

They hurried down to the cottage, and Everett watched as Rosie swung her flashlight up onto the porch, expecting to see the dogs huddled there. He was disappointed when they weren't.

Her shoulders slumped. "I really thought they'd be here."

"Maybe we should go back up to the Cove," Everett offered. "Get warm and try again."

"I can't go back without them," Rosie said.

"They're out here somewhere. We'll find them."

"How do you know that?" she asked. "You show back up here

out of nowhere and you just want me to take your word for it? What are you doing here, Everett?"

But he wasn't listening to her. He was looking past her at the small crack in the door of the cottage. "Rosie," he said.

"I'm serious," she continued. "I told you to go back to New York. You should have listened."

"Rosie."

"They'll be announcing the winner any minute now, and here you are, just another reminder that everything could fall apart . . ."

"Rosie!" Everett grabbed her by the shoulders and turned her around to face the door. "Look," he said. "Your door is open. Do you think they could have gotten inside?"

"What?" Rosie asked. She squinted through the snow.

"Look at your door," Everett repeated.

She looked and then bolted up the steps of the porch and into the house. From where he stood, he could hear her shriek, "Bonnie! Clyde! You two are in SO much trouble!"

Everett grinned to himself and then followed her inside.

Rosie was on her knees in the living room, hugging the two corgis, who by now were both struggling to escape her grasp.

She glanced up at him, and this time, she didn't look nearly so upset with him.

"How did they get inside?" he asked her.

Rosie stood up. "The door doesn't latch if I don't lock it before I leave. The dogs know they can scratch at the door, and most of the time, it'll open."

"Like I said. Smart."

"So," she said, looking at him. "What are you doing here, really?

I know you didn't come back just to help me find the dogs. Did you even go back to New York?"

"I did," Everett replied. "I went back to New York the day you told me to go."

"And what?" Rosie asked. "You just missed Texas so much you had to come back on Christmas Eve?"

"No," he said. He took a deep breath. "I missed you."

Rosie took a step back from him. "Everett . . ."

"I got the present you sent me," he continued. "I got it yesterday. Thank you."

"I bought it before . . ." she trailed off. "I bought it before everything . . . happened. I didn't want to keep it."

"You could have returned it," he replied. "You didn't have to send it to me."

"You hurt me," Rosie said, her voice soft.

"I know. I know I did, and I'm so sorry."

"Why are you here?" she repeated. "I need to know why you're here."

Everett wanted to go to her. He wanted to reach out and take her in his arms, but he knew she wasn't ready for that. So he shoved his hands down into his pockets and said, "I didn't expect any of this when I first came to this place. I figured I'd come in, do my job, and go home. It was just supposed to be one sale. A means to an end, and I wasn't expecting . . . you."

When Rosie didn't say anything, he continued. "It was a fight with myself every day. Do my job and ignore what I was feeling for you or ignore my job and get to know you. I wasn't trying to hurt you, but what I thought I wanted and what I ended up wanting were two different things, and after that night, that fucking amazing night, Rosie, I just wanted to be with you."

"Then why did I hear you telling someone that you wanted us to lose the contest?" Rosie asked. "Why would you *say* that?"

"Because I didn't know what else to say," he confessed. "I couldn't very well say, 'Oh, I'm sorry, I think I might be falling in love with my client, and I quit.'"

Rosie took a step closer to him. "Why not?"

"Because I was a coward," he admitted. "Then I went back. I went back to New York and I got my old job back and I thought it would fix everything."

"And?"

"I hated it," he replied. He laughed hoarsely. "All I could think about was you. I wondered all the time what I was missing here. I just wanted to be here with you, and then I got your gift, and I thought . . . I don't know." He ran his hand through his damp hair.

"You thought you could come back here, explain yourself, and I'd forgive you?" Rosie asked.

"Sort of."

She laughed. "Well," she said. "You did help me find the dogs."

Everett wrapped his arm around her waist and said, "That counts for something, right?"

"It might."

"Rosie," Everett continued. "There's something else I want to talk about."

Rosie pulled away from him and motioned for the dogs to follow her. "It can wait," she replied. "Whatever it is that you have left to say can wait. They're announcing the winner right now, and I've got to get back."

"It's important," Everett said.

"It can wait!" Rosie called over her shoulder. "Come on, or we're going to miss it!"

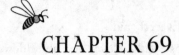

CHAPTER 69

Rosie

Rosie led Everett, Bonnie, and Clyde back up to the Cove. She was almost positive she'd missed the announcement of the winners, and when they walked through the door to a nearly silent house, she felt a pit grow in her stomach. If they'd won, they'd be celebrating. The jubilance she'd felt only minutes ago with Everett dissipated. Even if he was no longer interested in buying the Cove on behalf of the Lake Queen, that didn't mean that they were safe.

Rosie took a deep breath and entered the living room where everyone was standing up, gathered around her laptop. She couldn't see it or hear anything, but nobody was celebrating.

She cleared her throat and everyone turned around to stare at her. Mary and Joe made their way over to her, and Rosie could see that Mary had been crying. This wasn't good.

Before Mary could open her mouth to speak, Rosie flung her arms around her and said, "It's okay. We can figure something else out."

Her aunt hugged her back and then the strangest thing happened. Mary laughed.

Rosie pulled back to look at her, confused. What was funny?

"We don't need to do something else," Mary replied.

"What do you mean?" Rosie asked, the pit in her stomach rising to panic. "We can't give up! We can figure this out!"

"Oh, for God's sake," Joe said, stepping closer to Rosie. "Your aunt means we won! We won the contest, you silly child!"

"We won?" Rosie asked. But her question was drowned out by cheers and shouts from the crowd.

Suddenly, everyone was buzzing around her, hugging her and congratulating her, and she realized her aunt's tears were tears of joy, and despite her best efforts, she began to cry, too.

"Merry Christmas!" someone shouted.

"It's a damn Christmas miracle!" Irene hollered back, raising her glass in the air.

"Sissy's already called to congratulate us," Mary gushed. "She said we were her favorite from the start, and she's going to be coming back after New Year's to do a special edition just on the Cove. Can you believe it?"

Rosie couldn't. She felt as if she were walking in a dream. There was no way this could be real. She'd nearly convinced herself that they'd lose. After all, it was such a long shot.

"Everett?" Joe asked, just noticing him. "My boy, what are you doing here?"

"You'll have to tell the Lake Queen we appreciate their offer, but we respectfully decline," Mary said, hugging him.

"I don't work for them anymore," he said simply. "So I doubt they'll listen to anything I have to say."

Rosie gawked at him. "You didn't tell me that," she whispered.

"You didn't give me the chance," Everett replied.

"None of that matters right now," Uncle Joe said, clapping Everett on the shoulder, a knowing twinkle in his eye. "It's Christmas Eve. It's time to celebrate."

CHAPTER 70

Rosie

Rosie and Everett stayed in the living room by the fire long after everyone left and her aunt and uncle, her mother and Rick, and the other guests had gone up to bed.

"I didn't realize there wouldn't be any rooms available," Everett said. "I underestimated how popular the Cove has become."

"It was the coverage on the website," Rosie said. "But everyone here is fairly local. We'll have to wait and see how it goes after the holidays."

Rosie spread out three blankets onto the carpet in front of the Christmas tree.

"We could just go to your cottage," Everett said, his grin slightly wicked.

"I always spend my Christmas Eves at the Cove," Rosie replied, smacking his hands away from her. "And since there

aren't any rooms left, I guess we'll just have to sleep down here."

"It's not a bad place to sleep," he said. "When I was a kid, my sister and I used to sneak down and wait up for Santa. We always fell asleep waiting, and we'd wake up in the morning to more presents than we could open. I always wondered how my dad managed to sneak in and leave everything without waking us up."

"It wasn't your dad," she said. "It was Santa."

"Oh, right." Everett laughed. "Santa."

"So, what was it you wanted to talk to me about?" Rosie asked him as she finished setting up the bed on the floor.

"You were right," he replied. "We can talk about it later. Your aunt and uncle need to be there for it, anyway."

She furrowed her brow. "Okay. Then why don't you tell me about quitting your job."

He laughed. "There isn't much to it," he said. "I quit, and I'm not going back." He walked over and sat down next to Rosie on the blankets.

"To New York or to the Lake Queen?"

"I have to go back to New York, at least to tie up some loose ends," Everett said, looking over at her. "But how would you feel if I spent more time here?"

Rosie looked over at him. "With me?"

"If I have a choice in the matter, yes," he said.

"You're going to give it all up? To be here with me?"

Everett moved closer to her and brushed a stray strand of hair out of her eyes. Outside, the snow continued to come down in wet clumps. "Yes," he said.

Rosie knew that she wouldn't wake up in the morning to a blanket of fresh snow, it was Texas, after all, but right in this moment, the world felt so small and perfect. She leaned in to him and brought her mouth to his.

"I missed you," he breathed into her ear. "I think I missed you before I knew you."

Rosie pulled him down, allowing his weight to press into her, covering her. She knew what it meant to miss someone you didn't even know. That's how she'd felt her whole life until recently. Now here he was, the person she hadn't even realized she'd needed until it was nearly too late. Maybe this Christmas was just the beginning of a life she thought might never get started.

CHAPTER 71

Rosie

"So this man came to buy the Cove?" Rosie's mother asked at Christmas breakfast the next morning. "But instead he . . . bought you?"

"It sounds gross when you say it like that," Rosie replied, wrinkling her nose.

"To be clear," Everett spoke up, "no money was ever exchanged for any type of goods or services."

Rosie punched him in the arm. "You're not doing a very good job of making a good first impression," she said.

"Well," Everett said. "There was something else I wanted to talk about, and I was going to wait, but maybe this will help my case a bit."

"What is it?" she asked.

He got up from his seat and walked over to his briefcase, which he'd set near the front door the night before. He reached down inside and took out a thick folder. He brought it over to the table and set it down in front of Joe and Mary.

"I have a proposal I'd like to make," he said.

Mary, who'd been watching him carefully since he stood up, cocked her head to one side and said, "Well, out with it."

"I'd like to invest in the Cove."

"What do you mean, *invest*?" Rosie asked.

Everett sat down across from Mary. "We don't have to talk about this right now," he said. "But I think I have a good offer."

"We're done with offers," Rosie replied before either her aunt or uncle could say anything. "You don't even work for the Lake Queen anymore."

"This isn't on behalf of the Lake Queen. It's on behalf of myself."

"I don't understand," Rosie said.

"Keep talking," Joe said, speaking up at last. "Let's hear what you have to say."

Rosie looked confusedly from her aunt and uncle to Everett. She thought they'd put the matter of Everett and the Cove to bed . . . quite literally, last night. Now she was looking at him and wondering if maybe she'd missed something.

"The money and publicity from the contest is fantastic," Everett said, glancing over at her and giving her a small smile. "But it won't last forever. I think we all know that. It's enough to get you on your feet, make some small changes, but ultimately, you're going to need . . . more than that."

"How do you figure?" Joe asked.

"I've run the numbers," Everett said, sliding the folder toward him. "This is what you'll need for long-term success."

Joe pulled a pair of reading glasses out of his shirt pocket, put them on, and looked down. After a few minutes, he sighed. "The boy's not wrong, Mary."

"I can help with that," Everett continued. "Let me bring my money, and my expertise, to the Cove. I want you to be successful. I want you to—" He looked over at Rosie again. "I want *us* to be successful. That is, if you'll have me. If you'll let me."

Rosie pulled the folder over to her and took a look. He'd worked everything out, down to the last nickel. He'd written plans for everything they would need, including advertising costs and a remodel. There was an entire five-year plan.

She felt a lump in her throat and had to fight tears. He'd thought of everything. She reached for his hand under the table and when she found it, soft and warm, she squeezed it hard.

"Are you sure this is what you want, young man?" Joe asked, glancing from Rosie to Everett and giving them a knowing smile.

Everett, not taking his eyes off Rosie, said, "It's all I want, sir. It's all I want."

EPILOGUE

One Year Later

The Turtle Lake Farmers' Market took place the third Saturday of the month at Corgi Cove. It wasn't quite the scale of the market in Austin, but it brought in vendors from all over, even the Hot Goat Farmer and Rosie's friend Miranda, who was now Mrs. Hot Goat Farmer.

The whole thing had been Everett's idea, an initial ploy to bring more business to the Cove. In the six months since it had begun, however, the farmers' market had taken on a life of its own, and Everett marveled at the sheer magnitude of it.

"Here," he said, taking a basket of beeswax products from Rosie's hands and handing it to a customer. "Let me get that for you."

"I'm fine," she said, slapping his hands away. "It's not that heavy."

"Oh, let him help," Katherine said. "He's trying to be useful."

"He's supposed to be helping Uncle Joe at the Cove," Rosie replied. "He's not supposed to be here, hovering over me."

Katherine looked down at the small, barely there bump that was visible beneath her daughter's sunflower-pattern overalls. "He's just worried."

Rosie rolled her eyes, but couldn't help but smile. She knew that. Everett was constantly worrying over her these days, and she had to admit that it was very cute.

"Mom," she said. "You're supposed to take my side in all things. I'm pretty sure that was part of the deal when I let you buy a vacation house here."

"Oh, you let me?" Katherine laughed. "You're going to want me around soon enough, just you wait."

Rosie reached out and gave her mother a quick peck on the cheek. "I already want you around. Who else is going to help me with the bees?"

Katherine laughed and started off toward Rick, who at the moment looked to have gotten into an argument with the vegans.

"I love this," Rosie said, leaning up against Everett.

The contest and subsequent windfall of publicity had helped the Cove more than she ever expected. In the days following the announcement, they'd done interviews with news stations, and even a couple of national publications carried the story. Naturally, business picked up, and hadn't even suffered a hit when they closed months later for several weeks of renovations. Bonnie and Clyde, the Cove's official mascots, were also enjoying their own slice of fame, picking up a spokes-dog gig for a Texas-based dog food brand.

But it had been Everett who'd helped make the success last, just as he'd promised. He'd jumped in with both feet to make sure everything went to plan, and now his life was entirely with her in Turtle Lake, in their little cottage, surrounded by the ones they loved most—each other.

He leaned down and brushed a light kiss over her belly and said, "I hope this kid is every bit as stubborn as you are."

"She will be," she replied, waving at her aunt Mary, who was standing on the front porch of the Cove, surveying the scene with pride. "But her family will be here to remind her that life is the most surprising just when you least expect it."

ACKNOWLEDGMENTS

Thank you to Lucia Macro for being an amazing editor and, ultimately, my friend. Thank you for having confidence in me as a writer, for your patience, for your honesty, and for teaching me so much about what it means to love my craft.

Thank you to Asanté Simons for your absolute patience in the face of probably the most annoying writer on the planet. I appreciate all of the times you were so kind to me when I asked silly questions. I am so grateful, and I hope all of your writers know how lucky they are to have you as their editor.